THE
ORIGIN
OF THE
WOLF

DANNY
BEESON

The Book Guild Ltd

First published in Great Britain in 2024 by
The Book Guild Ltd
Unit E2 Airfield Business Park,
Harrison Road, Market Harborough,
Leicestershire. LE16 7UL
Tel: 0116 2792299
www.bookguild.co.uk
Email: info@bookguild.co.uk
X: @bookguild

Typeset in 11pt Minion Pro

Printed and bound by CPI Group (UK) Ltd, Croydon, CR0 4YY

ISBN 978 1835740 309

British Library Cataloguing in Publication Data.
A catalogue record for this book is available from the British Library.

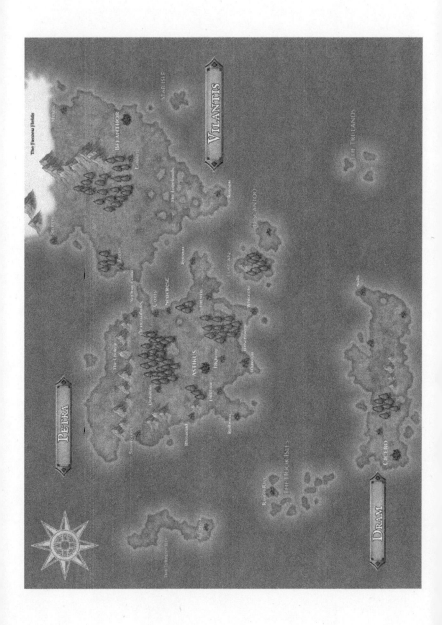

Chapter 1

Seaweed on the Rocks

Gently, he rocked back and forth. Back and forth. The wind carried a lullaby of rolling waves to his ear, soft and sweet. It filled his head with hazy dreams that drowned out all else. He stirred a little and smiled. A mistake. Water rushed into his open mouth, cold and sudden, filling him. Killing him. His smile faded. He coughed and fought, limbs lashing against the darkness all around him. Panic boiled his brain as he lost all sense of which way was up or down, left or right. Still the water poured in. Finally, after a futile fight, he was still.

The fishermen came, as always, before first light, emerging from the safety of the dunes to once again face the fury of the sea. There were twelve in all, lugging three small boats between them across the stretch of pale white sand. They were hard men, tall and strong, the type that grew full beards within a day of shaving and had arms thicker than most trees. They worked in silence, heaving the sturdy wooden craft towards the waves. Their nets lay balled in the bottom of the boats, ready for the fertile waters beyond the breakers.

Today the wind was cold and fierce as it blew hard from the north. It drove sand down the beach and whipped it into the men's faces, slapping against their cheeks and stinging their eyes. Ahead, the waves rolled towards them in swirling crowds, ever shifting and changing, charging forth with untamed fury to pound against the sand only to retreat again to repeat the process. It was a bad day for fishing, all the men knew it, but they pressed on regardless. The men of Seacrest were not so easily dissuaded from their task. Their families had fished these waters for generations. Shielding their eyes from the sand, they trudged closer to the wild water, heaving the boats along with them.

Their leader was named Drel, a tall man with wild grey hair and a beard to match. He was the village chief, the descendant of the founding father of their village, and their most revered fisherman. Every day, he chose the spots and the fish would come. So it had been for twenty years. Every man amongst them trusted Drel without question and he had never once led them astray.

A shout, off to his left, made Drel pause and the rest of the fishermen followed suit, gratefully letting the boats grind to a halt in the sand. The words that were said had been lost, whipped away by the wind, but he knew it had been meant for him. His men were not ones for idle chatter, especially on a day like this. He turned, shielding his face from the biting sand grains, and saw a figure lumbering towards him. It took him several seconds to recognise the figure as Franz, one of the more senior fishermen, well liked and reliable. Though not the most intense thinker, he was respected for his size and strength along with his unwavering devotion to the village and their way of life.

2

He was at least a foot taller than Drel but now hunched forwards with the wind, his broad shoulders forming a wall as he huddled close to his leader.

"Somethin' in the wa'er!" he boomed against the wailing air. He pointed up the beach. "Think it's a man."

Squinting, Drel did his best to pick out where his friend was pointing. Eventually he spotted a pale shape, an unmistakable shape, at the water's edge. As he watched it was tossed up the shore by a wave and then dragged back along the sand as the water receded. Without thinking, Drel released the boat and began to run.

It was hard going, fighting his way up the beach, the wind pushing him back so that the soft ground gave way with every step he took. By the time he reached the body, Drel was panting hard, his bad knee throbbing. Above him, dark clouds were beginning to blanket the sky with the threat of rain.

The man was as naked as the day he was born and lay face down in the sand, his legs still gripped by the surf, so that with every wave the sea rose to try desperately to reclaim him to its icy depths. Fortunately the tide was retreating and the water falling further and further short. The man's arms were up beside his head as though he had fought to drag himself free of the waves before succumbing to exhaustion. His face was turned away and hidden from view by thick black curls but that was not what caught Drel's eye, not what made him freeze in his act of rescue. Instead the fisherman's eyes rested on the three jagged cuts that ran across the man's exposed ribs. Drel had lived long enough to see such wounds and know they were not made by blades. They were made by claws.

3

Franz, appearing silently beside him, cursed at the sight. The sound startled Drel into action and he stepped closer to reach down and feel the man's neck for a pulse. Silently he waited, his fingers pressed against the cold, pale skin. He was about to give up and pull away when he felt a brief flutter. Life still stirred within.

"Alive!" Drel declared. By now all twelve men stood around the body, intrigued by the stranger that had washed up on their shore. When Drel reached under the man's arms and began to pull him out of the surf, the men only watched him, as if afraid to step forwards.

"Grab 'is legs and 'elp me get 'im clear of the water!" their leader demanded, and reluctantly two of the men moved to assist him. Away from the hungry waves, Drel rolled the man onto his back. They all gasped.

"Fuck!" repeated Franz, eyes wide beneath his knitted cap.

Almost every inch of the man's body was covered in wounds. Most were like those on his ribs, three close claw marks running in jagged lines, but there were others too, hard and straight cuts that looked to have been caused by a sword or knife. Together they formed a criss-crossing pattern of red and pink lines across his pale, sea-shrivelled skin. In the faint morning light the man looked more of a corpse than most corpses Drel had seen. Yet still he fought on, clinging to the little life he had left, though Drel did not know for how much longer.

"Let's get 'im up. We need to take 'im back to the village," Drel ordered. When no one moved he stood and glanced around in confusion, unsure if the men had heard him against the winds.

4

Franz stepped closer and put a big hand on his shoulder. "Drel, look at 'im. No way 'e is going to last. Even Momo cannot save 'im." The big man stared down with a mix of confusion, pity and disgust etched across the small portion of face visible between his cap and his beard.

"Then we make what time 'e 'as left as comfortable as we can!" Drel shouted back. "We ain't leaving 'im, so 'elp me!"

After a lengthy pause, the men reluctantly stepped forwards to help and soon they were carrying their find back towards the village as quickly as they could, trudging across the long stretch of white beach in stony silence. Their boats stayed where they had dropped them, left to the mercy of the wind and sand, silent observers to all that occurred. Suddenly, the heavens opened and rain began to beat down onto the beach, quickly drenching everything. Thunder rolled in the distance, an echoing boom carried across the waves towards them. Behind them, the sea roared in its vast fury.

With age came a lack of sleep and Momo was as old as they come. Despite the dawn having not yet broken she had been awake for several hours and was currently sitting in her wooden rocker by the fire, her thin frame wrapped in blankets as she waited for her tea to boil in the small pot hanging from the mantle. Sleep had once been her friend, scarcely enjoyed and always sought after, but now it was more of a curse, a prelude to what waited for her when her time was finally done. She avoided it as much as she could.

With gnarled fingers, like withered twigs, she slowly lifted the pot and poured the steaming liquid into a mug on the table beside her. Setting down the pot, she sat and picked up the mug, enjoying the warmth that seeped through it into her hands. She blew on the tea, her breath shallow and ragged, before taking a cautious sip. Beside her the flames danced and crackled as they devoured fresh kindling with glee. Shadows pranced around her small wooden hut, moving to the fire's tune. Outside, rain began to lash against the shutters as it rolled in from the sea.

She had just finished her second sip of tea when a sharp knock at the door broke through the hammering of the rain. Momo raised an eyebrow but did not get up. It was early for visitors but then perhaps that depended on who the visitors were.

"Come in but make it quick!" she ordered, tongue no less sharp than it had ever been in her younger days.

Immediately, the door flew open and the fishermen rushed in, Drel at their head. They were soaked and heavy raindrops ran down their sealskin coats to drip onto the floor. Momo was surprised to see them; even in this rain they should have been out fishing by now, and the concerned look on Drel's face did nothing to lessen her unease. That man did not scare easily. Then she spotted the body they were carrying between them and her eyes widened. She put down her tea and slowly rose to her feet.

"Put him on the table." She gestured to the long wooden dining table across the room and the men moved to obey, clearing the surface before laying down their burden. The men stepped back but made no move to leave. Momo pushed past them.

"Out! Won't have you standing there gawping. Go home!" There was no debate in her tone and all except Drel and Franz did as they were told.

"What happened?" asked the old woman when the door had shut behind the last of the fishermen. She was already examining the body in front of her, eyes roaming over the injuries.

"We found 'im on the beach, washed up," Drel explained. "At first we thought 'e was dead but I felt a pulse, only faint but there."

Momo nodded agreement without checking for a pulse herself; she had been a healer long enough to know the difference between a person and a corpse. Her eyes evaluated the man's wounds with practised precision, her hands moving gently to probe the skin here and there. The man made no move or sound at her touch, lost in his own sea of darkness.

Drel peered closer at one of the cuts. "What do you think 'appended to 'im? These wounds are not shark bites, more like claws. Wolf attack perhaps?" Not two days ago the fishermen had seen a pack of wolves prowling a beach just up the coast and the image was still fresh in Drel's mind. One more worry to add to his list.

"Certainly not! When have you known wolves to carry knives?" The old crone pointed to some cuts on the man's thigh. "These are man-made, probably a sword by the size of them."

She turned and began to shuffle towards her medicine cabinet in the kitchen, a tall wooden bookshelf that seemed to house everything except books. A small stool stood nearby in case she had to reach the top shelf but now she elbowed Franz instead, pointing up at a leather bag that sat gathering dust at the very top. "Was he awake when you found him?"

"No, Momo, 'e was like this. Cold."

"Was he wearing anything?" she asked as she began to remove things from the bag and lay them out on the table in front of her. When Drel shook his head, she sighed and paused, eyes locked on the man in front of her, withered hands frozen halfway through unwrapping a bandage. Drel watched as her eyes studied every detail of the man's face, taking in every inch of his features. Her own face was filled with suspicion and just a hint of unease.

"Momo, are you alright?" he asked gently, sensing her sudden unease.

Snapping back to the present, Momo waved a dismissing hand. "Yes, yes, of course. Fetch Ellen for me, I will need her eyes. Then leave us. This will take time."

The men both nodded and shuffled out, leaving Momo alone with the stranger. Once again she paused, mind churning as she examined the man for any distinguishing features. Indecision spread through her like a fog, clouding her mind to which path she should take. Her heart was beating faster than it had in years and she had to grip the table to stay upright. She had seen the wounds of battle before and, with the country currently at war, it should not have fazed her, but for some reason the sight of this man filled her with pure dread, a deep dark feeling that made her stomach cramp and her pulse thunder in her ears.

She wanted to save this man and it was her duty, not only as a healer but as a human being, to try everything she could to do just that, but there were two sides to every

8

war, allies and the enemy. Without a sigil or house crest it was impossible to tell anything about who he was or where he came from, impossible to tell if he was friend or foe. Momo reached up and rubbed her temple with trembling hands.

The sound of the door opening made her jump and she spun round to see Ellen entering, shaking rain from her golden hair.

"You sent for m…" She froze as she saw the body and Momo watched her expression, intrigued. She had expected disgust or caution but instead she saw only pity in the young girl's eyes. It was that look that made up her mind.

"Stop staring, girl, and fetch me warm water! We have work to do!" After a silent prayer she rolled up her sleeves and set to her task.

The man woke for the first time late the following day, while Momo was sitting in her chair with a tea in her hand, staring at the flames with distant eyes. She had not long risen from her own bed having watched her guest through the night before being replaced by Ellen at sunrise. Rustling sheets and a groan alerted her to her charge's state and she rose slowly (at her age you did nothing quickly) and ambled towards his bedside.

He was lying in the wooden bed in her second bedroom with the sheets pulled back, his body plastered in bandages over the many wounds she had stitched up. The room was small and cramped and with the curtains partly drawn it felt warm and stuffy despite the cold of the day outside. As she arrived, he gave another low groan before finally summoning the strength to open his eyes. He stared around from beneath a stray lock of black hair before his gaze settled upon her. His breathing was ragged and he ran his tongue slowly over his dry, cracked lips.

"W… water?" he croaked in little more than a whisper. Momo nodded in silence and disappeared, returning a moment later with a small mug of fresh water that she gently pressed to his lips.

Once he had drank the mug dry he nodded. "Thank you." He began to look around again though his movements were stiff from the stitches Momo had made along a cut on the side of his neck. "Wh… where am I?"

"Safe," she replied simply as she continued to watch him with avid interest, empty mug in hand. "The men found you washed up on the beach. Do you remember how you got there?"

He tried to shake his head but then winced in pain. "No," he replied after several deep breaths. His face was a ghostly white that matched the bandages that circled his head, contrasting sharply with his hair.

"What do you remember? Your name?"

"My… my name… is Lyncon." He fell silent as his eyes glazed over and his mind seemed to drift to other places. Momo let it happen, content to watch as Lyncon searched for memories in his wounded mind. When he spoke again his voice was thick and his words slow. "I… I was hurt. There was noise all around, people… screaming, shouting. It was so loud." He paused again, gathering his strength. "I remember fighting, battle. There was blood, so much blood. I… I could smell it, everywhere, overpowering."

Momo's face was lined with concern but she did her best to keep her voice steady. "Then what? Do you know how you got into the water?"

"No." He thought for a moment. "There was a bright light and... and a noise like thunder. Then... just... nothing." He sighed and let his eyelids droop, clearly exhausted from the effort.

Momo stood still and silent, staring intently at the wounded man before her, as if seeing him for the very first time. Then she turned slowly and made her way to the kitchen where she retrieved a small bottle from the old leather bag. She poured a dose of the liquid into the mug and then set the bottle back. As she returned to Lyncon, she swirled the liquid around in her hand, the mug trembling just a little. Carefully, she sat down on the wooden stool beside his bed.

"Drink this. It will help your pain." She offered him the mug, which he took reluctantly, sniffing the liquid. He coughed as the foul stench caught in his throat and nostrils.

"What is it?" he asked through more coughing.

"No questions, just drink." One look at the old woman's face told him there was no point in arguing. After a deep breath, he downed the liquid in one go, wincing at the taste.

Momo nodded. "Good."

"Thank you... for helping me," Lyncon said softly.

Momo raised a single eyebrow. "I just put the stitches in and bandaged you up, nothing more. You did the rest, more than most men could." She gave him a searching look. "You should be dead. I have been a healer for fifty years and I have never seen anyone heal so fast." She gently reached out and touched one of his wounds, a small cut that was now almost completely gone. Her face was etched with an almost childish wonder as she marvelled at what she saw.

"Where am I? What is this place?"

His questions snapped Momo from her trance and she shook her head, face returning to its usual hard and weathered look. "Safe. That is all you need to know. Now sleep! You need your strength." For a second, she thought he would argue but then a flush suddenly swept over his features and he blinked several times, fighting to keep his eyes open. He opened his mouth to shout but no words came out. Slowly, his eyelids forced themselves shut and within seconds he was asleep.

Leaving her patient behind, Momo shut the door and leant back against it, finally releasing a breath she had not realised she had been holding. She took a moment to calm herself, working her mind through what she had just heard and what must now be done, before fetching her cloak. She had need to call a council meeting. There was much to discuss.

It was almost dark outside by the time the meeting assembled in Drel's home. The golden sun was just falling below the horizon and cast long shadows over the small village. Beyond the dunes, the sea was calm, lapping gently at the beach. Gulls wheeled lazily through the sky and soon would drop to the earth to rest their wings and roost for the coming night.

They were convened, as always, in the dining room. Drel sat at the head of the long wooden table, sipping at his ale, lost in thought, as the rest of the village council helped themselves to food and drink. Momo took the place of honour on the chief's immediate right while Franz sat to his left, loudly chewing on a chicken leg, grease dripping into his beard.

Beside Momo was Ellen, the young girl who cared for and helped Momo as she learnt the secrets of medicine and healing. Though not a member of the village council, the girl rarely left the old woman's side and was allowed to attend to help see to her needs. She never spoke during the gatherings, mostly just sat with her hands in her lap, head down and face covered by her mass of golden curls.

Across from Ellen sat Harris, the village's wealthiest and only merchant. He was a short man with a bald head, a large belly and a larger ego. Few liked him, so he mostly kept himself to himself, but he was a useful man to keep close. He had business connections all over the land and his frequent trips to the nearest towns always brought back plenty of news and gossip. Despite his greedy and cunning nature, Drel knew Harris was loyal to the village. He loved Seacrest more than most and it only took one look at his face when he arrived home from a long trip for Drel to see that. He may not like the man but he knew his worth and valued his insight.

Finally, seated directly opposite the chief, was Drel's own mother, Karis. Though not as old as Momo she was still advanced in years and her neat grey hair and wrinkled skin showed it. After becoming a widow almost twenty years ago, she had stayed in the village and guided her son through the many trials of leadership. Like Harris and Momo, she had the benefit of a formal education received from a childhood spent away from the village and as such her words were revered and always welcome. Drel finished his drink in one long gulp and set it down with a thud. The room quietened as he began to speak.

"Momo 'as called a meeting and you no doubt all know why. Yesterday morning we found a man washed up on the beach, injured but alive. We bought 'im to Momo to try and save." He rubbed his jaw and glanced at Franz. "In truth, we did not think 'e would make it, 'e was a mess… but Momo believes 'e will pull through and we need to discuss what 'appens next."

The old healer nodded. "This morning the man woke for the first time. He was delirious but I managed to question him somewhat. He claims to have no idea where he's from or how he got here, says he can't remember anything. I got little more out of him other than his name: Lyncon. When he started asking questions of his own I gave him something strong to knock him out again, give us time to meet and discuss what to do with him."

The others looked confused, while Drel, who had spoken to Momo privately beforehand, remained unmoved, watching each one of them closely in turn.

"What do you mean?" Harris asked after a long pause.

"The wounds the man suffered were 'orrific, cuts and slashes all over 'is body, worst I 'ave ever seen. Most looked like claw marks but some seemed to 'ave been done by a blade," Drel said gravely.

"You mean he was attacked?" the fat man asked, suddenly a little more startled.

It was Momo that answered. "No. I believe they were wounds from battle."

14

The room fell deathly silent as its occupants took their time to digest what had been said. The great war between Petra and Vilantis had been raging for several years, with both sides suffering victories and grave losses. The war of elves versus men had cost many lives with battles fought all over the Petran continent. Though stories of the conflict inevitably reached Seacrest, the tiny village had remained untouched and untroubled. Both the human capital city of Astikus and the elven capital of Belanthor were very far away and news of the conflict always felt like stories, tales of a distant land in another place. Now, it seemed a fragment of the war had come to this small corner of Petra as the shadow of the conflict and its consequences loomed over them all.

"He said his name was Lyncon?" Karis asked Momo after a lengthy silence. The old woman nodded. "Did he give a family name?"

"No."

Karis pursed her lips and shook her head. In Petra a family name was important; it carried honour and status. Holton, the name she and her son bore, had been the name of the family that led Seacrest for centuries, since its very beginning when it had been founded by a group of fishermen and their families. To all those that lived here, the name meant strength and wisdom. However, in other parts of the world this was not the custom; some did not even have family names at all.

"Do they use family names in Vilantis?" Franz asked, his deep voice echoing around the room.

"Some of the humans there do but the… others…" Karis shrugged. "I don't know."

"And is 'e... one of them?" the big man asked slowly, looking at Momo.

The old woman scowled. "One of what? An elf? No of course not! My eyes may not be what they used to be but I know an elf when I see one!" Franz flinched away at her outburst, genuine terror in his eyes. Drel did his best to hide his smile in his beard.

The big man still looked confused. "If 'e is 'uman then 'e must be from Petra!"

Drel shook his head sadly. "Men fight for both sides in this war, not just ours."

"So who does our man fight for?" Harris asked, looking worried.

"That's our problem. We don't know." Drel sighed. "This man is a stranger and possibly even a danger to our village. We must decide what to do with 'im."

"What to do with him?" The fat merchant looked perplexed but Drel sensed he knew what was coming; he just wanted to hear the words.

"If this man is a soldier of Petra then it is our duty to King Renthor to let 'im recover and send 'im to the nearest barracks or outpost to return to 'is unit. If we do not we would be tried for letting a soldier die." He paused, looking at each of their faces in turn. "But, if 'e is a soldier of Vilantis, our enemy, and we make 'im better, stronger, then 'e could become a danger to Seacrest and its people." He trailed off, letting the silence do the talking for him as he poured himself another drink.

"And what exactly is the alternative to healing him?" Karis asked, her eyes locking with her son's gaze.

"We end 'is suffering. The man will..."

"His name is Lyncon!" Ellen suddenly slammed her fist down with such force it made the cups rattle. She stood and turned to Drel with eyes of cold fury, her hair swept back, giving an untamed look. Colour shone in her cheeks. "If you are going to discuss killing a man at least have the decency to use his name!"

Drel should have been angry but instead he was simply speechless. He had never known such fury from the girl, usually a timid and shy little thing. Now standing before him she looked like a Valkyrie, wild and fierce, her fists balled at her sides as her eyes shone with defiance.

"Ellen! Leave us!" It was Momo who broke the stunned silence. She did not look up at the girl as she addressed her, instead staring at the wine in her cup as she swirled it slowly between her leathery fingers. Her voice was as hard as iron and gave no room for debate.

For a moment the girl froze, staring, open-mouthed, at the healer. When she made no move to leave, Momo lifted her head and fixed the girl with a stare that made her almost physically recoil, her resolve and anger withering under the old woman's power. Ellen pushed back her chair and stormed out, not once looking back. A hushed silence descended on those that were left.

Momo cleared her throat. "I am sorry for her. He is her first patient and though I have taught her not to get attached…" She shrugged.

Drel gave a heavy sigh and shook his head. "The girl is right. I am trying to remain detached, rational, but we are talking about a man's life, Lyncon's life. We must not forget that. No matter our reasons, this is a decision that cannot be taken lightly."

"Is there really no way to tell which side he is on?" the merchant asked.

"Other than simply ask 'im? No."

"He may not be truthful," Momo admitted. "We are all human here and if he is from Vilantis he may have already figured out he is not there now. He could simply lie to us all, bide his time and then flee when he is strong enough. If the king's men found out we let an enemy soldier escape, we would all hang." She glanced at the men across from her. "Though for some perhaps that would be a blessing."

"So how do we settle this?" Harris asked. He was clearly fearful, sweat lining his brow, and had flinched when Momo had mentioned hanging. "It seems we are damned if we do and damned if we don't." He paused and cocked his head slightly, as if he were considering what to have for lunch. "Perhaps we should end his suffering. Best for everyone."

"Except for Lyncon!" Karis retorted, looking disgusted but not in the least bit surprised. "This is not some bad investment you are ending but a man's life. Will you be the one who carries out this sentence that you can so easily pass?"

Harris wilted under the older woman's stare and bowed his head, muttering quietly under his breath. Momo smiled as she watched the rich man squirm and gave an approving nod to Karis.

"We will vote." Drel's voice left no room for argument. "All those that believe ending Lyncon's life is the best decision, raise a 'and."

Franz slowly raised one of his huge hands, staring defiantly at the women. Harris quickly followed suit but did not meet anyone's gaze.

18

Drel nodded. "And those that think 'e should live."

Both women raised their hands in unison, sharing a smile.

Everyone now turned to look at Drel intently as they awaited his casting vote. He ignored them and instead focused on the decision before him. Never, as chief, had he been faced with such a huge dilemma that could yield such terrible consequences for his village and the people he cared for. To balance one life against others made him feel sick to his core and he kept his hands on the table to stop them from shaking. He took a deep breath and finally settled on what he believed was right.

"Lyncon lives. We will get 'im well and then I will speak to 'im and decide what to do after that."

Chapter 2

Seacrest

It had been over a week before Lyncon learnt that the village was named Seacrest. By then he was up and walking, unaided, his wounds now little more than pink scars that gave only the occasional ache as he wandered amongst the various buildings that made up the village. Physically he was growing stronger every day but mentally he was broken. He was prone to terrible headaches that left him feeling weak and dizzy, while his memories of before were either hazy or missing entirely. Momo had warned that, while his body had healed incredibly quickly, his mind would take longer. It just needed time, to rest and to remember.

For the first few days of his recovery Lyncon saw only Momo and Ellen. As he had lay in bed, often delirious with pain, they had taken it in turns to watch over him and re-dress his wounds whenever needed. Both women were kind and gentle but also stern and had refused to answer any of his questions about where he was, leaving him confused and often frustrated. Momo especially would grow very serious when he asked her, the colour draining from her weathered face as she disappeared out the door. In the end, Lyncon learnt it was simply best not to ask. He was at the mercy of his two hosts and relied on them completely; it was neither polite nor wise to upset them.

On what Lyncon believed to be the fourth day, he had woken to find that his pain was all but gone. Slowly, he had stretched out each limb and found their movements free of the fiery pain that had burnt the night before. Eventually, he had risen from his bed and padded silently out of the cramped hut to sit on the porch and gaze up at the stars. He had planned neither to escape nor to explore. He had only wanted to be outside, feel the breeze on his skin and listen to the crickets that chirped from amongst the dunes.

It had taken him several minutes to realise he was not alone. Turning, he had found Ellen sitting on a rocking chair at the far end of the porch, watching him with her big brown eyes. She looked startled but not afraid and the moonlight gave her pale face a ghostly beauty, framed by her tumbling golden curls. He had been about to say something when Momo appeared, looking distraught, and whisked him inside in a whirlwind of wrinkles. He was ordered back to bed and told to stay there. Despite his feeble protests, the old woman would hear none of it and gave him a look that suggested she could soon bring back the pain he had lost. Reluctantly, he had done as he was told.

Finally, on the seventh day in the village, Lyncon was told to get up and dress in clothes Momo had already laid out for him. They were plain and made of rough wool but they fit him well enough and it was nice to wear something new. Momo gave him a once over before she let him leave.

It was time for him to meet the chief.

"So, Lyncon, are you well?" Drel asked from the other end of the long table. Between them sat the remains of breakfast, mostly empty plates and bowls, though some still held bits of fruit or the worst of the bread. It turned out Lyncon had a ferocious appetite and he had just finished his third plate of sausages and eggs. He laid down his fork and licked his lips before replying.

"Yes, thank you. My wounds barely trouble me at all."

Drel nodded slowly, noting carefully how Lyncon spoke with no discernible accent. Once again his eyes swept over the face before him, the strong jaw, modest nose and pale grey eyes that saw with such eager intensity, all framed by masses of shoulder-length black curls that cascaded down in untidy waves. Stubble covered the man's jaw and neck but Drel was surprised to find it had not grown at all since he had fished Lyncon from the sea a whole week ago. The face looking back at him was ordinary, unremarkable, and somehow that only worried Drel more.

"Good. I am glad you are finally up." He paused as if uncertain if he should say more. "Momo says you 'ave 'ealed very quickly. Quicker than she would ever believe possible."

Lyncon paused for a second. He was still getting used to the people's accent in the village. Finally, he smiled. "Clearly she underestimates her own ability. She is a remarkable woman and I cannot thank her enough."

"Mmm yes, she is certainly something, though perhaps not all 'ere would agree with remarkable." He studied Lyncon carefully as he sipped his tea.

"I am told this village is called Seacrest." He smiled. "It is peaceful here. I like it."

22

Drel, who had unwillingly stiffened at the name, forced a smile. "Yes, we try to keep it like that. We are mostly fishermen, working the sea, but a few of us are farmers and merchants too. Some travel but most stay put. This is our 'ome and we 'ave everything we need."

The stranger nodded. "Of course. I am also told that it was you who found me? Out on the beach?"

"Yes, myself and the other fishermen. We found you as we were about to go out, washed up in the surf. We could not leave you there, so took you to Momo in the 'ope she could do something."

"Then I owe you my thanks. You saved my life and I am eternally grateful." He bowed his head in respect.

Drel raised a hand as if to push away the gratitude. "Nonsense. We only did what any man should do." He paused and caught Lyncon's eye. "Momo tells me your memories are… vague and jumbled. Do you know 'ow you got into the water? Ended up on our beach?"

Lyncon did not reply immediately, instead seeming to consider the question before slowly shaking his head. "No. I remember… a battle, people screaming and dying, fighting all around me. Then there was a sudden brightness, a burning light that filled everything. After that there is nothing until I woke up here."

"And what about before?"

"Before what?" Lyncon asked, puzzled.

"Before the battle, the fighting. Where did you live and grow up?"

Lyncon frowned and his eyes clouded over like a sudden storm, soon to produce lightning. He began to answer then stopped himself, his confusion growing ever deeper. Across the table, Drel could see the turmoil inside his guest, the inner struggle that was playing out before him. Here was a man at war with himself, fighting a battle with his own mind to remember the things that made him who he was. The chief suddenly found himself feeling a pang of pity for the lost soldier, coupled with a desire to free him from his struggles. For now though, Drel pushed his better nature aside and stayed silent. He knew how much he could lose if he got this decision wrong.

After several minutes had passed, Lyncon looked up slowly with an expression of hurt that struck Drel deep in his chest. "I don't remember." His words were weary, defeated.

"It is no matter. In time they will return, I know it." The chief found himself giving the stranger a reassuring smile as pity overcame him. He could hear the pain in Lyncon's words, the weight of the unknown. Despite everything he had debated before this meeting, he knew then he could not turn him away, not when he was so obviously lost. He sighed, glancing briefly around the dining room at all he was risking.

"For now you will stay 'ere, to rest and recover your strength. You will 'ave to work, everybody does, but I do not think that will be any problem for you." He forced a grin onto his face and nodded to the toned muscles that lined Lyncon's arms.

Lyncon gave a grateful smile. "Thank you. I will do whatever is needed of me. It will be good to spend some time outside."

Drel nodded and rose, rounding the table to shake Lyncon's hand. "Excellent. I will tell Franz to put you to

24

work as soon as 'e can." He crossed to the door and opened it for his guest. "Tonight you will stay with Momo but after that I will see to it that you are 'oused elsewhere. Momo may be patient but I know what too much time in 'er company is like."

The two men shared a laugh and Lyncon nodded his thanks before strolling away. Drel watched him from the door as he disappeared down the hill and back into the village. Even after he was lost from view the chief remained where he was, standing on the threshold, the wind tugging at his clothes and beard as he surveyed all below him, face creased with worry.

That evening Momo made the seemingly ever-steepening trek up the winding path to Drel's house. The wind had dropped and a splattering of stars shone overhead, a breathtaking masterpiece painted on the darkest of canvas. Momo ignored them; she had seen them all before. The air was cold and her bones hurt. She had no time for such trivial niceties.

Reaching the large stone house, she did not knock but instead strode straight in, slamming the door behind her before collapsing into the chair nearest the fire. She was thankful it was already roaring and warmed her brittle hands against the flames. The room was dark and empty but she could hear footsteps and voices coming from the rooms above where Drel and his family slept. The old woman sighed as she removed her scarf and shawl. She would not have said no to tea but there was none brewing. She gave a disapproving shake of her head and settled into the chair to wait.

Drel appeared moments later, descending the stairs with two mugs of steaming tea in hand. Momo took the mug offered with a nod, struggling to suppress a smile. Drel sank into the chair opposite her and sipped his drink with a serious expression. Knowing where his thoughts lay, she did not interrupt him, instead sipping her own drink and leaning closer to the fire.

"I suspect Lyncon is from Vilantis," Drel said suddenly from the gloom, firelight dancing across his face as he fixed Momo with a hard stare.

"And why would you say that?" asked the healer, not turning away from the flames. Behind them both, shadows danced to a merry tune across the walls and ceiling, flickering one way, then the other, performing a show known only to them.

"Firstly, the speed of 'is recovery is unnatural. I think it is elven magic."

"Or perhaps I am a better healer than you give me credit for!" Momo grinned at him but Drel ignored her.

"Secondly is the way 'e speaks; there is no accent. I 'ave 'eard tales that elves speak without accents; perhaps it is the same for men in Vilantis?"

Momo raised a questioning eyebrow. "It seems to me that you are basing your suspicions on a lot of tall tales and children's stories."

"But you do not disagree?"

The old woman shook her head slowly. "I don't know about accents but that man is not like us. I have travelled all over Petra in my many years on this earth and met none like him. The way he healed, it could only be sorcery and I suspect it is far beyond what any human mage can wield."

"Then what do we do?"

Momo sighed. She was used to giving guidance and secretly revelled in the way people stopped and listened whenever she spoke. As a woman in a man's world, it had taken her a great deal of time to earn the respect of all those around her. In the past she had been relentlessly shunned and overridden in the medical surgeries she had worked in. As a young woman she had fought to be heard, through both actions and words, and now her status and respect here were her reward for all those years of labour.

This, however, was different. Drel was no longer looking to her for advice or guidance; he was looking for answers, answers that could shape the entire fate of the village and all that lived there. Looking into his eyes, she could see the doubt that divided him, kept him up at night as he turned the dilemma over in his head. She shuddered despite the heat of the flames. Power was not always welcome. Outside, the wind suddenly howled, like a wolf calling to the moon.

"We do nothing," Momo said finally, her voice little more than a whisper.

Drel blinked twice in astonishment. "What?"

"We do nothing," the old woman repeated, with more than a little impatience in her voice.

"The man is an enemy of the entire country! The king would want 'im dead. We cannot just let 'im live 'ere with us!"

"Why not? Do you really think King Renthor will be visiting us anytime soon? Will he question everyone that lives here to see if they are his enemy?" Momo's tone was sharp, her face creasing into a familiar frown, but it softened a little when she caught Drel's exhausted expression. "He does not know where he came from, does not remember. If we say nothing of our suspicions then perhaps they will never be confirmed as true."

"But what if 'e remembers?"

"Then we remind him how we saved him, rescued him from the sea and gave him food and a warm bed. Healing the mind takes time, patience, and by then he may feel at home here, perhaps even have friends." Her voice trailed off as she let her words hang between them.

Drel looked at her with eyebrows raised. "What are you suggesting?"

"You have lived here all your life, Drel, everyone is your friend, so if I told you that you were from Vilantis, that you were the sworn enemy of our king and an imposter in these lands, would you kill me? Would you kill Franz or Ellen? Just because you were not born in the same country."

"No."

"Then why would it be any different for Lyncon?" Momo gave a sly smile but hid it behind her mug as she sipped her now cold tea.

Drel stared at her for several seconds before settling back into his chair to think, one hand absentmindedly stroking his beard. Momo watched him patiently, saying nothing. Eventually he sighed and downed his drink in one large mouthful, no doubt wishing it was something stronger.

"Very well. We shall do as you say, treat 'im as our own and pray that it is enough. The fate of the village may well depend on it."

28

"The chief 'as told me to put you to work. After a week lying around, I think it is about time." Franz gave an unfriendly grin and rolled his huge shoulders. "Let's see what a 'ard day's work does to you." He gave a brief booming laugh and shook his head. They were outside Franz's house, a small stone building near the well at the centre of the village. A woodshed leant against one wall, and Franz turned and disappeared inside.

Lyncon gave a low sigh, acutely aware of the dislike that emanated from the villager. Seacrest was a close-knit community made up of families that had known each other for generations. A lot of the villagers eyed Lyncon with suspicion whenever they saw him, their stares and hushed whispers following him until he was well out of sight. Outsiders, it seemed, were mostly treated with hostility and scorn. Ellen had assured him it was nothing personal, change was not welcome in Seacrest and always treated with disdain, but Lyncon sensed that Franz was different. Franz seemed to be taking Lyncon's presence here very personally and he feared what that might mean.

The fisherman returned from the shed carrying a huge axe, which he tossed at Lyncon without warning. He gritted his teeth in obvious annoyance when Lyncon caught it easily.

"Go to the woods past the cornfield, ask for Julian. There will be work for you there, 'e will know what to do with you." Without waiting for a reply he turned and strode away, muttering curses under his breath that he no doubt thought Lyncon couldn't hear.

Lyncon set off through the village at a leisurely pace. He had no idea where these woods were but, luckily for him, Seacrest was not a large village and he doubted it would take him long to spot them. Made of ten small stone residences and perhaps a dozen wooden ones, the village was arranged in a semi-circle, radiating out from the chief's larger dwelling that sat on the small hillock in the centre. To the east the village was flanked by the sand dunes that led to the beach and the dark blue sea beyond, while to the west were gentle rolling hills and green fields. The only road cut through the village from north to south, a wide mud track worn into the earth from years of passing carts and roving tradesmen, and ran along the coast between the cities of Corin and Reevan, though both were many miles away. Most days the road was empty and the few merchants that did pass through never stopped.

Despite its small size, Seacrest was almost always bustling with activity. Both men and women worked hard to provide for their families as children ran and played in the mud between the houses or amongst the sand dunes. Most residents were either fishermen or farmers but there was also a carpenter and a few hunters that would take their bows and scout the hillside or forests looking for game. It was a chaotic and noisy place, children and animals openly roaming the streets, but also oddly peaceful and at ease, the residents settled and content with their way of life.

After a brief meander between the buildings, Lyncon spotted a small patch of trees across one of the larger fields and, hopping over the gate, he followed the narrow path that had been beaten through the waist-high corn. The sun shone down on him with ever-growing heat as it rose towards its midday peak, while gulls wheeled lazily in the cloudless sky, calling to one another as they surveyed the world below them. Lyncon shouldered the axe and continued across the field, the rough tunic he had been given already beginning to stick to the sweat on his back.

Soon Lyncon heard voices along with the rhythmic beat of several axes striking wood. In front of him the corn stopped as the field ended in a steep bank about ten feet tall that flattened out into the small woodland beyond. After climbing the bank, Lyncon found three villagers working on the trees, all with their backs to him. A horse and cart stood nearby, the cart half loaded with logs from trees they had already felled. The horse, a tired-looking brown cob who had been happily chewing on the grass around a nearby stump, raised its head as he approached and began to stamp its hooves as it moved against its harness. Noticing the animal's agitation, the three men stopped and turned to meet the new arrival.

For a moment there was tense silence as the villagers took in their new help. They were young but all three were broad-shouldered and strong, bodies built from full bellies and hard work. All had the beginnings of beards emerging from their jaws. Their eyes were cool and unwelcoming, examining the stranger with a mix of distaste and curiosity.

Finally, one of the men stepped forwards, halting a cautious distance from Lyncon. "Franz send you?" It wasn't really a question but Lyncon nodded anyway. "What's your name, Outo?"

"Lyncon."

The villager nodded slowly as he rested his axe against the side of his leg and regarded Lyncon carefully. "I'm Julian. Those two are Artur and Bjorn." He gestured behind him to the two men still silently staring at him, axes gripped firmly in calloused hands. "You look strong enough. You felled trees before?"

"I… I don't think so, no."

Julian gave a puzzled expression but shook his head and continued. "OK. We'll put you on the little ones. Nothing to it really, a couple of swings at the base and they should be over pretty easy. Watch."

With a casual step, he strolled to the nearest tree and planted his feet. Pulling back his arms and twisting his body, he drove the axe into the trunk, sending bark and splinters falling to the floor. The trunk was barely half a foot thick and, after several hard strikes, the wood groaned and snapped, the tree tumbling onto the grass with a rustle of leaves and a soft thump.

Julian turned back to him with a wry smile. "See, easy. You can start over there." He pointed to a knot of smaller trees that stood at the edge of the woods, some fifty metres away, before turning back to his friends and resuming the boisterous conversation Lyncon had so rudely interrupted.

Silently, Lyncon moved to where he had been told, avoiding going too close to the cob, who was still neighing in his direction. Approaching the first tree, he adjusted his grip on the axe handle and placed his feet apart in a solid stance. Loosening his muscles, he pulled back his arms and swung the axe as hard as he could. The blade struck the tree and just kept going, powering straight through the trunk and out the other side with a satisfying crack. For a moment the tree was still, as if frozen in shock by the strength of the blow, but then it dropped and fell to the forest floor with a crash of snapping branches. Satisfied, Lyncon moved to the next one.

He had just felled his fourth tree when he paused, noting that the other men and their axes had fallen silent. Turning, he found all three villagers were looking at him with mouths hanging open, stunned.

"Did I do something wrong?" Lyncon asked when none of them spoke.

Slowly, Julian closed his mouth and walked over. Glancing at the trees he placed a firm hand on Lyncon's shoulder, face cracking into a huge grin that made him look several years younger. "Clearly I misjudged you, Outo. I think we are going to be very good friends. Are you thirsty? We 'ave a little wine. Let's sit and drink, get to know each other."

Two weeks later and the woods were cleared. The job had been done quicker than expected thanks to Lyncon's help and even Franz had seemed to show a glimmer of grudging respect for the young men's sudden efficiency. Over the course of their work, the three villagers had soon taken a liking to their new, hardworking friend. They were fascinated by his seemingly immense strength as well as his lost memories and mysterious past. All three had lived in Seacrest all their lives and to them the outside world was a huge and foreboding place.

Since that first day, the young men had taken to calling him Outo, which meant stranger in the old tongue, and would often laugh and joke about his memory and his lack of knowledge of village life. At first Lyncon didn't know how to take it, unsure if they were being cruel, but when one of them stood up for him against Franz he soon realised it was all in good faith and that they really did seem to like having him around. They were almost always joking together, their laughter carrying across the village, much to the disapproval of many of the elders.

One sunny afternoon, Lyncon and Julian had been tasked to help rebuild one of the walls that ringed a field on the edge of the village. After lugging stones up from the beach all morning, the pair had started at one end of the wall while Bjorn and Artur began at the other. With any luck, they planned to meet in the middle by nightfall.

It was a scorching day and the sun beat down from on high, the air hot and heavy. Julian had shed his top and was now working in shorts and boots alone, sweat trickling down his torso and arms. Lyncon remained covered for longer, conscious of the few scars still visible, but his shirt soon became plastered to his skin, wet to the touch, and he relented and tossed it aside.

After carefully placing a stone in the wall, Julian straightened up and retrieved his canteen. He unstopped it and took a deep gulp, drinking long. He watched Lyncon as he worked, his eyes tracing the zigzagging lines that covered his body. Aware of the other man's gaze, Lyncon placed his own rock and turned to face him.

"Do you remember any of them?" Julian asked quietly, still not looking away from the scars.

He glanced down at the pale ridges, glistening with sweat. "Luckily, no I don't."

Slowly, Julian reached forwards and traced a scar, a long straight slash that cut across Lyncon's ribs. "This was a sword or knife. It is too straight for anything else."

Flushed, Lyncon stepped away. "If you say so. As I said, I cannot recall."

34

"But don't you want to remember? Each of these scars tells a tale, a story of adventure in a far off land!" Julian's eyes were alight as he stared intently at Lyncon.

He shrugged. "Or perhaps I was just a very clumsy fisherman who hit his head and fell off his boat, washed up here." An image of the sea flashed through his mind, the dark waves turning him over and over. He shuddered and quickly pushed it away.

"You were no fisherman; you know that as well as I do. You were something different... something more." He turned to stare out across the fields towards the woods and distant hills beyond. A singular cloud passed overhead, throwing them into sudden shade. Lyncon was grateful and sighed in relief as he sat down on the grass. Julian seemed not to notice, eyes fixed on the horizon. After several minutes he spoke again. "Did you know that I 'ave never left the village? Not once in my whole life and I am almost twenty-five. At one time I thought this was all I needed: friends, family, food on the table. But now... now I'm not so sure." He trailed off.

Silently, Lyncon unstopped his own canteen and took a swig of the lukewarm water inside. He dried his mouth with the back of his hand before asking, "Is it because of me?"

"No... and yes." Julian finally turned to look at his friend. "What's it like out there, Outo? The rest of the world?"

"I don't know... my memories..." He trailed off when he saw the look of disappointment on Julian's face. With a sigh, he tried to think of what little he could recall. "It... it's big, bigger than you can ever imagine, full of people living so many different ways of life. It can be ugly but it can also be immensely beautiful. I… I remember visiting a place with buildings made of the purest white stone, their surface shining in the sunlight. I remember the way the light danced across the surface, filled with what seemed like joy. It was truly breathtaking."

Julian nodded, a smile touching his lips. "I think I want that, to see the world, the beauty it 'as to offer. I feel… suffocated 'ere. Small."

"Be thankful for what you have: a home, a family that loves you. Not all are as lucky as you."

Julian caught the tone of Lyncon's words and raised his hands apologetically. "I'm sorry. I meant nothing by it…"

Lyncon dismissed the apology with a wave of his hand. "It is fine. It is not wrong to want more from life, Julian, but it is unwise to be ungrateful for what one already has."

A smirk slowly formed on the villager's face. "Say, with words like that perhaps you were a poet in your past life?"

Lyncon grinned back. "Ha, perhaps. Fetch me a lute and I'll try playing you a tune but I suspect you may want to cover your ears."

Both men burst out laughing and remained that way for some time. By nightfall, the wall was still unfinished.

Now that he was fully recovered, Lyncon had moved out of Momo's house and into the small wooden house that Julian's family lived in. It was cramped but comfortable, and Julian's parents were very welcoming. While he was happy to leave the old woman, with her watchful eyes and short temper, it meant less time with Ellen and he found that he missed her dearly.

During the time he had been bed-bound, the young woman had been nothing but kind and gentle with him as she tended to his needs. They had chatted often and Ellen had been the first of the villagers to treat him like an equal, without suspicion or fear. While he had no doubt that it was Momo who had saved his life, it was Ellen that had truly made him feel better with every gentle, bubbly laugh or radiant smile. It was not until after he had moved that he realised how much he missed her company, and his constant work meant he saw her very little.

One sunny afternoon Ellen walked by the house carrying a large basket of washing while Lyncon was busy fixing a fence at the front of the small garden. He rose from his work as she approached, dropping his hammer onto the grass.

"Hello, stranger. It is good to see you." He smiled at her with genuine fondness, feeling a heat rise in his face.

Ellen, however, seemed flustered as her eyes darted around, not knowing where to look. "Erm… yes… good to… see you too," she mumbled.

Lyncon raised an eyebrow in confusion but then remembered that he was shirtless. While Ellen had, of course, seen his body when she had tended his wounds, it would no doubt start some village gossip for a young woman to be seen talking to a half-naked man, especially him. With a gasp of realisation, he spun and snatched up his shirt from the ground, pulling it on and clumsily attempting to do up the buttons, fumbling every one.

"Sorry," he muttered, the red in his cheeks not just from the heat of the day.

She shook her head. "It is fine. How are you?" Her eyes remained fixed on the floor, as if her shoes had become the most interesting thing around.

"Excellent, thank you. I have no pain at all and my scars are fading more and more each day."

"Yes, I saw."

"Er... yes. Sorry about that I..."

"Oh I wasn't complaining." She put down her basket and gently reached forwards to do up a button he had missed in his haste to cover up, the tips of her fingers just brushing his hot skin. She glanced up at him, catching his eye for just a moment as she gave him a shy smile, then she turned in a whirl of hair, picked up her basket and was gone, leaving Lyncon to stand open-mouthed at the gate.

The sound of slow clapping brought him back to his senses and he tore his eyes away from Ellen's retreating figure to find Julian watching him from the porch, a grin spread across his face.

"Careful. You stare any 'arder at 'er backside and your eyes will pop right out of your skull," he said with a laugh.

"Fuck you," retorted Lyncon but he was grinning too. He returned to his work but not until after one more longing glance in the young woman's direction.

Harris was the only villager who ever left Seacrest regularly to travel to another town, the only one who had contact with the outside world. Once a week he would load up his cart with grain and baskets of fresh fish and rumble his way out of the village, heading south on the road to Aberson. He would return that same evening with his cart empty of fish and instead laden with barrels of ale or salted meats along with sacks of brightly coloured vegetables from the south that the villagers could never grow themselves. He would stop his cart in the middle of the village and sort everything he had brought, distributing the goods to those that had given him goods to sell. Most villagers merely wished to sell what they had made to buy what they needed, few cared about coin or profit and they never asked Harris the prices he had bought or sold the goods at. Judging by the cut of his clothes and size of his house, he was as shrewd as any businessman and this system worked in his considerable favour. Once his work was done and the goods were sorted, he would park his cart beside his house and disappear inside, not to be seen again until his next run or if called upon for a council meeting.

It was as the merchant was returning from one of these weekly ventures that Lyncon was struck by an idea and that evening he strolled across the village to the merchant's house. Though he had never been before it was certainly hard to miss. Set apart from all the other buildings, the house was huge: two storeys made of polished grey stone bricks neatly cut and arranged in rows topped off with a tiled red roof. The windows were large and plentiful, the glass always clean. Through them, Lyncon could see lavish curtains made of thick green velvet. They were all drawn firmly shut.

Stepping up to the green timber door, Lyncon grasped the brass knocker that was shaped like a fish swimming in a circle, as if trying to eat its own tail. He gave two sharp knocks. Almost immediately the door swung open and a slight, middle-aged man appeared in the doorway. He was meticulously well groomed and dressed in a crisp white shirt and navy trousers. He smelt faintly of lemongrass.

"Can I help you?" he asked, pronouncing the words without a hint of an accent.

Lyncon, having been convinced Harris lived alone, was momentarily too shocked to answer. "Err... yes. I would like to speak to Harris."

The man eyed him carefully, his gaze seeming to linger on his exposed arms and the scars there. Then he nodded. "Wait here." Without waiting for a reply, he turned and disappeared inside the house, leaving Lyncon loitering awkwardly on the doorstep. After several minutes the man reappeared looking noticeably flustered.

Casting Lyncon a sudden glare, he spoke in a stiff tone. "He will see you now. Follow me."

Lyncon followed the man through a short, narrow hallway that then opened into a lavish living room decorated in rich shades of red and orange. Harris was waiting for them, lounging on one of three plush couches that surrounded a neat wooden table. He was wrapped in a soft white robe of fine silk and held a large glass of wine in one hand. On seeing Lyncon he gave a thin smile and gestured with his other hand for him to sit. The other man left them to it, slipping silently through another door Lyncon had not noticed.

"Wine?" the merchant asked, gesturing to a jug on the table before him.

"No, thank you."

Harris nodded, his jowls imitating him in double time, and took a long swig from his own drink. He eyed his visitor carefully over the lip of the glass as he drank.

"What is it I can do for you, Lyncon?" he asked after a moment's silence. His voice was businesslike, flat and to the point. His words were pronounced perfectly and Lyncon guessed that, like Momo, he had been educated outside of the village.

"I wish to accompany you when you next leave for Aberson; myself and Julian."

Harris considered the request as he swirled the wine around in circles in his cup. "I travel alone." The merchant's voice had hardened, though his expression remained fixed. "Why would you want to come with me?"

"Julian is my friend and he has been good to me while I have been here. I thought I should repay him and I know he wants to see more of the world. To leave the village, for a time at least, might be good for him and I thought you could help."

The merchant laughed suddenly, as if he had been nervous about what Lyncon might say. "A favour for a friend? Is that all? Here I thought…"

"You thought what?" Lyncon asked as the merchant trailed off into silence.

Harris waved a hand dismissively. "Nothing." He paused to sip his wine again. "As I said, I travel alone." He gave Lyncon a stare that stilled the protests he had been about to make. "However, you have piqued my curiosity. An outsider, an unknown entity in the village, in my home; I would certainly like to learn a little more about you." His eyes ran over Lyncon in a way that he did not appreciate. "You were a soldier, correct?"

Lyncon stiffened. "I don't know. My memory…"

"Ah yes, your memory loss, so very unfortunate." His eyes fell on Lyncon's scars. "Perhaps you were not a soldier but with all those scars you must have been good in a fight… or at least involved in a few. I am confident it would all come back to you. The body remembers even when the mind does not." He sipped his wine, never taking his eyes from his guest.

Lyncon raised an eyebrow, suddenly hesitant. "What do you want from me?"

Harris gave him an unpleasant smile. "Lyncon, I am a merchant, a peddler, and I can tell you that everything in this life is an exchange. Life and death, hot and cold, day and night; all are simply deals that have been struck, the world bartering one substance for another. Nothing is ever free." He paused, resting a hand on his expansive belly. "Our trade is simple. I take you and your little friend into town and in return you help me with a small problem of mine. Some… debt collecting that I need taking care of. Nothing a man like you can't handle."

Lyncon eyed his host warily. Despite the merchant's soft voice and easy smile, he got the feeling that Harris had not made his fortune from being a man of kindness and second chances. There was a glint in his eyes that he did not like. "What do you mean by debt collection?"

"Precisely that." He shrugged. "A man owes me money and is refusing to pay. I simply need you to persuade him to change his mind and give me what is owed."

"How exactly?"

"Any way you like. The means are not important to me, only the outcome." Harris grinned and leant forwards, carefully placing his empty glass on the table between them. His eyes gleamed in a way that made Lyncon's skin crawl. "So, do we have a deal?"

Chapter 3

There and Back Again

"Are we almost there?" asked Julian as his eyes roved over the forest on either side of them with obvious disinterest. Sitting beside him in the cart, Lyncon sighed quietly to himself. In the front, Harris was not so subtle.

"No, Julian, we are not, so please be so kind as to shut up!" The fat man shook his head and turned back to the horses as they pulled them steadily onwards.

Undeterred by the outburst, Julian continued with his questioning. "When will we reach Aberson? Will it be soon?" He paused as if struck by a sudden thought. "Does Aberson 'ave walls? Is it a castle? Does it…"

"Enough!" spat Harris, his cheeks an alarming shade of red as he turned to glare at the young villager. "No more questions! You will see it when we get there but, for now, we shall have silence. Understood?"

"Uh fine. Whatever you say." Julian sighed and slumped down further into the cart, one arm draped lazily on top of a crate while the other arm dangled over the side. Next to him Lyncon gave a wry smile and continued to stare at the back of his hand, carefully tracing the pattern of a scar that ran in a crooked line from his wrist to the base of his thumb.

Over the next hour they left the woods and began to wind their way steeply up the side of a hill, the road meandering back and forth beneath the clear blue sky. The wind had picked up and blew keenly across the hillside, chilling the air despite the heat of the day. They passed no one on the road except for two small children playing with a ball in front of a farm, a grizzled sheepdog keeping one beady eye on them as it lay in the shade of a wall.

As the horses finally drew them over the crest of the hill, the view opened up before them and there was Aberson, nestled in the valley below. The town was huge, a sprawling mass of wooden lodges and stone townhouses. Smoke billowed from a hundred chimneys in dark grey plumes like fingers stretching to the sky. Even from here Lyncon could hear the shouts of men and the cawing of gulls as both flocked to the settlement.

While the town had no walls or castle, it was granted some protection by its location. Tucked into a meander, the river offered a natural moat on three sides, the wide waterway glistening in the sun despite its muddy brown tinge. The docks were busy with boats of all sizes as they moved up and down the river on the mile stretch between the town and the open sea. A lone bridge carried the road further south, on to the city of Reevan many miles away.

"It's bigger than I ever imagined," muttered Julian, wide-eyed. "There are so many people."

Indeed the town was busy. Where before the road had been quiet, Lyncon could now spy at least ten wagons of various sizes moving towards the town, destined for the markets within. If he strained his eyes he could just about make out the minute shapes of people as they milled through the streets, browsing the stalls that cluttered the sidelines.

"Aberson is the only market town for miles," Harris informed them without looking back. "It's always busy but few people actually live here."

They joined the steady procession of carts destined for the town and trundled down the hill between wide fields of green. The road levelled out as they reached the floodplain and the sounds of the town began drifting to them more clearly on the wind, shouting and arguing punctuated by the occasional snatch of laughter or song. Oddly, Lyncon found himself a little nervous, sweat beginning to bead on his brow, but he kept his thoughts to himself. Beside him, Julian's head was on a swivel as he stared in fascination at everything around them, clearly trying to take in every detail of this whole new world.

"What?" the villager asked when he caught Lyncon smirking at him.

"You. If your jaw was any lower it would be scraping the road!" He burst out laughing while Julian thumped him in the arm.

"Don't you find it exciting?"

He shrugged, suddenly uneasy again though he was not sure why. "Not really. It feels... familiar but I don't know why." He glanced around. "I think I prefer the village."

"You've been here before?" Harris asked, suddenly twisting in his seat to eye Lyncon with curiosity.

"I… I don't know. I don't think so but I think I've been to some place similar. The noise, the smells… I don't know." He sighed and shook his head.

"Hmm, I see." The merchant muttered to himself as he turned back to the road.

Julian stood up and peered past Harris as the town's streets grew ever closer. "I can see lots of stalls, selling things. Is that what we will do?"

Harris gave a snort of contempt. "Never. I sell my goods privately. My deal is already arranged, no need to haggle like these amateurs." He eyed the other merchants with something close to disgust as they began to pass between the first stalls.

A sudden breeze blew directly into their faces and the three travellers were hit with an overpowering mix of odours, not all of them pleasant. Julian coughed and all three of them wrinkled their noses in disgust. "Oh, I didn't think it would smell… ah… like that." He sat down hard, covering his nose with his sleeve.

"The smell of human progress. You better get used to it," Harris remarked with a chuckle but he too had covered his nose, with a white handkerchief he had conjured from his pockets.

They moved through the town at a crawl. The main street was chaotic and cramped as wagons pushed through the bustling crowds busy perusing the many brightly decorated stalls. The air was filled with noise and the smells of a hundred different foods cooking at once. As they passed, Lyncon saw merchants selling books, swords, spices, clothing and musical instruments. One stall was even selling live animals, the merchant gesturing

46

to a pen of goats and several chickens locked in tiny cages as he shouted his prices to anyone who would listen. On multiple occasions they passed heated arguments between buyer and seller, always filled with angry shouts and the pointing of fingers. One argument broke out into a full-on brawl and Harris had to yank the cart to a halt to avoid running over the two men as they fought in the road, rolling in the dirt. After a string of expletives, Harris moved the wagon around them and they continued on. Lyncon rubbed his temple, a dull ache beginning to form behind his eyes.

After a long slog punctuated by frequent stops while Harris seemingly cursed everyone in the town, they turned off the road and through an open gateway into an empty courtyard. They were surrounded by tall stone buildings that blocked out the rest of the town and the sudden quiet was startling compared to the hubbub of the streets they had just passed through. A man sat on a stool outside the largest of the buildings, a lit pipe stuffed into the corner of his mouth. As they brought the cart to a halt and jumped down, he stood and opened a large sliding door that revealed a warehouse beyond, its depths hidden in the gloom.

Harris turned to the young men. "Wait here." Then he shuffled over to the man to greet him with a smile and a handshake.

As he waited, Lyncon rolled his shoulders and stretched his back; sitting in the cart for hours had done his body no favours. Julian was the same, stretching his legs as he winced at the sore muscles. His friend caught his gaze and grinned like a child, full of feverish excitement. Lyncon barely stifled a laugh.

As Harris talked, Julian moved forwards towards the horses, patting their necks. The beasts had pulled them all morning and yet barely looked to have broken a sweat as they lazily eyed the courtyard floor, searching for food. Lynçon approached them too and was raising his hand to pat the nearest animal when it suddenly neighed and began to buck, violently pulling on its harness in an attempt to flee as it eyed Lyncon with unforeseen terror, nostrils flaring. The panic of the first horse spooked the second and both animals began to frantically stamp their feet against the flagstone floor. In shock, he leapt back while Julian fought with the reins, desperately trying to calm the beasts.

"What the hell are you two doing?!" demanded Harris as he returned to the cart, grabbing the reins from Julian and whispering to the horses to calm them.

Julian raised his hands. "Nothing. Something spooked the 'orses. It was not our fault."

"Well stop standing about and get the cart unloaded! Put everything in the warehouse over there." He indicated the open door behind him where the man stood by watching them. When Lyncon moved to do as he had been told, Harris grabbed his arm. "Not you. You have another job to do. Remember?" His words were low and his gaze met Lyncon's, challenging him to disagree.

"Of course." He nodded and followed Harris as he pulled him out of Julian's earshot.

He bent forwards so his forehead was almost touching Lyncon's chest. He could smell a mix of perfume and sweat drifting from the large merchant. "Listen carefully. Derry over there works for the man who owes me money; a man named Clifford Uller. He will take you to Uller and then

48

I want you to get what I am owed." He reached into his robes and produced a dagger in a plain-looking sheath. "Take this but keep it hidden. They won't allow you a sword, so this is the best I can do."

Lyncon eyed the weapon with distaste but took it anyway and strapped it to his belt. He untucked his shirt; the fabric hung over the dagger and hid it from view. Though he did not own a weapon of his own, the feeling of it against his hip felt familiar and oddly comforting. Lyncon shivered at the thought of what that might mean.

"I don't know how this is going to go but do whatever you need to do to get my money. Try not to kill anyone if you can; murder raises too many questions. Just get the money and get out." Lyncon, shocked by the ease of which the merchant spoke of murder, was about to object when Derry strolled over, eyeing the two men suspiciously. Harris' gaze flicked once to Lyncon's belt before he turned and gave the workman his best smile. "Derry, this is Lyncon. He will accompany you to see your boss."

The man nodded slowly, pipe still shoved to the corner of his mouth, as his gaze flicked between the two of them. His face was old and weathered, the craggy skin broken by two bushy eyebrows that seemed to be constantly on the move. A sword hung at his belt. When he spoke it was in a slow drawl. "This way, then. He doesn't keep waiting."

"Lyncon, where are you going?" called Julian as his friend turned to go.

He gave him his best reassuring smile. "Harris has a job for me. I won't be long."

Julian grunted. "Long enough to miss all this 'eavy lifting, no doubt." He shook his head in disgust. "Typical!"

Lyncon grinned and shrugged before turning back to follow Derry.

Stepping out into the street, he was immediately hit by the madness of it all. Down on the ground, away from the height and safety of the cart, the street was chaos, a bustling throng of bodies that threatened to wash him away like a spring tide. People were everywhere, moving from stall to stall like locusts as they shouted about their wares or argued a sale. Lyncon waded through the crowds, getting jostled and pushed as he struggled to keep up with his sullen guide, who seemed to be able to predict the movements of those around him, sidestepping and dodging like a dancer. The overwhelming sense of confinement, the closeness of so many people, made fear trickle down Lyncon's back and he fought to control his breathing as his heart thundered in his chest. As he threw himself to one side to avoid a cart that rumbled past him, Lyncon prayed they did not have to go far.

Derry stopped at the door of a small stone building with an alleyway running down one side. The building was plain and ordinary, smaller than most and windowless, the thick stone punctuated only by a large door made of solid oak. The local turned to Lyncon and stared at him intently. He was a similar height to Lyncon with short black hair and wide shoulders. His expression was blank and the angle of his nose said he was no stranger to a brawl.

"Wait here," he ordered. Then he was gone, slipping through the door and disappearing inside, promptly shutting the way behind him. Lyncon was left standing on the busy street unsure what to expect next. He focused on calming himself. He was wholly aware of the weight of the knife on his belt and his hand strayed to touch the top of the hilt through his shirt. The weapon felt comfortable to wear and that made him shudder again. He snatched his hand away when the door sprung open and Derry beckoned him inside.

He was surprised to find himself in the gloom of another warehouse, though this one was much smaller and almost completely empty, nothing in it besides a few dusty wooden crates. At the back of the room stood three men, watching him approach. Torches on the walls cast a flickering light over their unfriendly expressions. Another man leant on a small door in the wall to Lyncon's left, which he judged led out into the alleyway he had seen as he arrived.

As Lyncon neared, one of the men stepped forwards. He was tall and slim with oily hair combed back above an intense, pointed face. Lyncon guessed this was Clifford Uller. His eyes examined Lyncon with open distaste as he picked at something in his teeth with a splinter of wood. He spat before speaking, throwing the pick into the dirt.

"So you're the one Harris sends. I can see why." His eyes roved over Lyncon's arms as he nodded to himself. "I am not surprised the fat fuck didn't come himself. He always was a coward."

"Just give me what you owe and I can leave." He tried very hard to keep his voice firm and level. He kept his face blank as he heard Derry bar the door behind him.

Clifford's face broke into a grin and he chuckled softly to himself. "What I owe? Ha, tell me, what exactly do I owe? Did Harris tell you the sum?"

Lyncon paused. His mind picked over what Harris had told him and he realised that the merchant had never told him the amount. Instead he had simply convinced him that Clifford must pay. A cold chill ran down his spine as he remembered that unreadable glint in the merchant's eyes.

Seeing his face, Clifford laughed, a horrible cackling sound. He turned to his men. "Looks like the village simpleton has finally caught up to the rest of us." He stepped back as his men advanced. "A shame it is too late to save him."

It was Derry that attacked first, swinging a right hook from behind, aimed at Lyncon's head. He heard the fist travelling long before it connected and reacted instinctively. He crouched, letting the punch sail over him, and pivoted on the balls of his feet before striking Derry with a left hook just below the ribs that drove the air out of his lungs and sent him staggering back into some of the crates.

Lyncon had no time to celebrate as he was caught by a jab to the cheek as he turned to face the other men. While he stumbled backwards, his attacker pressed the advantage, stepping closer to land more strikes, but he was too eager and his next shot was obvious. Lyncon caught his arm, pulled the man even closer and then drove his knee up into the man's groin. The attacker gave a grunt of pain as his eyes bulged in their sockets. Lyncon swung and struck him hard on the chin with a right hook that sent him collapsing to the floor in a heap.

Lyncon turned at the sound of footsteps to see one of the men, the one with a long scar down his face and who had been guarding the door when he arrived, shoulder barge him in the chest. He was driven backwards into the wall, his head striking the cold stone, and for a moment his vision was speckled with specks of bright light. His headache flared inside his skull and he felt an odd warmth flowing through his veins. Gritting his teeth, he ignored it and returned his focus back to his attackers.

Scar-face straightened up and threw a punch that connected hard, crashing into the side of Lyncon's skull. Tasting blood, Lyncon brought his head back around and spat, sending a plume of crimson spittle into his foe's face. With the man momentarily dazed, Lyncon seized his chance. Knocking away the hand pinning him to the wall, he struck with a vicious uppercut that almost lifted Scar-face off his feet. With a push, Lyncon sent the man stumbling backwards to collide with Derry, who had just regained his feet.

The final foe was a young man who seemed nervous. His movements were jerky and unnatural and when he threw a punch it was half-hearted, almost timid. Lyncon blocked it easily and struck a quick right jab to the young man's throat. He collapsed clutching his neck as he gasped for air.

Lyncon had just begun to think the fight was over when Derry rose and turned to face him. The man's expression was still one of boredom but now his eyes were alive and watchful, darting backwards and forwards. After a pause to catch their breath the two men stepped closer.

The thug swung his right hand, which Lyncon blocked, but too late he realised it had been a trick. As soon as Lyncon committed to the block, Derry shifted and unleashed a left jab that caught him on the jaw. Still moving, he followed the punch with an uppercut to Lyncon's stomach, the blow driving the air out of his lungs. Wildly, he struck out and hit his attacker behind the ear, only a glancing strike but enough to daze him a little and force him to step away.

Seizing the moment of respite, Lyncon crouched and snatched up a plank of wood that had broken loose from one of the crates. Gripping it tightly, he swung the makeshift weapon as hard as he could and the wood connected with Derry's left knee with a sickening crunch. The man let out a piercing scream as he collapsed, clutching his knee. A second strike to the temple silenced him.

Panting, Lyncon turned to Clifford Uller, who had pressed himself up against the wall as if hoping to merge into it. His eyes were wide with fear. As Lyncon approached, he suddenly lunged for the side door, but Lyncon caught him by the collar and threw him back against the wall. Whimpering, he slid to the floor.

"Stop! Please stop!" he muttered as he rummaged through his pockets and retrieved several gold coins, which he threw at Lyncon's feet. Oddly he recognised them as golden grouse, the most valuable coin in Petra, though he had never seen one in Seacrest. "Take them! I don't care! Take them all!"

Lyncon stared down at the grovelling coward and felt sudden rage build inside him. His head was pounding harder than ever and his entire body felt hot, as if lit from the inside by a blazing fire. Clifford could have given him the money and walked away. Instead he had tried to kill him, end his life for the sake of the coins he was now desperate to get rid of to save his own skin. He clenched his jaw as he glared down at the man beneath him.

"Get up." His voice was soft but left no room for debate. When Clifford did not move, he stepped closer. "I said get up!"

Reluctantly, the merchant did as he was told, sliding up the wall, his eyes still glued to the floor. "Take the money. Please…"

Lyncon looked at him with open disgust. "How many times have you done this before? How many men have you ordered killed just to line your own pockets?" His heart was racing as he spoke and his blood burnt. There was a deep throbbing in his temple that seemed to vibrate through his entire skull. His hands were shaking.

"Please… don't…" Uller's words were cut off as his cheek began to spill blood from the three ragged cuts that had opened there. His eyes bulged in shock and terror as his hands shot up to clutch at the wounds. His gaze drifted to Lyncon's hand just in time to see it smash into his nose, connecting with a resounding crack and knocking his head back against the wall. With a thud, Uller slid to the floor, unconscious. Lyncon stood above, frozen in shock as blood dripped from three of his fingers. Inside him the fire dimmed and went out, his heart slowing to its normal beat.

After several long moments Lyncon finally released the breath he had not known he had been holding and looked down at his hand. His fingers were slick with blood but he had no clue as to how they could have sliced open the merchant's face. Crouching, he examined the wounds, three jagged lines that ran through the flesh at equal distances apart. He froze with sudden recollection as he stared at the wounds. Slowly, he reached to pull his shirt up at his left hip. Beneath were three scars, the lines identical in size and spacing to those in Clifford's flesh. He recoiled as his breathing quickened and his heart began to race once more. Quickly he gathered up the coins and fled the warehouse, not once looking back.

As Lyncon walked back into the courtyard, he registered the look of surprise that flashed across Harris' features and had to stifle a smile. Instead he ignored the merchant entirely and heaved the large sack he was carrying onto the cart. Julian, who had been shutting the warehouse doors, stopped to watch.

"Where have you been?" asked the fat merchant as he strode over.

Lyncon shrugged without turning. "Around."

"Did you do your job?"

"What job?" he asked, feigning ignorance as he finally turned and met Harris' gaze. Both men were aware of Julian watching them intently.

The merchant's face had turned an ugly shade of purple as he seethed in anger. "Don't play games with me! Where is my money?"

"Oh yes of course, the money. Here you are." After fishing them out of his pocket, Lyncon dropped three silver stags and eight bronze boar coins into the merchant's greedy hand.

Harris' eyes bulged. "Where are the rest?"

"The rest? You never told me how much I was collecting, so I presumed that was all of it." The merchant's face grew redder still and he was about to protest when Lyncon tossed the dagger at him. Luckily for Harris it was still in its sheath. He fumbled the catch and dropped the weapon at his feet. "You can have that back too; I didn't need it." He turned back to the cart and produced another dagger from the sack he had brought with him. "Besides, I have my own."

Shaking his head, Harris withdrew to the warehouse to lock the doors while Julian walked back to the cart and climbed up next to Lyncon. "What was that all about?" he asked, eyeing his friend suspiciously. "You 'ave been gone a long time."

"Harris needed me to collect a debt for him, that's all. I did as was asked." He shrugged.

"Then why do you look like you 'ave been in a fight?"

"We had a... disagreement but soon straightened it out."

Julian stared at him for a moment, as if searching for answers in his face. After a while he just shook his head and sighed. "Well you left me to lift all the 'eavy stuff. You can unload it on your own when we get back!" he grumbled as he rolled his stiff shoulders.

"Ha, I suppose I owe you that much."

Behind them Harris climbed up onto the front of the cart with a huff and urged the horses into action. Once again they trundled back out into the streets. As they passed one stall, a strong aroma of spice wafted over them and Lyncon spied Julian licking his lips. Reaching over, he grabbed the sack he had brought and pulled it towards him. He rummaged around and eventually pulled out a small jar; he tossed it to his friend.

"Here, try one of those."

"What are they?" Julian eyed the contents with a mix of curiosity and suspicion.

"Spiced crickets. I picked them up from a stall on my way back." He laughed when he saw his friend's expression. "Don't pull a face. I tried some; they're delicious." He took the jar back and unscrewed it before popping one of the bugs into his mouth and grinning.

Julian took the jar and slowly removed another cricket. They were whole and coated in a bright red powder that stuck to his fingers. The smell of spice was overpowering.

"Be careful. They are hot."

After a moment Julian shrugged and popped the cricket into his mouth before chewing furiously as it crunched between his teeth. Almost instantly his cheeks turned crimson and his eyes bulged. Leaning over the side of the cart, he spat the cricket out into the street, panting like an overweight farm dog in summer sun, while Lyncon watched on, howling with laughter.

Lyncon stretched and yawned, his eyelids as heavy as boulders. Beside him Julian was already dozing, his chest rising and falling, with an occasional snore escaping his lips. Harris sat stock still and silent, focused on the horses and the road ahead. Around them trees pressed in on both sides, casting long shadows as the sun slowly drowned in the horizon.

The attack happened suddenly and without warning. From the bowels of a nearby tree a dark shape sprang forwards, huge claws lunging towards the horses. The beast caught the nearest horse on its back leg and clamped its pincers into the flesh. Panicked, the animal began to buck and kick as it neighed in fright and Harris had to fight with the reins as the cart swerved from side to side. Both passengers were awake instantly.

The creature was on the opposite side to Lyncon and as he turned he could see only a singular claw, several feet long, swipe up through the air and crash into the side of the cart. The force of the blow tipped the cart sideways, up onto one wheel. Lyncon held on with all his strength as it tipped alarmingly and some of the barrels and sacks tumbled past him to land in the road with a thud. Harris too went tumbling, losing the reins as he fell to the dirt. Then the momentum faded and the cart began to right itself again, falling back onto two wheels with a bone-shaking crash that sent several more barrels spilling over the side. With a cry of alarm, Julian went with them.

At the sound of Julian's cry the creature whipped around and released the horse, now aiming instead for Julian as he lay winded in the dirt. As the creature neared, it raised its claws and caught hold of his leg. The villager cried out in pain as he tried, unsuccessfully, to twist away. Sensing what was about to happen, Lyncon drew his dagger and threw himself from the wagon, landing hard on top of the creature's dome-shaped body. The impact caused the beast to hiss in pain as its legs buckled and it sank to the floor, releasing Julian in the process.

Still on the beast's back, Lyncon scrambled for a handhold. The creature was shaped like a huge crab, a large domed shell with four spindly legs and those two huge pincers protruding from the sides. The top of the shell was covered with moss and dirt, clearly the monster's camouflage of choice. Instinctively, Lyncon drove the dagger down hard at the beast's body. With a piercing screech the blade slid across the shell before it caught in a ridge and snapped clean in two. Silently, Lyncon cursed the merchant who had sold him the weapon.

The crab was enraged by the attack and began to shake violently as it regained its footing, desperate to throw Lyncon off. Discarding the useless dagger, he clung on as best he could but the shell was too smooth, the moss breaking away in his hands, and he slid from the creature's back into the grass at the side of the road. The beast rounded on him at once, claws raised to strike a deadly blow, but as it struck Lyncon rolled out of reach, tumbling further from the road. The crab followed, scuttling across the grass after him. It lunged with one of its claws, aiming for his neck. Raising both his hands, Lyncon caught the claw before it could crush his windpipe and focused all his strength to hold it at bay just above his skin. The beast hissed in anger and began beating at him with its other claw, striking hard against his ribs until he felt something crack. As he gasped in pain, his grip faltered and the claw clamped mercilessly around his throat.

Choking, Lyncon clung to the claw as he tried desperately to force it back open. The smooth sides were difficult to grip and as they pushed down harder against his windpipe he felt his vision begin to blur as his lungs screamed for air. Looking up, he saw the creature's beady red eyes peering out at him from within its shell. He lashed out with hands and feet but the blows did nothing. The crab simply hissed at him and continued to squeeze.

As his mind began to reel from lack of air, Lyncon felt a warmth take hold of his body, the same warmth that had shot through him in the warehouse when he had faced Clifford. It filled his body, pulsing through every muscle fibre, reaching every inch of his being. Gritting his teeth, he clutched the claw again and began to force it apart. At first it didn't budge and continued to choke him but then, slowly, it began to inch open. Lyncon felt his strength growing and he pressed on, dragging the claw apart as the crab began to beat at him in a desperate panic. He ignored it, instead focusing fully on the claw. He prized it off his neck and kept going, pulling until finally the claw snapped and shattered into two pieces in his hands. The crab gave a shriek of pain as it recoiled, its injured arm dripping blood across Lyncon and the grass around them. Discarding one half of the claw, he turned the other half in his hand and thrust it, point first, into the creature's eye. The whole beast shuddered as it flailed around in a feeble attempt to get away. Then it toppled over and was still.

Exhausted, Lyncon dropped the claw and pushed himself up onto his knees. He was coated in blood, thick black liquid that looked like ink and gave off a sharp, almost salty smell. He was panting, his grateful lungs working like billows as they greedily took in air. A sharp pain in his side suggested he may have broken at least one rib. The warmth that had engulfed his body began to fade, the lightning that had crackled through his every nerve blinking to nothing. Slowly, he got to his feet and limped back to the cart.

Julian was lying with his back against the wheel. He had a cut on his head from falling from the wagon and was rubbing his leg where the creature had grabbed it. His eyes were wide with shock and he was muttering to himself, though Lyncon could not tell what he was saying.

He crouched down beside his friend; his ribs giving off a sharp stab of complaint. "Are you alright?"

"You... you killed it?" he mumbled, mouth barely moving as he stared at the creature's corpse.

"Yes, it's dead."

"Thank you," Julian whispered, turning to look at him. "You... saved me. It was on me and... it was going to... to kill me." Without another word, he suddenly hugged Lyncon hard, gripping him almost as tightly as the monster had. Despite the searing pain the embrace caused in his ribs, Lyncon didn't protest.

Chapter 4

The Feast

"A rootcrab? On the road? Impossible!" proclaimed Franz as he towered beside Drel's chair in the dining room.

"It was definitely a rootcrab. Saw it with my own eyes," Harris confirmed from his own seat. Behind him, Lyncon and Julian stood silent.

"Saw it, yes, but it seems you did not do much to 'elp." Drel raised an eyebrow as he sat at the head of the table, studying Harris with an unfriendly gaze.

The fat man's cheeks turned an ugly shade of purple as he stammered his excuses. "I... I had to get the horses under control. It was... all so fast, I panicked..."

"Enough! It does not matter." Drel shook his head as if angry at himself. "You are all safe and that is what is important." He turned to look at Lyncon. "It seems that is mostly thanks to you."

Lyncon bowed awkwardly. "Thank you but no thanks is needed. I simply did what anyone would do to save their friend."

Drel studied him in silence for a second before nodding slowly and rising from his chair. "A noble sentiment. Come."

Lyncon stepped forwards. He did not expect the embrace he received from the chief, strong and friendly but above all accepting. When Drel broke away he placed a hand on each of Lyncon's shoulders and smiled at him.

"I will admit that when we found you I 'ad my doubts about what we should do. We do not like outsiders and most often they bring pain or unrest... but you, you 'ave been different. I am glad you are 'ere and would like you to stay. Seacrest is your 'ome now, if you want it."

He smiled at Lyncon's stunned expression. Harris and Julian both looked shocked, while Franz seemed to have gripped the back of the chair a little tighter with each word spoken.

"Thank you, sir. I would like that a lot," he replied in a quivering tone, his smile stretched as wide as it would go.

"Excellent." He removed his hands from Lyncon's shoulders and spread his arms. "To celebrate we shall 'old a feast in your 'onour. Tomorrow evening we will dine and drink to welcome you to our family and thank you for your bravery." He turned back to the table and retook his seat. "Now, forgive me but there is much to prepare. Go rest, you 'ave earned it."

The three men made to leave but as they reached the door Drel called to them. "Not you, 'Arris. We need to talk."

The merchant's shoulders sagged but he turned and waddled slowly back to the table. Julian and Lyncon made a speedy exit, neither wanting to hear what would be said next.

The two friends strode down the hill into the village. As he walked, Lyncon felt eyes crawl over his skin, stares coming from every direction as they passed between the houses.

"Everyone is staring. Why are they staring?" Lyncon asked, feeling more than a little uncomfortable as they made their way down the street to Julian's house.

"I thought they always stared at you?" Julian countered.

"This is more than usual."

"Perhaps it's that 'ideous wart on your chin?"

Lyncon's hand got halfway to his face before he stopped himself. It was too late and Julian was already laughing.

"Fuck you!" he whispered, trying to suppress his own grin.

"You are too easy," the villager muttered as he wiped the tears from his eyes with the back of his hand. With a deep breath he grew serious again. "They stare because they know what you did. News travels fast in this village. You are a 'ero now." He clapped his friend on the back. "I bet even Ellen will know. Can't 'arm your chances."

"Really?" He paused, suddenly a little lost for words.

Julian grinned. "Of course! But we will 'ave to get you looking good for the feast. I will see if I can find you some of my old things."

As they approached the house, the door flew open and Julian's parents hurried out. His mother rushed to her son and smothered him in her embrace, tears already running down her cheeks and onto his shoulders as she leant into him. Her husband stood a few feet away, watching with a loving expression. Julian froze in shock for a second, standing awkwardly in his mother's arms, but then softened and gently hugged her back.

65

"It's OK, I am safe, Mother," he whispered into her hair. She nodded but continued to weep as she clung to her son.

"We 'eard what you did for Julian." The old man had shuffled to Lyncon's side and stared up at him with shining eyes. "Thank you for saving our son." He reached out and took Lyncon's hand, squeezing it tightly with his thin fingers.

Lyncon smiled back at him. "It was nothing. He would have done the same for me." Over his mother's head, Julian gave him a sceptical look and Lyncon had to fight back a smile.

Julian's father nodded. "We are glad you are both 'ome now. Come inside. Dinner is almost ready." He turned and ushered his son and weeping wife into the house. Lyncon followed, beaming; filled with an unfamiliar warmth that he thought might just be pride.

"I really don't think these fit," Lyncon mumbled as he pulled at the crotch of the slim black trousers Julian had given him to wear. "They're very… restricting."

Julian rolled his eyes. "Don't flatter yourself. I've seen you washing in the surf and it is nothing to go 'ollering about."

"That's not fair! The water is freezing!"

Julian laughed as he turned his attention back to buttoning up the elaborate navy shirt he had finally settled on. The other options lay in an untidy pile at his feet. "A poor excuse, Outo."

With a sigh, Lyncon once again turned to examine his reflection in the small mirror they had borrowed from Julian's mother. Julian had given him the trousers along

66

with a thin shirt of fine cotton dyed a pale sky blue that ended in small cuffs of subtle white lace, woven to resemble clouds. The clothes were thin and light but also a little itchy and Lyncon had to keep pulling on the neck of the shirt as it slowly cut off his air flow. He had tried to keep the top button undone but Julian insisted it was against tradition and Lyncon had relented. Any traditions that made a man feel deliberately uncomfortable should be abolished, in his opinion, but he kept that firmly to himself. Like most of the villagers, Julian and his family honoured tradition above almost all else and took it very seriously.

Shaking his head, Lyncon sat down slowly on the bed, conscious of the way his thighs strained against the seams of the trousers, and began to pull on his boots. They were simple, made of thin brown leather that was aged but not shabby, and he was glad that these felt at least a little familiar.

Seeing his friend's dismay, Julian gave up with his shirt and walked over. "You look good." He nudged Lyncon with his elbow and winked. "You look like a man even Ellen could love."

Lyncon raised an eyebrow at him. "If I didn't know better I would say you were jealous."

"Of Ellen's affections? No, no. We 'ave never quite seen eye to eye." He paused, his smile slipping just a fraction. "But perhaps you are right, perhaps I am jealous of you, for other things. Is that so bad?"

He frowned. "Why would you be jealous of me?"

"You are a 'ero. The man who saved his useless friend's life. Everyone loves you now; they respect you. I am just the boy who fell in the dirt."

Lyncon stood and met Julian's gaze with a steady one of his own. "Julian, I did not want to be a hero. I did what I did to save you, to save my friend. All this, the feast, the attention, I don't want any of it." He gave his friend a mischievous smile. "If it helps, I can tell the ladies of how you risked your life to distract the beast and save the cart?"

Julian was silent for a moment but then laughed. "That would be most kind. I am sure it would be of great 'elp." He turned to the mirror, examining his reflection as he took a deep breath. His next words were little more than a whisper. "I... I 'ave never done... it before. With a woman."

Lyncon slapped him on the back. "Well consider yourself lucky, at least you know for certain. I can't even remember."

Julian's laughter echoed around the house and tears began to form in his eyes. "Can't remember? Really? You must not 'ave been very good!"

They had planned to walk to the feast together, just the two of them, but were quickly joined by Artur and Bjorn, who showered them with questions about all they had missed. Both men were dressed as extravagantly as they were and seemed just as uncomfortable in the frills and lace. The four friends talked endlessly as they strolled towards the feast, all of them battling unruly collars or ill-fitting waistlines as they went.

It was a pleasant evening and the air was warm from the blazing sun that had long since hidden behind the horizon. Above, a thousand stars twinkled in a patchwork of light against the growing black. Beyond the dunes the sea rolled gently against the sand, nature's ceaseless lullaby.

Since none of the buildings in the village could hold everyone, two long rows of wooden tables had been arranged on the square of grass that sat in front of Drel's house. Torches and candles had been lit and shadows danced amongst the women as they moved around setting the tables with plates and mugs. The benches were already half full of eager villagers, all dressed in colourful, mismatching garb, laughing and joking as they helped themselves to drink.

The four friends made for the nearest space but a shout stopped them in their tracks before they could sit down. Harris strolled over to them dressed in a crimson shirt tastefully decorated in golden lace. He seemed to Lyncon like he was the only one in the whole village who looked comfortable in his clothes.

"Lyncon, Julian. You two are to sit at the end of the table. Next to Drel." He smiled without a hint of warmth. "It is, after all, a feast in your honour."

Bidding farewell to their friends, they followed Harris to their assigned places, the two seats closest to the chief's large wooden chair that stood empty at the head of the table.

"Enjoy the feast," Harris muttered as he turned to leave.

"You're not staying?" Julian asked as they sat down.

"I will join later." He waved a hand. "Someone has to oversee all of this and it will most certainly not be Franz." With that he strolled away up the rise to the chief's hut.

"Ignore him. He acts as if it is all such hard work but secretly he relishes it."

The woman that had spoken sat opposite them; on what would be the chief's immediate right. She eyed them both steadily from beneath neat grey hair that was twisted into an elegant bun. Though clearly old she sat with dignity and an easy authority, her wrinkled face kind but firm. She was dressed in an elegant green gown with a modest necklace of sparkling gold around her neck. The hands that gripped her wine cup were thin but sure, confident in their movements.

"You must be Lyncon?" she asked with a warm smile. "I have heard a great deal about you." She turned her attention to Julian who was busy assessing the various jugs set on the table between them. "There is wine or ale, take your pick. I would recommend the wine but I know you boys love the ale." She laughed, a light, forced sound.

Julian licked his lips. "Ale for me. What about you, Lyncon?" He grabbed the nearest jug and poured himself a generous cupful.

"I... I suppose if Lady..." He looked at the woman across from him, who was still smiling.

"Karis."

"If Lady Karis recommends the wine then I had better start there."

Julian gave his friend a funny look but poured the wine anyway. "Suit yourself," he muttered before downing almost all his ale in one mouthful. Lyncon decided to just sip his own drink. The liquid was sickly sweet at first but then became suddenly bitter as it disappeared down his throat, causing him to purse his lips. However, it tasted better on the second sip and even better on the third.

Karis smirked at him as she watched him drink. "You like it?"

70

"I think so," he said, smiling back at her over his cup.

"Excellent. Drel will be pleased."

They were interrupted by the arrival of Momo and Ellen. The old healer walked over slowly, leaning heavily on a gnarled stick Lyncon had not seen before. She was dressed in her usual grey cotton but looked to have tidied her hair a little and had a dark blue shawl draped over her bony shoulders. When she reached the table, she seated herself carefully beside Karis, sighing with relief when she finally sat down. Without a word of greeting to anyone, she poured herself a cup of wine and downed it in one, smacking her lips as she slammed the cup down. Then she raised her eyes to study her three companions, ignoring Ellen as she sat beside her, her gaze glued to the floor.

"Good wine. Not quite as good as brandy but it will do." She paused, her beady eyes flicking from one face to the next. "I heard the tale of your run-in with the rootcrab, very well done." She nodded to Lyncon. "I also hear Drel has offered you a place here, to stay permanently."

Lyncon felt himself blush a little and looked down at his drink as he replied. "Yes, that is right."

After a long pause the old woman chuckled. "Very good. Seems the old man is growing soft." The healer turned her attention to the empty chair at the end of the table. "Speaking of which, Karis, where is your son? I have not come to sit here with my teeth chattering while he fiddles with his breeches."

Karis smiled pleasantly. "He will not be long. When I left him he was just checking the food was still on schedule."

"It better be. I'm famished," blurted Julian, before realising who he had spoken to and blushing deep red.

Momo gave him a wry smile as she poured herself another cup of wine before passing the jug to Ellen. The girl poured her own drink in silence.

Around them more and more villagers were joining the tables while those already seated glanced towards Drel's hut, eager for the food. Children ran around freely, chasing each other between the crowds.

Drel appeared in the doorway to his house and strode confidently down the hill. He wore a loose black shirt with silver cuffs and buttons. Across his shoulders was strewn a deep purple cape that fell to just below his hips. His hair and beard had been combed and trimmed and he gave an almost regal impression as he moved towards them. When he reached his chair, he pulled it back but did not sit. Instead he stood in front of it and surveyed them all as quiet descended on the crowd.

"Welcome, my friends. It 'as been a long time since we last 'eld a feast like this. Too long. These past years we 'ave retreated from the world, from the war. There 'as been little to celebrate, so little to be thankful for. We 'ave become suspicious and mean when once we were welcoming. We forgot the old ways, of kindness and friendship, even towards strangers. It took Lyncon 'ere to show us that." He smiled down at him. "This young man, a stranger to us, risked 'is life to save one of our own. Tonight, we 'onour 'im and welcome Lyncon into our village." He filled a cup before raising it in a toast. "To Lyncon!" All around him the villagers echoed his cry while Lyncon sat awkwardly in silence. Julian grinned at him and punched him on the arm. Even Ellen chanced a look but quickly averted her eyes, blushing, as he smiled back at her.

72

His cup empty, Drel set it down with a thud. "Let's eat!" he roared and the crowd burst into cheers, none louder than Julian.

As the cheering and laughing continued, a line of women began to stream from Drel's hut, each carrying a large tray or steaming bowl. Immediately Lyncon was overwhelmed by the bombardment of different scents that hit him, the rich aroma of roasted pork and the salty tang of fresh fish and prawns. As the plates were set down, he had to concentrate to stop himself dribbling and his stomach growled in eager anticipation, making Julian howl with laughter while Lyncon covered his blushes.

With the tables now full, the women took their seats and everyone began to eat, piling plates high with all manner of culinary delights. The night air was quickly full of the sounds of clinking cutlery and the slurping of wine as the guests gorged themselves in simple bliss.

After all were finished, the women cleared away the plates and dessert was served, a fine collection of freshly baked cakes and pastries that smelt of syrup and sugar. More wine and ale was also brought out to replace the many jugs that already stood empty.

While Lyncon, not possessing much of a sweet tooth and already feeling very full, picked absentmindedly at a small bowl of grapes, Julian had piled his plate high with pastries and cakes and was now happily munching through them, crumbs spraying from his mouth with every bite.

"Are you not eating these?" the villager asked in between mouthfuls, indicating a small plate of neat lemon tarts. "They are delicious."

73

"I can tell," Lyncon replied with a grin. "I am too full to eat another mouthful but I have a feeling someone will eat them." Julian grinned as he plucked one from the plate and popped it into his mouth, spilling crumbs all down his shirt. Ellen gave a brief laugh at the sight before blushing hard and averting her gaze. Drel watched the exchange from behind his cup, grinning.

"More wine, Lyncon?" Karis asked, raising the jug to pour for herself.

"Thank you." Once his mug had been refilled he raised it in a toast and took a long, deep drink. This was his third or maybe fourth cup and the liquid was becoming more and more agreeable with every mouthful. He could already feel a strange warmth in his fingers and toes, while his head felt light and a little fuzzy.

"Was the food to your liking?" Drel asked him in between bites of an apple he was slicing with a small knife.

"Yes, thank you. It was all delicious." Behind him Julian nodded his agreement, sending more crumbs tumbling onto the table.

"Very good. It 'as been a long time since we 'ave feasted like this."

"It shows," commented Momo as she threw down her spoon, the tart she had chosen only half eaten. She eyed Julian in open disgust before turning to the chief. "The pork was overcooked."

"Come now, Momo, there is no need to be so cruel. The chefs did an excellent job."

"Not with the pork!" The old woman stared at each of them in turn, daring anyone to disagree. Finally she nodded. "But it is good to see everyone happy for a change, especially in these dark times."

Drel stiffened at the comment and fixed the healer with a fierce look. "Let us not talk of such dreadful things. Tonight is for celebration. For thanks."

"Yes, to thank Lyncon here for saving this one's hide." She indicated Julian with a dismissive wave of her hand before she turned her eyes to Lyncon. "Tell me, how did you kill a rootcrab? I saw one once and they are fearsome creatures. It must have taken some skill to kill it."

Lyncon suddenly felt very uncomfortable under the old woman's gaze. He took a long sip of wine before he answered. "I guess it was more luck than skill. It all happened so fast. I didn't have time to think."

"Modesty. I am sure there was some skill involved. I don't think anyone else here could do what you did and even that giant oaf Franz would struggle to match a rootcrab's strength. Yet you did." She raised her eyebrows. "You must have been some soldier before all this. Am I right?"

"Momo!" barked Drel, scowling.

"Would you like some more cakes?" Ellen asked, desperate to distract the old woman.

The healer scowled at her and shook her head. "No I would not! Do not treat me like some senile old fool!" She sighed suddenly as her shoulders drooped and she seemed to sink into her seat. "But I am tired. It is time to go. Lyncon, would you escort myself and Ellen back to my hut? I would feel better with a strong man watching over us."

His eyes widened in shock and he quickly glanced at Ellen, who avoided his gaze. "Er... of course. It would be my pleasure."

The three of them rose from the benches and walked slowly away, Momo leaning on her stick with one hand while Ellen held her other. Glancing back, Lyncon spotted Drel and his mother sharing whispered words, heads pressed together. Julian was still eating but gave him a mischievous wink and a thumbs up.

When they finally reached the hut, Momo climbed the wooden steps by herself and turned to face them. "Thank you both, I will be fine from here." Her eyes met Lyncon's. "Enjoy your feast but afterwards, think on this. The world is at war. You may not have a side now and may not want one but once, as with every soldier, you pledged your allegiance to someone. There will be a time, in the future, where you will have to choose again. I pray you choose well." With that she turned and disappeared inside, slamming the door behind her. Lyncon stared after her, open-mouthed, her words weighing heavily on his mind.

For a moment the pair stood in awkward silence broken only by the sounds of the revelry that drifted from the feast.

"I am… sorry about her. She can get very fierce when she drinks." Ellen's eyes fluttered briefly up to his from beneath her curly blonde locks.

Lyncon smiled. "It's OK. Momo is Momo. She does not need drink to be fierce and nor does she ever sugarcoat her words." They both laughed as they turned to walk back to the feast. "How are you?"

"Fine. She keeps me busy, as always."

"Good," he said, unsure what else to reply.

Abruptly, Ellen stopped and turned to face him. "How did you kill it? The rootcrab I mean?"

76

He paused for a moment then shrugged. "I told you, it was luck. It all happened so fast I can barely remember. I guess I just saw Julian was in trouble and knew I had to help."

"You did it to save your friend?"

"Yes, of course."

"And for no other reason?" she asked slowly, staring up into his eyes.

"What do you mean?" he asked, confused.

She said nothing and stared at him for several more seconds before finally answering. "You did not do it to gain favour? To impress us?" She paused. "To impress me?"

"No," he said sternly but then his face broke into a grin. "But did it impress you?"

A twinkle of mischief flared in her eyes as a smile crept onto her face. "Perhaps." She shrugged, still smiling, and linked her arm with his. "Let's get back to the feast. Before people start spreading gossip about the two of us."

Striding forwards with Ellen, Lyncon felt burning desire flow through him. Being this close to her he could smell the sweet scent of her perfume in the air and as they walked her hair brushed gently against his shoulder. His heart was thundering in his chest as the warmth he had felt earlier grew. He took a deep breath to try to clear his head and focused on walking in a straight line.

Back at the feast, Lyncon resumed his seat while Ellen paused to talk to a group of girls, all of whom cast admiring glances in Lyncon's direction. Drel and Karis were gone but Julian remained and quickly poured his friend a drink as he sat down.

"What 'appened with Ellen?" he asked with obvious excitement.

77

"Nothing," replied Lyncon, though he could not help a smile spilling onto his face. He downed his drink in one go and Julian quickly poured him another.

For the next hour the two men sat and drank and laughed. They were alone at the end of the table for a while until Artur and Bjorn joined them and the four friends were soon telling jokes and stories galore. By the time the tables were cleared of the last few jugs of drink and pushed back to make room for dancing, Lyncon was feeling more than a little unsteady. The drink had numbed his mind and his movements were wild and clumsy. The heat he felt burning in his stomach had escalated to an inferno and he was unable to feel the tips of his fingers or toes.

As the elder villagers struck up a tune on a selection of dusty-looking instruments, the men roared with triumph as the first of the women got up to dance, skirts billowing around them. Soon almost all the women were on their feet, laughing and smiling as they twirled together.

As soon as one song ended another began and the women moved to grab at the men on the sides, picking a partner and pulling the reluctant but grinning men into the seething mass of dancers. More and more joined the dance and it did not take long for Lyncon's group to be picked on too.

Bjorn was first to go, the hulking blonde picked by an equally large woman with hands the size of Lyncon's. She grinned at them all and slapped Bjorn hard on his backside as she ushered him onto the dance floor. Lyncon and the others howled with laughter as they watched their friend stumble back and forth as he attempted to join in.

A trio of girls approached their table, eyes alight with excitement and cheeks flushed from dancing. Each held out a hand as an invitation to join them. Julian and Artur were more than happy to oblige and leapt from their seats quicker than Lyncon had ever seen them move, grins plastered to their faces. He himself remained seated, uncertainty twisting a knot in his stomach.

The young woman staring down at him was pale-skinned with fierce eyes bordered by waves of silky black hair. Her features were sharp but beautiful and she smelt faintly of lily or lilac. Her smile was sure but sweet and she stood with her shoulders back to further display breasts that were already threatening to burst free of her figure-hugging bodice. Torchlight danced across her face, echoing the movement of the villagers behind her.

After a brief pause, Lyncon rose awkwardly and took her hand. Raising it to his lips he kissed it gently and then let go before sitting back down again. The girl glared down at him, eyes as cold as the harshest snows, but then she noticed Ellen walking towards them, saw the look on her face, and her gaze softened.

"I can see we are each destined for another," she said. Her voice was as smooth and sweet as honey. "Goodnight." Lyncon bowed his head as she turned and disappeared into the crowd.

Ellen stopped beside Lyncon and stared down at him, puzzled. "You refused her hand?"

"I did." He locked eyes with her and smiled. Slowly she smiled back and then reached down and took his hand before pulling him to his feet. Together they joined the twirling mass of dancers.

Lyncon soon suspected that he was not a natural dancer, even without the alcohol. His steps were clumsy and wild as his arms swayed of their own accord. His head was throbbing from the drink and he was soon covered in sweat from both the exertion of dancing and the rising heat that was burning in his stomach. More than once he was overcome with a wave of nausea but he fought it off and kept moving.

Despite his poor effort at dancing, Ellen seemed to be enjoying his company. She smiled and laughed at his missteps while spinning her crimson dress like an elegant flame. Every step she took was so sure and perfect and Lyncon envied the ease with which she moved around him. Her hair, which had been neatly pinned earlier, was now free and trailed behind her in golden waves that danced to their own rhythm. She was beautiful and Lyncon was addicted to her, mesmerised by her smile and hypnotised by the wiggle of her hips. The heat in him roared and he forgot all about his own dancing, which actually improved slightly as a result, as he got lost in her eyes.

After what felt like an eternity of bliss, the song ended and the dancers all paused to cheer and catch their breath. The musicians began another tune, this one slow and soft. The villagers began to couple up, the men taking the women by the waist as they began to slowly circle the grass. Ellen and Lyncon did the same, him delicately holding her hips while she linked her arms around his neck and rested her head on his shoulder.

"You dance like an outo," she whispered, giggling.

"Really? I thought I was doing rather well."

"No but I think there is still hope for you." She pulled away to look at him. "I am sure I could teach you."

He smiled. "I would like that very much."

They were silent for a moment as they slowly spun to the music; each admired the other.

"Can I kiss you?" he finally asked, feeling heat flush his cheeks.

She rolled her eyes but smiled. "I was beginning to think you would never ask."

He threw his head back and laughed, more from exhilaration than humour. His body was on fire, liquid heat pumping through every sinew, numbing his limbs. A surge shot through him like lightning and he groaned as the whole world seemed to wobble and distort. There was a moment of immense pain, his mind lost in a sea of fog, unable to control his body. Then he bent forwards and ripped out her throat with his teeth. Blood flowed hot. Far away, someone screamed.

Chapter 5

The Massacre of Seacrest

Lyncon woke to find blood on his hands. He groaned feebly. His head was pounding as if something was trying to burst out of his skull and the pain made him dizzy. He clenched his eyes shut and tried to move but pain flowed through him and he soon gave up, taking ragged breaths as he lay face down.

He was lying on sand, the coarse grains grating against his naked flesh. Above him gulls circled, cawing loudly, as the sun shone with a burning heat that beat down upon his exposed back. Somewhere nearby waves lapped against the shore in their own carefree rhythm.

Slowly, Lyncon sat up and forced himself to open his eyes, shielding them from the bright sunlight with his hand. His body felt tired and sore, his muscles aching beneath his skin and making his movements stiff and painful. Eventually his eyes began to adjust to the light and he saw his hands. Looking down he saw his body was covered in blood; his arms and chest were nearly completely red. He knew immediately it was not his own.

As his heart began to race, he staggered to his feet and stumbled towards the village. He tripped, his legs falling from beneath him, and collapsed back into the sand. His skin glistened with sweat as it ran in rivulets down his back and arms, tracing new waterways through the blood. A cloud passed overhead and he shivered.

Undeterred by the effort, he gritted his teeth and began to crawl forwards on his hands and knees. The exercise made him cough, his throat as dry as the sand beneath him. He reached the edge of the village, the beach giving way to rough grass, and paused, panting. With a grunt he pulled himself to his feet, digging his toes into the dirt, and wobbled forwards. He had not gone far before he reached the first body and his strength vanished. He sank to his knees, head bowed, panting breaths quickly turning to sobs.

The body was a young boy who must have been no more than ten years old. Lyncon recognised him from around the village, remembering him running and playing with the other children, but did not know his name. He was lying on his back, his empty eyes staring up at the gathering clouds. His stomach was split open by several ragged gashes and his guts were hanging out, sagging against tiny hands that had desperately fought to keep them in. The boy's face was frozen in a grimace of terror and pain, mouth open in a soundless scream. The grass beneath him was drenched with blood. From the roof of a nearby hut, several gulls eyed the body with greedy curiosity.

Hot tears stung Lyncon's eyes as he bent double, sobbing over the body. The gulls, growing ever braver, swooped down to the grass and began to creep towards the boy, watching Lyncon intently. Silently, one began to pick at the boy's arm, its sharp beak piercing the flesh with ease. When Lyncon noticed, he sprang up, flailing his arms in the air as he shouted.

"Away, you monsters! Get away!" His voice was thick with grief.

As the gull took to the sky to circle above him, Lyncon noticed others gathered on another body nearby, three birds pecking feverishly at the remains. Releasing a scream of anguish he staggered towards them, hatred fuelling his body. Again the birds scattered, fleeing the wild kicks aimed at them, but only for a moment. They rose briefly and then fell onto another body to continue their feast, their bloodstained beaks tearing at the soft, lifeless flesh.

In a frenzy, Lyncon gave chase, banishing the birds with his waving fists. He chased them from one body only to see them converge on another. Heedless to his own failings, he continued, tears flicking from his cheeks and blurring his vision as he lashed out at anything that moved. Eventually he collapsed, exhausted, his whole body shaking as he wept into the grass.

Time had no meaning now, it was irrelevant, and he simply lay there, face down and crying, as the gulls feasted on the dead all around him. Though the sun baked his naked skin, he was shivering uncontrollably, his whole being cold with pain. Eventually he struggled to his knees. To his left lay a severed head, its empty eyes staring directly at him as the mouth hung open at an unnatural angle. The scalp looked to have been completely ripped free of the skull and the white bone shone in the harsh light. Lyncon stared into the lifeless eyes, the dead orbs seeming to peer into his very soul, and fresh tears sprang from his own. Then he turned to the side and threw up onto the grass.

When he was finally empty and his throat was raw, he spat, and wiped his mouth on the back of his hand. His head hurt a little less now and he took several deep breaths to steady his shaking limbs before plucking up the courage to stand. An image of Julian laughing at the feast flashed through his mind and he took a determined step forwards. He knew he had to search the bodies, had to find his friend.

Seacrest was like a battlefield. Bodies lay everywhere, strewn in and amongst the buildings like the forgotten toys of a careless child. Blood, long dried in the heat, covered almost everything in its deep red and the thick stench of death hung heavy in the air. Nothing moved save for the birds and flies, hard at work feeding on the remains. The place had an unnerving stillness about it, as if the village itself was frozen in shock from the atrocities that had occurred the night before.

Lyncon floated around the village like a ghost, numb, stepping over corpses or dismembered limbs as he wandered the streets in a daze. He moved from one body to another, checking faces, recoiling at the ones he recognised. Those that lay face down he rolled over, their limp forms cold to touch. After a while he gave up and simply wandered past. His eyes were empty, mind devoid of all real feeling as he walked amongst those he knew he had slain.

Finally he reached the site of the feast, the place of such happiness that had now become the epicentre of pain. Here the bodies were numerous and lay in piles, limbs twisted into grotesque shapes that made them seem inhuman as they littered what had been the dance area. The long tables were still positioned at the edge of the space but the furthest from him now lay on its side, the ground beneath it covered with shattered wine jugs and uneaten food. The musicians lay together, still clutching their instruments. The smell here was at its strongest, an acrid scent of rotting flesh and dried blood. Flies buzzed in their hundreds as they gorged on the bodies, watched over by droves of gulls.

Lyncon paused as he took in the scene with little understanding. Bile rose in his throat and he forced himself to take several deep breaths, which did little to help considering the putrid air. He wiped his eyes on the back of his hand and stumbled onwards.

He found Artur first, lying on his back with both legs missing, replaced with ragged red stumps. Bjorn was nearby, his body leaning against the table with his guts pooled around him. The birds had picked at his bowels and an overpowering stink of shit stopped Lyncon from wandering too close. Instead he moved towards two bodies in the centre of the circle, a man and a woman. He knew who they were even before he reached them.

Ellen lay on her side, face pressed into the grass as her hands clutched at the bloodied remains of her throat. Julian was beside her, arms stretched out towards her. His face had been split in half with the left eye and lower jaw completely missing, replaced by limp strands of red flesh that hung down like vines. The grass around them was stained a deep crimson, the colour matching Ellen's dress. Lyncon's legs crumbled beneath him and he knelt at his friend's side while fresh sobs coursed through him. Collapsing, he gave in to the exhaustion of grief.

When he next opened his eyes it was darker, the day beginning to wane as evening drew in. The lapping of the waves was louder now, driven closer by the tide as it devoured the beach. The clouds had multiplied to almost completely cover the sky and drifted overhead, silent and unperturbed by the scene below them as they continued their ceaseless journey. A wind had arisen, blowing in from the sea, and its cool salty touch had roused him from his grief. He felt something soft and cold against his cheek and recoiled, tumbling backwards, as he realised his head had drooped to rest against Julian's shoulder, the dead flesh touching his own.

After several deep breaths to try to slow his pulse, Lyncon stood up. He was weak and tired, while each of his limbs seemed to weigh several tonnes. His headache was gone but he still felt sick, his empty stomach leaving him with a hollow sensation. He reached up to rub his eyes but froze when he remembered the state of his hands, each digit coated in blood, the dried flakes lodged under his fingernails and caking his knuckles. A sudden image flashed through his mind, a man raising his sword, striking out, standing firm against the great hulking beast that faced him. With a deep sigh he turned and walked up towards the chief's house on the hill.

The door to Drel's house hung open on one hinge, the wood splintered and rent with deep claw marks. Inside the room was a mess of shattered furniture and broken bodies. Crimson pools dotted the stone floor and the air was thick with the stench of death and shit. The fire in the grate was long dead.

Karis was slumped against the wall, head bowed and eyes closed, a dribble of blood running from the corners of her mouth. She was holding hands with another woman Lyncon did not know but he guessed was a servant. Despite the blood she looked almost peaceful, as if she were napping just for a moment and would any second wake to start tidying the mess around her. The thin red line across her throat told Lyncon that she never would.

Drel was in the centre of the room, his body sprawled across the floor. His left arm was missing at the shoulder and the side of his skull had been caved in, with grey matter oozing from the cracks. His right hand still clutched his bloodied sword, the knuckles white in their death grip. Beside him lay the body of a child. Lyncon could not tell if it was a boy or a girl but the chief had clearly been trying to protect it from the attacker, his body draped over the child in a human shield. Lyncon quickly averted his eyes, instead moving them back to the weapon in Drel's hand. Reaching down, he prised the handle from the chief's grip, and then he left, closing the door behind him as best he could.

Slowly, he staggered to the healer's hut. Here the door was missing with only a few splintered remains hanging from the frame. Inside, the old woman sat motionless in her chair, her bony fingers curled around a knife handle that protruded from under her ribs. Lyncon quickly retreated. He had seen enough.

Alone, he sank to his knees. The air was still and unnaturally silent, as if all feeling and warmth had been sucked from the world. All that remained was a shadow, an empty patch of soulless buildings and joyless land. Seacrest was gone, replaced by a dark and hollow imitation, a memory drenched in suffering and blood.

His vision was blurred as he began to dig a small hole in the dirt with the tip of the sword. It was hard work, his body numb and his arm heavy, but he kept at it, gritting his teeth as he began to pant. Tears fell before him, wetting the soil.

Finally, when the hole was deep enough, he turned the sword and inserted the handle into the ground, packing the loose soil down around it. Now the weapon stood upright on its own, the blade pointing to the sky. Lyncon knelt before it, the tip just below his chin. A ray of sunlight burst through the clouds and the edge of the sword glinted up at him, urging him on, eager for more blood.

"I'm sorry," he whispered to no one. He closed his eyes tight, the lids wet with tears, and pulled back his head.

"Lyncon!" A voice called to him but he ignored it. "Stop, Lyncon!"

He did not dare open his eyes. He felt a sudden sharp pain and then nothing.

Chapter 6

A Friend of the Woods

Though the ground was favourable, the going was slow and Fenrir was growing impatient. The rain had started as the night drew in and, despite the trees doing their best to shelter them, he was soaked through. His hood was heavy and clung to his head while fat raindrops kept falling from the rim in front of his eyes to land on his boots. He cursed the weather in old elvish, whispering under his breath. A deep groan from the trees silenced him at once and he quickly bowed his head for forgiveness.

Quickening his own pace, he pulled on the reins of the horse behind him and the beast gave a snort of disapproval. It did not like its unresponsive passenger, hanging limply over the saddle, but Fenrir had convinced it to carry the limp body with a few gentle persuasions. Even so, the horse was unruly and in no mood to be rushed.

After another tedious hour they began to near their destination. The Haren Forest was a vast place and they were deep in its heart, miles from the edge, in territory few humans had ever properly explored. Fenrir was not concerned; he knew the way, the earth guiding him on the path home as it always did. Haren was one of the last few wild areas of Petra, untamed and undisturbed by humans, the perfect hiding place for an elf and a monster.

Finally they reached the elf's home. The forest opened out into a small clearing that sat at the base of the remnants of a huge white tree, a gigantic twisted skeleton, stripped of its bark and leaves, bare branches reaching for the sky like gnarled fingers of bone. It had been a special place once, full of life and a deep, ancient power. Now it was hollow, dead, and the sight always caused Fenrir a pang of sadness that struck him to his very core.

A small hut made of mismatching planks of wood and clumps of dried earth stood amongst giant roots emerging from the ground. It had two windows, both shuttered, and a narrow wooden door with a chimney poking out from between the roots that snaked over and around the dwelling in an almost tender embrace. It was not a lavish place and nor was it very homely but in that moment, as the rain beat down upon him, it had never looked so inviting, and Fenrir rushed forwards to get indoors, almost forgetting his companion in his haste.

Hoisting the body onto his shoulders, the elf bid the horse farewell. It trotted off amongst the trees but he knew it would not go far; it sensed safety here and was curious about them both. Straining, Fenrir carried his guest inside, careful of the doorframe as he squeezed them both through. He set the human down on the bed and sighed with relief, shaking off his cloak to hang it by the fireplace. With creaking joints he began to stoke the embers in the grate back to life, adding fresh kindling until he could see new flames begin to rise.

"Tea. That is what this weather calls for," he muttered to himself as he walked to the small kitchen in the corner and hurriedly filled the pot with water before hanging it above the fire. When the water was boiling he added some leaves that he carefully extracted from a small pouch by the door. With a quick stir, the air was soon full of the heady smell of herbs and earth. Helping himself to a cupful, he gave another sigh and paused to study the man on his bed. He was drenched, wrapped clumsily in Fenrir's spare cloak and breeches, his body covered in streaks of blood that had run in the rain.

"It's alright, Lyncon," he whispered. "You can rest. I will make this right."

Lyncon woke to the sounds of battle, the sharp clash of steel and the shouts and screams of men. His head was spinning as images raced through his mind, death and bloodshed, fear and terror. He sat up suddenly, the rough woollen blanket sliding from his sweat-slickened skin. The screams continued, echoing around him, but as he desperately looked he could not see their source; the unfamiliar room was empty.

He kicked his legs free and staggered to his feet, swaying alarmingly. The room was gloomy, a cramped wooden box full of simple furniture and a fire glowing happily in the grate. He spotted light coming through from under the door and stumbled towards it, pausing with his hand on the doorknob. Slowly, he placed an eye against a gap in the wood. Beyond the door a battle raged, men fought and died while other creatures moved between them, hideous beasts slashing with claws already coated with blood. He

92

could smell the killing, the death. It choked him, filled him. His head was pounding and he felt his stomach lurch.

With a vicious push he threw the door open and charged into the light, lips pulled back into a feral snarl as he stepped out onto a battlefield that wasn't there. Instead he found himself in a grass clearing, surrounded by dense forest. Behind him loomed a huge dead tree, its wood as white as bone, the hut he had been lying in dwarfed by its size. A horse stood nearby, eyeing him warily as it chewed on a tuft of grass. He blinked sunlight from his eyes and covered his face, rubbing the memories away with a hand.

"So, you're finally awake." A figure emerged from the trees carrying an untidy bundle of logs under one arm. As Lyncon studied the figure, flashes of memory surged through his mind; armoured faces like the one before him, shouting, screaming, dying. His breath caught as he suddenly realised that he was looking at an elf and that he had known elves before, as both comrades and friends.

The elf was tall and slim with skin that was an alarming shade of white, as pale as the tree that towered above them. His hair was black peppered with grey and short, shaved close to the skin. He wore a simple brown tunic of hard-wearing fabric with a plain leather belt and dark green trousers that were splattered with mud. A small knife hung from the belt at his hip.

"I'm glad you're up, just in time to help me with the firewood."

For a long moment Lyncon was simply too stunned to reply. His body was frozen as his mind grappled with his new memories, racing to process everything. Eventually he managed to snap back to the present enough to splutter, "Who... are you? Where are we?"

The elf froze, staring at Lyncon as if seeing him for the first time. He padded silently towards him and stopped only inches away, staring hard at Lyncon's face.

Up close the elf's appearance was even more striking. His eyes were huge; two round orbs that seemed to fill his face and hold inconceivable depth, the iris a mixed shade of blue-green. The ears were small, pointed and almost completely flat against the side of his skull. The nose and mouth were the most humanlike, thin and sharp, set above a pointed chin and strong jaw. They stared at each other in silence for a long time, both examining the other.

"Who are you?" Lyncon asked again.

"You really don't know me?" the elf asked, eyes narrowing slightly in suspicion.

Lyncon shook his head. "I... don't know. I... lost my memories..." He trailed off, head bowed.

"Lost your... memories," the elf muttered, hand stroking his chin as he considered this. Then he gave a small nod and strode past him to a pile of logs that lay beside the door to the hut. "Bring the wood," he called over his shoulder before setting down his load and disappearing inside.

Without knowing what else to do, Lyncon did as he was told and wobbled over to the wood pile. The aroma of split bark filled his nostrils as he carried a large bundle back towards the hut, the logs scraping against his bare chest and arms. Dropping the logs with the others the elf had carried; he stepped back inside.

The elf was crouching by the fire, feeding a fresh log into the flames. He paid no attention to Lyncon as he strode over and stood above him.

"Who are you?" he demanded impatiently.

"Tea first. Then we can talk."

"No! Answer me now! I need to know!" Lyncon roared, sudden rage bubbling inside of him.

The elf sighed but did not get up. "Seems human impatience has rubbed off on you. Hardly surprising, I suppose. You can teach a pig to eat at your table but show it a field of shit and it will dive in with glee." Shaking his head he reached down and picked up a heavy iron cauldron that he hung by its handle from a hook above the fire. It was already full of water. After removing something from a pouch, he sprinkled it into the water and straightened up, finally turning to face his guest. "Sit. Let us have tea and talk." When Lyncon did not budge, he scowled. "Then at least put a shirt on!"

After a moment of resistance, Lyncon relented and pulled on the loose shirt that had been left at the foot of the bed for him. He sat down on a stool, blowing air through his teeth in frustration. The elf sat opposite and began to unlace his muddy boots.

"You really do not remember me?" he asked suddenly, not looking up from his feet.

"Should I?"

The elf laughed, a harsh sound, short and hard. "Oh yes. Very much so."

"Then tell me who you are!" Lyncon balled his fists as he stared at the elf.

95

He looked up at Lyncon, studying him, those big blue-green eyes drinking him in, missing nothing. "My name is Fenrir."

Lyncon had hoped for a sudden surge of memories upon hearing the name, images of his past flooding back to him, but instead all he got was more frustration. The name meant nothing to him. He did not know it. He rubbed his temple. "You say you know me and yet your name means nothing to me."

The elf scowled. "Perhaps you are trying too hard to remember."

Fenrir rose and went to the kitchen, returning with two clay mugs. He handed one to Lyncon before turning to the pot and removing it from the hook. Setting his mug down, he poured himself a tea and then waited for Lyncon to offer his own cup. Warily, Lyncon did so and felt the warmth of the liquid seep into his hand through the clay as the elf passed it back to him, full almost to the brim.

"How much do you remember?" the elf asked as he sat back down.

"Of what?"

"Anything. Your life." He waved one hand dismissively as he sipped his tea.

"Very little, lots of vague images that don't make much sense. Occasionally I remember words or names but often I don't know what they mean." He paused, thinking of the battle he had re-lived only minutes ago. It had felt so real, so familiar. "I remember a battle, fighting… people dying."

The elf nodded, eyes never leaving Lyncon. "Do you know what you are?"

Lyncon furrowed his brow. "What am I?"

Fenrir ignored him. "What happened in Seacrest?"

"S... Seacrest?" Images suddenly flared in Lyncon's mind. Bodies and blood littering the sand. Julian, Momo, Ellen. All dead. He saw them all as the memories came rushing back in a wave that hit him so hard it almost physically hurt. He bowed his head and gave a deep moan of anguish. Tears dripped onto the wooden floor at his feet as grief enveloped him. Nausea swept over him like a tide.

"I did it. I killed them all!" he wailed, voice quivering as he buried his face into his hands.

"I know."

"What am I?" he whispered into his hands, tears leaking through his fingers.

Fenrir looked across at him with a pained expression, his tea forgotten. "You're my fault and I'm going to help you."

Lyncon sprang up, tears flowing freely as he stormed out of the cabin. "No one can help me! I don't deserve it! I'm a monster!"

After the massacre, Seacrest stood silent for three days, populated by only ghosts and an ever-growing number of gulls. On the fourth day a convoy arrived made up of an odd assortment of worn carts and large covered wagons driven by teams of oxen. The people on the wagons were just as strange, a mixture of men and women, all shapes, sizes and ages. A short man, dressed in faded white robes, stepped down from the first cart. He was old and moved very slowly, leaning heavily on a gnarled wooden staff taller than he was. The birds that had ruled the village until now took to the air as one and fled, all without a sound.

The old man led his band of misfits and castaways into the centre of the village. There, he raised his hands and spoke in a language so old that only a few alive still spoke it. Thunder rumbled in response as the clouds suddenly darkened from grey to black. A lightning bolt crashed down from the heavens and struck at the old man's feet. Where it hit, the ground began to split and open up, fissures darting away in every direction, and from these rents the Essence came, clouds of pain and misery, the memory of the blood that soaked the soil. It rose into the air and the Crooked Man feasted on it. A power as old as time itself, the only power that could sustain him.

His followers gathered closer to their saviour, their Leeraar, and began to feed from him, inhaling the strength that he gave them as he continued to chant. Soon they were all gorging themselves, insatiable and relentless. Some turned to fucking, stripping and rolling in the dirt wherever they had stood. Others fought or ran around shouting, revelling in the pleasure of the power they were being gifted. Most simply wept tears of pure joy as they devoured the memory of death.

In the castle overlooking Astikus, Petra's capital city, Evanora awoke suddenly and sat bolt upright. Books lay open across the desk in front of her, research from the night before. With shaking hands, she closed them while rubbing her cheek where it had been resting against the paper.

"I hear you," she whispered to herself. "I hear you."

After jumping up, she crossed to the door and threw it open, stepping out into the corridor. Her footsteps echoed off the cold stone as she strode down the familiar empty hallways. At this time of night the castle was almost completely silent and the darkness seemed to press in at every window. She ignored it. The peace would not last. She was about to break it.

She strode into the king's chambers without a moment's thought and was greeted by a large bald man with his sword already drawn. When he saw her he scowled and lowered his blade.

"Evanora! What are you doing barging in here? Do you know what time it is? The king is asleep." He growled in a deep gravelly voice.

"Of course I don't know what time it is and neither do I care, Amos. Wake the king. I must speak to him immediately."

The big captain did not move. "He will not appreciate being disturbed. Is it really urgent?" He paused, looking at the floor. "He has guests again."

Evanora rolled her eyes at the big man's awkwardness. "I don't care if the whole of fucking Astikus is in there; I need to speak to him." With her impatience getting the better of her, she added, "If you will not fetch him then I shall wake him myself."

"No." He raised a hand and sighed. "Wait here."

She nodded and turned away as Amos knocked lightly on the door to the bedchamber before disappearing inside. Now alone, she crossed the lavish chamber to a large mirror that hung between several portraits of the king in various bold and noble poses. The reflection that greeted her was one of dishevelment and fatigue. Her long black hair was a knotted tangle, while her round eyes were sunken and ringed with dark bags. Her lips had lost their usual bright red gleam but she fixed that easily with a small lipstick that she kept in a pouch on her belt. Her robes, the traditional Petran blue she was forced to wear, were lined with creases but she did her best to ignore them.

She was trying and failing to unknot her hair when the door to the bedchamber behind her opened. In the mirror, Evanora saw two girls and a boy run from the room, all in various states of undress, clutching clothes to their chests. She guessed they were all no older than eighteen but her concepts of human time and age were always unreliable.

Shortly after, Amos entered the room followed closely by King Renthor of Petra. He had wrapped himself in a grand-looking silk robe but his chestnut hair was unruly and his eyes were tainted by sleep. That did nothing to lessen his look of scorn. Seeing him, Evanora felt the usual hatred bubble up inside of her but kept her face an emotionless mask.

"What is it, elf? Can't you see I was asleep?" He sat heavily in one of the armchairs beside the fireplace. The fire itself was little more than embers now. Amos stood close behind him.

Evanora crossed the room and sank into a seat opposite him without waiting for permission. She smiled apologetically at the fat man across from her. "I am sorry, Your Grace. It is urgent."

The king sighed heavily. "Well, go on then. Spit it out," he barked.

"Of course, Your Grace." She paused, choosing her words carefully as she pushed her feelings to one side. She had to be careful how much she revealed. "When you first… acquired my services you asked if there were more like me, more who could access the Essence like I can. I told you there were but I did not know where so you tasked me to find them. I have been searching ever since, with the help of Amos and his men. Now, I think I have found one of them."

The king was silent for a moment, eyes fixed upon hers. "Are you sure?"

"Yes, Your Grace."

"Do you know where they are?" She was silent for a time and the king shook his head in frustration. "Speak!"

"The vision was fleeting. I only saw a glimpse of where he is."

"He?" The king raised a hand to stroke the stubble on his chin.

"Yes, Your Grace. It was an old man… crooked. He was the one summoning the Essence."

The king nodded, a smirk touching his lips. "Almost like a wizard from the stories. Did he have a pointy hat as well? A beard?" He waited for them to laugh but then sighed when neither of them did. "You said there were images of where he was. Tell me." He turned to Amos. "Fetch paper and a quill. Write down what she can remember."

The big man did as he was told at once, retrieving the writing materials from a drawer and setting them on the nearest table. The show of immediate obedience from the captain made her shudder inside.

"I saw a village, houses made of wood and thatch. There was sand, dunes on the horizon, and the sea beyond. I could hear the waves crashing." She paused, face fixed in concentration. "The village was empty. Something bad had happened there, something terrible. The Essence was tainted... rotten."

"And this old man was... using it? As you do?" the king asked.

"Yes and no. He wasn't using it the same as I do. He was... summoning it and absorbing it somehow. Like he was feeding off it."

All three were silent as they considered what they had learnt.

"Anything else?"

She shook her head, looking at the floor. "No, Your Grace."

The king stood abruptly, scowling again. "Well it's not much but it is a start. Amos, get your men to find out if there are any coastal villages that have had some sort of disaster recently, perhaps a storm or plague. Mention nothing of this Crooked Man. No one is to know." He crossed to a lavish dresser in the corner and poured himself a generous drink, a large measure for any hour. "Elf, I want you to keep listening out for him. If you get another... vision then I want to know immediately. Understood?"

Evanora nodded solemnly. The king smiled, an expression without an inch of warmth.

"Good. Now get the fuck out of my chambers!"

As Evanora strode silently back to her room, she forced her contempt for the king aside and reflected on the feelings that had come with her vision, the cold dread that had gripped her as sights and sounds bombarded her mind's eye. It had been terrifying, to be so helpless, and yet it had also been exhilarating. She had felt the power the Crooked Man could wield, felt it touch her own and sing, surging through every inch of her being. At that moment she had seen everything so clearly: the empty village, the storm raging above, the Essence rising from fissures in the earth to greet the man who stood, arms aloft, in front of his people. She had seen him as clearly as if she were standing in front of him. A face from her past and one that she knew she would see again.

Chapter 7

The Werewarg

Lyncon walked through the woods without any care for where he was going. It was past noon now and the sun was blazing high in its arc, its warmth touching his skin but not his soul as sunlight streamed between the leaves above. With vacant eyes he wandered amongst the trees, fallen twigs and leaves crunching beneath his boots as he ventured further into the half-gloom of the forest.

He had left Fenrir behind and the elf had made no move to follow him nor utter a word of protest. He had simply sat motionless, staring after him with a tired expression on his pale face. That seemed like so long ago now. The hut was far behind him, the past, a memory.

Lyncon stopped, leaning heavily against a tree to steady himself as a fresh wave of heartbreak rolled over him. Images of Julian, both alive and dead, flashed through his head and he screwed his eyes tightly shut in a futile gesture. His breathing was sharp and ragged, coming in unsteady bursts as his heart raced along inside his chest. He forced himself to focus and try to control it, tame it, and eventually his pulse began to slow. After a long time he opened his eyes and straightened up. When he pulled his hand from the tree it stuck a little and, peering closer, he saw small holes in the bark where his fingers had been. Claw marks. He turned and reeled away.

"What am I?" he whispered to the gloom. His only answer came from the wind as it stirred the canopy, causing the leaves to chatter and snigger, as if the forest itself was mocking his plight. A cloud passed in front of the sun and the rays of light began to fade, one by one, leaving the forest in near darkness. Everything suddenly began to feel very close as the hulking trunks around him seemed to lean forwards, pressing in. He shivered despite the warmth in the air.

Lyncon skirted around the nearest tree and froze mid stride. In front of him, no more than thirty feet away, stood Julian. He was leaning against a tree, smiling at him, still dressed in his navy shirt from the night of the feast, hair neatly combed.

"Outo!" he said with a grin, his tone cheerful. "What are you doing out 'ere? Are you lost?" He gave a brief laugh, a happy sound that filled Lyncon with both love and despair.

"J… Julian," he muttered. "You're alive." With his heart thundering he charged towards his friend, arms outstretched, tears already wetting his cheeks. Julian didn't move, just kept smiling, watching him intently. He had almost reached his friend when his foot caught on a root and Lyncon went sprawling forwards into the leaf litter, landing with a soft thump, his face pressing down into the damp earth.

"Oops. Did you take a little tumble?" Julian asked from above him. He laughed again but this time it was cold and piercing, more like a scream, and it turned Lyncon's blood cold.

Slowly, he lifted his head from the dirt. Julian stood nearby, leering down at him with a madness burning in his eyes. As Lyncon watched, Julian's face began to melt and droop while his laugh became a horrible gurgling sound, the sound of a man drowning. Blood bubbled from his mouth and ran down his chin to fall at his feet. The left side of his face suddenly fell away to reveal a hideous hole, a mush of brain and shattered bone. His eyes glazed over and then popped from their sockets, falling to the forest floor with two dull thuds. Still he laughed, a gurgled scream of pain and malice and death. Lyncon dragged himself to his feet and backed up, not daring to take his eyes away.

A hand appeared suddenly on his shoulder, making him jump, and he twisted around to find Ellen standing behind him, staring with sorrowful eyes, the savaged remains of her throat dripping blood down her pretty dress. She smiled at him, a slow, horrible grin that made her wound stretch into a grotesque red imitation. Then she screamed so loudly Lyncon's knees almost buckled in pain as the sound bounced around his skull. Covering his ears and with a scream of his own, he turned and bolted, heedless to which direction he went.

He fled as fast as he could, charging through the trees at a ferocious speed. Branches whipped past him as he ran, Ellen's screams still echoing in his head. His breath came in painful gasps but he willed himself to run further, faster, until his legs eventually gave way and he stumbled to a halt.

Panting hard, he bent double with his hands on his knees as he sucked in great lungfuls of air. The clouds above had thickened and the gloom of the forest had grown, making the air feel dense and stale. His heart was pounding in his chest and when he straightened up black spots swam in front of his eyes. He ran a shaking hand through his untidy hair, slick with sweat.

He sank down next to a tree, sitting with his back to the bark and finding some reassurance from the solid feel of it against him. Forcing images of Seacrest out of his mind, he closed his eyes and tried to steady his heart. Round and round their faces swam, Julian and Ellen, savaged and mauled. He had done that, the monster in his heart. Guilt weighed upon him like an anvil, crushing his every thought. It consumed him, eating at him from every side as he remembered what he had done, the lives he had ended. He did not deserve peace, forgiveness, or even his life. Abruptly, a new darkness took him, more complete than the blackness of his own misery, and he fell into a troubled sleep.

It was a long time before Lyncon awoke. When he did it was slowly, tentatively unwrapping his arms from around his head and opening his eyes. The forest was silent and empty all around him. It was darker now, the sun sitting low on the horizon, and he wondered how long he had been asleep.

He pulled himself up and stretched his sore muscles. His cheeks were soaked and he was still shaking but his heart was calm and he felt at least a little better. He took a deep breath, rubbing his temple. He was so occupied by what had happened it took him several moments to realise he was being watched.

From behind a thicket of wiry bushes dotted with small curved leaves, a large pair of amber eyes stared out at him. As Lyncon locked his gaze with theirs, a low snarl emanated from the creature. He backed away, hitting the tree behind him, as he fought to control his fear, to fight the panic that flooded every inch of his being. He had no weapon, nothing to defend himself with. He was unarmed and alone.

Still growling, the creature stepped forwards out of its cover. It resembled a tabby cat, only much larger, its powerful limbs and long body knotted with thick muscles, tensed and ready to pounce. Its fur was brown speckled with black, matted and coarse. From its mouth two long fangs projected down either side of its lower jaw and ended in sharp points that curved slightly back. The beast's fierce orange stare was fixed upon him, unwavering.

For a moment they just stared at each other, predator and prey, each preparing themselves for this dance of death. Around them the forest was silent, as if the trees themselves were holding their breath, anticipating the outcome. Then, with one final snarl, the beast sprang forwards and the dance began.

As the creature flew towards him, Lyncon flung himself sideways, rolling across the leaf litter as the cat crashed into the tree trunk, claws scraping against the bark. It roared in frustration and spun to chase him, leaping again. This time Lyncon stood his ground and, pulling back his right fist, he swung at the beast. His fist landed, connecting with the side of the creature's head, but its momentum carried it forwards and it struck him on the left shoulder, its claws slicing his shirt and gouging into the flesh beneath. Both fell to the floor with a cry and rolled apart.

The cat was first to its feet, hissing in a low, menacing tone. Lyncon rolled away, clutching his bleeding shoulder, the pain pulsing with every breath he took. The beast was readying for another leap when a voice cut through the forest.

"Stop," shouted Fenrir, bow raised. "Leave him!"

The animal paused briefly, as if considering the request, then, with a roar, it sprang towards the elf instead. It had barely left the ground before an arrow pierced its heart and sent it tumbling into the leaves. After two ragged breaths it was still.

Lyncon got slowly to his feet as Fenrir stalked over to him. "Thanks."

"Are you hurt?"

He looked down at the cuts in his shoulder, the bleeding somehow already beginning to slow. "Nothing serious."

The elf gave him a disapproving look and shook his head. Then he walked to the cat. Squatting down he carefully removed the arrow and wiped it clean on a nearby shrub.

"Help me carry this." He gestured to the cat. "Its meat will go well in a stew."

Reluctantly Lyncon did as he was told and, taking two legs each, they heaved the body between them and began to walk back to the hut, Fenrir leading the way while Lyncon tried to ignore the ache from his wounds.

"I remember being told elves could talk to animals? Isn't that true?" Lyncon asked as they skirted a thicket of brambles.

"It's true enough."

"So why kill it?"

Fenrir gave a brief laugh. "You can talk to humans; does that mean that they always listen?"

They sat and sipped their tea in silence. It had a sickly, sweet taste that Lyncon did not much care for but he drank anyway out of the need for something warm. Outside, the wind had picked up and Fenrir had closed the shutters, leaving them sitting in the flickering light of the fire.

"Tell me what happened at the village, everything you remember." The elf's words were slow and calm as he regarded Lyncon with those big round eyes. When Lyncon did not answer he pressed on. "Please, I am trying to help you. I know it hurts but…"

"I killed them," he whispered with a haggard expression as he stared down into his cup. "I killed them all. The entire village."

The elf nodded slowly, his face blank. "Yes, I know. What I'm interested in is why." He stroked his chin thoughtfully, eyes never leaving the man across from him. "It is obvious you were fond of these people, that their deaths have hurt you, so I'm trying to figure out why you did what you did. Was it ordered? Elves?"

"What? No! What are you talking about?"

Fenrir shook his head. "You are right. They would have nothing to gain from slaughtering a meaningless fishing village."

Lyncon's eyes locked with the elf's. "They were not meaningless!" he growled.

Fenrir raised his hands. "My apologies, I did not mean

the people. I only meant that the village would not be important to the war effort."

"So I am a soldier?"

The elf raised an eyebrow and laughed. "No, no. You are much more than that. You are a weapon."

"What do you mean?"

"What happened that night?" Fenrir demanded, ignoring Lyncon's question entirely. "Something must have caused you to change."

"Change?" Lyncon's mind was swimming in confusion. It was making his head hurt and he suddenly felt very hot in the little hut.

"What were you doing that night? Anything different? Something new perhaps?"

"No. We… we were just at the feast. What did you mean I'm a weapo…"

"Was there drinking? Did you drink?"

He nodded slowly. "Yes. There was ale and wine. I had… some but what does that have to do with anything?"

Fenrir nodded vigorously, drumming his fingers on the table as he spoke seemingly to himself. "Human alcohol is known to impede cognitive functions, causing the drinker to lose control if they have too much of it. This must have been what happened to you. It was something we never tested, an outside stimulus. We missed it in our re…"

"Shut up!" he roared as he shot to his feet and hurled the mug, still half full, against the wall, where it shattered with a resounding crash. "Shut up! Tell me what is wrong with me! Tell me what happened!"

At the sudden outburst the elf had frozen but he quickly regained his composure and shook his head, looking almost disappointed. Calmly, he whispered, "Look at your hand."

Despite his rage Lyncon glanced down and stopped. Fur was sprouting from the skin on the back of his hand. His nails were gone and instead had been replaced by curved claws, long and sharp. As he watched the fur began to shrivel, receding beneath the skin, and the claws withdrew into the tips of his fingers, transforming into untidy nails. Raising his hand he began to inspect it in disbelief at what he had just seen, his eyes roving over every inch of skin to check for any further changes.

"W... what was that?" he spluttered, still intently staring at his hand as if waiting for it to suddenly change again.

Fenrir sighed, a sudden sadness welling in his blue-green eyes. "You... you are not human, Lyncon. Not anymore, at least. You are a werewarg."

"What's a werewarg?" he asked, finally shifting his eyes away from his hand.

"Sit and I'll explain everything." He paused as Lyncon did as he was told then gestured to the cabin around them. "Before... this I was an elven researcher in Belanthor, a scientist and a good one. I specialised in experiments with rare and dark creatures we elves call Grezna. Elves can of course communicate with all living beings but Grezna are different; they cannot be tamed or reasoned with, and are often very violent." He stood and poured himself some more tea. He offered some to Lyncon but sat back down when he refused. "I worked for the Belanthor High Council, the collective leaders of the elven race. When war broke out between Petra and Vilantis, humans and elves, I was made head of a secret project. It was a project to make a new army we could use against the might of man. In pursuit of this goal, we created werewargs."

He paused but Lyncon said nothing, simply watching him intently as he tried to process what he had heard. "Werewolves are a fascinating species. They are strong and fast, heal incredibly quickly and their senses are far superior to even those of an elf. They are perfect predators and could have been the perfect weapons. There was just one small problem: they are impossible to control. They are wild and unpredictable creatures, prone to extreme savagery when transformed and madness when in their human form. To them, elves and men are no different; we are all just prey." He paused. "Hmm perhaps there is some logic in that somewhere." He trailed off, looking straight at Lyncon but yet not really seeing him.

"So… I'm a werewolf?" Lyncon asked, not really believing the words that were coming out of his mouth.

Snapping back to the moment, Fenrir scowled and shook his head. "No. You're a werewarg, completely different." He shook his head and sighed. "Under the supervision and observation of myself and my team, you were bitten by a werewolf. Left alone you would have become just like them, feral and ruled by the moon, but instead we slowed the transformation, allowing it to take hold gradually and giving your body time to adapt and learn to control the transformation."

"Control it? Control it?" Lyncon's eyes grew fierce as his shouts echoed around the cabin. Images of Seacrest raced through his mind, the scenes of death and destruction. It all began to fall into place, the pictures swimming into focus.

He had changed and killed them all. The beast inside him had erupted and slaughtered everyone he knew. "There is no controlling it! You made me a monster!"

The elf remained unfazed. "You can control it, you have just forgotten how." He paused to lock eyes with Lyncon. "I can teach you. I will teach you."

The flame of anger inside Lyncon guttered and died as he heard the sincerity and resolve in the elf's words. His shoulders sagged as he suddenly felt very tired. He rested his head in his hands and when he finally spoke it was in no more than a whisper. "Please help me."

The elf nodded. "Of course."

For a long time they sat in silence, neither brave enough to reach out to the other, burying their thoughts and feelings within.

Chapter 8

A Cabin in the Woods

"I think it is time for us to work on your control. See if we can help you remember what has been lost." The elf rose suddenly from the table where they had been eating a simple breakfast of berries and oats. Slinging his bow over his shoulder, he opened the door and strode outside without another word.

Lyncon rose too, his limbs heavy and stiff beneath him. He had slept badly in the little bed Fenrir had made for him, plagued by dreams that taunted and tormented him. There were so many questions bubbling inside of him that it was hard to shut off and sleep, especially when the elf refused to answer any that he had asked. He rubbed his eyes and followed Fenrir out into the clearing, blinking against the bright light of the morning sun.

"Usually we would give you an elixir for such things, dull your emotional responses while enhancing your senses, but the ingredients are native to Vilantis and impossible to replicate here. We'll have to make do without," Fenrir explained.

"What are we going to do?" Lyncon was in no mood for the elf's cryptic habits this morning. His head was already a tangled mess without Fenrir adding some obscure trial or challenge.

"We'll start with something simple." He stopped a few feet from a tree at the edge of the clearing and examined it as he spoke. "The claws are always the easiest part of the transformation, very little to change and a very useful asset. We believe it is related to survival instinct but that theory is untested. Regardless of why, they are a good place to begin."

After removing his bow from his shoulder, he nocked an arrow, took aim and fired it high into the tree trunk above. It stuck fast, quivering in the wood. He turned to Lyncon with a wry smile. "Fetch."

Lyncon merely gaped at him. "What? How am I supposed to reach that?"

The elf gave an impatient sigh. "I already told you. Claws!" He slung his bow back over his shoulder and began to stroll back to the hut.

"Wait! Is that it? I thought you were going to teach me something? Maybe about concentrating on my past or finding my memories!"

Fenrir turned and raised a questioning eyebrow. "What did you expect? Meditation? Lessons on finding inner peace?" He chuckled. "I created warriors, not monks. I cannot truly tell you how your transformation works, only present you with tasks to help it occur. Now fetch my arrow and then we can talk more."

With a heavy sigh of frustration Lyncon turned and stared up at the arrow, its shaft jutting from the tree some thirty feet above the ground. This was not what he had expected but the smug look on the elf's face as he disappeared inside had riled him and he wanted nothing more than to wipe that grin away. A new stubbornness began to take hold and he fixed the arrow with a determined stare. "You're mine."

Slowing his breathing, he stepped up to the tree and placed his hands on the trunk, feeling the rough bark beneath his fingers. He tried to remember back to when he had grown the claws whilst he had argued with Fenrir. He focused on the feeling in his hands, the wood and moss touching his skin, every rise and fall of the bark's uneven surface. When nothing happened he let out a low hiss of frustration and pressed his hands harder into the tree, trying to focus even further, but images of Seacrest loomed just below his thoughts, pictures of the damage these claws had already inflicted.

A squawk and sudden explosion of wings above him snapped him out of his focus. "Fuck!" he roared up at the bird as it soared away over the treetops. "This is hopeless."

In his frustration he punched the trunk in front of him, not hard but enough to hurt his hand a little. When he pulled his fist away, he saw his fist had left an imprint in the bark, about an inch deep. He stared at his hand in shock, flexing his fingers as if for the first time. A sudden thought struck him and he glanced back up at the tree, brushing his dark hair out of his eyes. Perhaps claws were not the answer. Perhaps old-fashioned strength would be enough.

He studied the tree again, this time focusing on the lowest, sturdiest-looking branch. Bending his legs he took aim and leapt, grabbing the branch with both hands. Quickly he pulled himself up and used the trunk to steady himself. Then he aimed for the next one.

It was the fourth branch that failed him. It held at first, long enough for him to pull his chest up to it, but then, with a sudden crack, it split from the trunk and Lyncon crashed back to earth with a heavy thump.

Winded, he lay in a heap, the branch draped on top of him. As he pushed it away he stared up at the arrow above him, still stuck fast, its unmoving stance somehow mocking.

Slowly, he sat up and flexed his aching muscles, rolling his bruised shoulders with a groan. There was no way he could reach the arrow without using claws to scale the trunk but he had no idea how to summon them. Both times they had appeared before he had been emotional, out of control almost, and he had not meant to do it. It had been natural, a reaction of body and not mind. To do it now, with a clear mind and calm focus, seemed impossible. Feeling hopeless, Lyncon stood and turned his back on the tree, walking off into the woods towards the stream that ran nearby.

From the window of the hut, Fenrir watched with an intense scrutiny. His expression gave nothing away.

For the next week every day was the same. After a simple breakfast, Lyncon would return to the tree to try to retrieve the arrow. Some days he would sit and think, almost meditating, while others he would huff and puff, throwing curses to the heavens in frustration and rage. Neither method did any good.

After a few hours he would slink back to the hut for lunch and Fenrir would give him jobs to fill the rest of the day. There was much to do around the forest. Besides the normal chopping of wood and carrying water, Fenrir would get Lyncon to help him to keep the forest happy and healthy. Occasionally he would allow Lyncon to ask some questions about his past, slowly filling in pieces of his missing memories. He would only ever answer a few before stopping, claiming he did not want Lyncon to become overwhelmed, but the only thing Lyncon ever became was annoyed. The two had fallen into an uneasy routine, busying themselves with physical tasks as they both tried to come to terms with everything that was going on. Despite their less than friendly relationship, Lyncon was glad to have the elf for company and spent as little time alone as he could.

It was a still, overcast afternoon when they found themselves picking their way through a dense patch of woodland in search of a distressed animal that had called to Fenrir for help. The elf led the way, as always, picking the best path through the countless trees and thick patches of gorse or bramble. Lyncon had spent his morning cursing the arrow, which refused to fall from the trunk into his hand, and his frustrations had still not yet fully subsided. He walked sullenly behind, silently cursing himself and shaking his hands in mute frustration.

The elf stopped abruptly and turned, frustration written all over his pale features. "Will you stop! Your sulking and trampling is very distracting!"

Lyncon scowled. "We were not all born with a light step."

"No but luckily for you I gave you one. Use it!" The elf turned away and continued his trek through the forest. After a moment of quiet muttering, Lyncon followed, his movements noticeably quieter.

"Why did you do that?"

"Because you were annoying me!"

Lyncon shook his head. "No, I mean why did you give me a soft step? Why would I need to be quiet on a battlefield?"

The elf shrugged. "Sometimes stealth might be necessary."

"You mean for assassinations?" Lyncon asked, scowling.

"I never said that."

He walked a few more steps, thinking, before asking, "Why did you use a werewolf? Where did the idea come from?"

Fenrir stopped and turned to face him, running a hand over his short hair as he spoke. "It was my idea. I… my… forget it."

He turned away but Lyncon held his arm. "Fenrir… please. I want to know. I… need to know."

The elf looked at him for a moment, big eyes locked with his, then he nodded. "My father was killed by a werewolf. He was protecting our village and one night it came out of the trees and cut him down. In the morning, after we found his body, I went out after the beast, intent on my revenge. I tracked it all day and when night came I found it in a cave in the very darkest corner of the forest. When I saw it, saw the power and strength it had, the feral rage, I was afraid. Here was a creature that knew death, knew how to take a life not just for survival but also for the pure pleasure of it. I shot it, two through the heart before it even knew I was there, but that image always stayed with me, that memory. When the High Council asked me to create a new, stronger soldier I knew the werewolf would be a perfect start and that, with a few refinements, I could make something truly special."

Lyncon stared at the elf, astounded. He saw a sadness in his features, almost grief, but also a spark of something like desire or longing. To dedicate your life to turning the very thing that killed your father into a weapon for good seemed wrong to Lyncon but it was clear it had given Fenrir a drive and determination that few could hope to match.

"I… I'm sorry about your father."

Fenrir gave him a brief smile. "It was a long time ago. Now come on, we have a job to do." Without waiting he turned and walked away, leaving Lyncon to stare after him and try to piece together what he had just been told.

The sun was fading fast when they reached their target, a young deer trapped up to its haunches in thick mud. Passing the rope they had brought to Lyncon, Fenrir walked across to the stricken animal, his feet never once sinking into the hungry mud below them. After a reassuring word in its ear, he tied the rope around the deer and Lyncon heaved it out onto the grass.

Free at last, the fawn bowed deeply to both its rescuers, placid eyes staring into theirs. Finally it trotted forwards and gently nuzzled Lyncon's hand before turning and bounding off amongst the trees. Lyncon watched it go with a mix of wonder and pride. Beside him Fenrir caught the expression and gave a gentle smile.

"We did well," the elf said as he looped the rope back over his shoulder. "She was grateful." Lyncon, still staring after the deer, only nodded. "Come. Let's start heading back."

Together the duo set off again back through the forest towards home. Around them birds chirped as they fluttered from branch to branch, the hustle of spring beginning to merge into summer. Lyncon watched as a robin, perched on the most slender of branches, burst into song, the power of its voice far outweighing its tiny form. It watched him as it sang, its beady eyes fixed on his passing, the voice never once faltering.

"In some ways the smallest of creatures are the greatest amongst us." Lyncon turned, not realising the elf had been watching him. "They do not demand the world bends to them but instead adapt to it, living their life in harmony with the forest. There is a purity there that very few reach, an elegance and understanding that our races could never achieve." His face fell, large eyes suddenly sombre. "It saddens me that we could never be as happy as that robin is now, never be as whole. For us, the joy of simply existing is lost amongst our thoughts of more selfish things. We are never content. Never." He paused, seeming to stare at the bird with something close to longing. "It took me a long time to realise that knowledge is not always a blessing."

As Lyncon watched he saw a great sadness pass over his companion's face, a heavy weight of age and the memories that came with it, past horrors and regretful deeds. Caught out by the sudden vulnerability, it took Lyncon a few seconds to respond.

"It is true we can do terrible things, hurt this world when we should be nurturing it, but can we also not do good? Would that deer have survived without us? Or the swallow we helped yesterday?" He paused. "The past can hurt but it can also grant us the knowledge and hindsight to become better. It should not be feared but learnt from."

Slowly Fenrir turned and stared at him. Then a smile crept onto his lips. "Perhaps some of that elven education remains within you after all." Lyncon smiled back and for a moment the two of them seemed almost like friends.

Above them, the robin continued to sing its merry tune.

"I want to know about the war," Lyncon asked in between mouthfuls of steaming stew. They had returned to the hut a little over an hour ago and were now tucking into a well-earned meal.

For a moment Fenrir did not reply, caught up in chewing. "What do you want to know?"

He shrugged. " Everything, I suppose. All I know is what you and Julian t…" His voice caught and he dropped his eyes to his bowl, spoon hovering in midair.

Spotting the look, Fenrir quickly pushed on. "Throughout time, elves and humans have rarely seen eye to eye. War is nothing new."

"But this one is different?"

He thought for a second, laying down his own spoon and scratching at one of those strange flat ears that Lyncon still struggled to look at. "Yes you're right, I suppose it is. This is the first war in history the humans are actually winning."

"Why? What changed?"

"They did." When he saw Lyncon's confused expression he sighed in frustration and rolled his eyes. "Elves have been around for a long time. We age very slowly and some of us live for thousands of years. Once, we ruled almost all the known lands, Petra and Vilantis was just one big kingdom. We built great cities and tended forests full of trees that grew just as tall as the white tree we now live beneath. When humans first appeared we welcomed them. They were young and primitive and we believed we could teach them our ways but we failed to account for one important thing: their mortality."

He picked up his spoon and ate another mouthful of stew while Lyncon waited patiently for him to continue, his own food now forgotten.

"Mortality is a difficult concept for elves. We do not fear our end; we have time to come to terms with and embrace it as a part of nature. Humanity does not. It is this fear, caused by the very briefness of their lives, which makes humans so dangerous, so volatile. They are emotional and unpredictable, desperately trying to outrun their own demise. As human numbers grew and they built cities of their own, they began to fight amongst themselves. Then they turned on us."

He pushed away his empty bowl before returning his attention to Lyncon. "At first we were not concerned. Humans were weak and we far outmatched them. However, they are quick to learn, adaptable, and soon became a threat we could not ignore. In response, a famous elf lord, now known as Balkin the Butcher, proposed a culling of human numbers to regain control of our lands. The other elf lords agreed and the first Great War began."

Fenrir stood abruptly and crossed to the fire where the pot of tea hung, keeping warm. He poured himself a cup, the firelight dancing across his face, shadows forming in every wrinkle. There was a stiffness about the way he stood that betrayed to Lyncon the shame he felt from this past, a feeling they shared. Lyncon felt a pang of sorrow then, a realisation that, although he did not often show it, Fenrir was almost as broken as he was.

"We don't have to talk anymore if you don't want to…"

"No." He shook his head, staring at the flames. "You deserve to know how you came to be."

Lyncon nodded slowly. "If you're sure. How many wars have there been?"

"That depends on who you ask. I would say at least five but some say more, others say it has only ever been one, coming in fits and starts. There are few, if any, that remember them all."

"When did this one start?"

"Five or six years ago, when King Hosban attacked the city of Dentonberg."

Lyncon frowned. "I thought Renthor was king?"

Fenrir nodded as he returned from the fire and sat back down. "He is; Hosban was his father. He was killed four years ago in battle and Renthor took the throne in his place."

Lyncon sat in silence for a moment as he chewed the last pieces of his stew, deep in thought. The food was cold but he barely noticed, instead turning over this new information in his head, tying it all together. Outside, rain had begun to fall, the drops drumming gently upon the shutters.

Finally finished, Lyncon laid down his spoon. "You said that this time men were winning; is that why you made me?"

Fenrir regarded him with empty eyes, the huge pupils staring steadily into his own. The elf's expression was one of contemplation.

"For the first time in history we were losing. King Renthor had gathered a great army after the death of his father and used his superior numbers to launch simultaneous attacks on the last elven cities in Petra, Dentonberg and Corin. Those that escaped the slaughter fled across the small strip of land connecting Petra and Vilantis known as the Neck of Corin. They were pursued by raiding parties and cavalry and hundreds were cut down as they made for the nearest towns or cities. Elven armies responded by pushing the humans back across the Neck and fortifying it, building a barricade across its entire length."

He sighed, a heavy gesture. In the half-light he looked older than this morning. "For a while there was calm, a sort of stalemate as neither army risked moving against the other. The king tried to use ships to move on Vilantis but lookouts spotted them easily and they were repelled. After losing half his fleet in the rough seas, Renthor abandoned the idea of a sea crossing. The war ground to a halt but it was not over."

Fenrir sipped his tea. Lyncon noticed his hand shake slightly as he lifted the cup to his lips. A sudden rush of wind brought a drumming of raindrops against the shutters.

"After the attacks, the Elven High Council knew the reprieve would not last. In desperation they turned to their academics, those that dealt in science and magic alike, to help find a solution. They ordered us all to come up with something to win the war, to save our homes from the merciless invaders and, like fools, we obeyed. Due to my knowledge of Grezna, I was put in charge of the Werewarg Programme." He gestured to Lyncon. "The rest you know."

Lyncon stared down at the table, absentmindedly scratching at its surface with his finger. Fenrir watched him intently with those big round eyes but said nothing more, the only noise between them the crackling of fire and the rhythm of the rain.

"Are there more like me?" he asked without looking up from the table.

"There were. When I left there were more than a dozen but who knows how many remain." Seeing this was not the answer Lyncon had hoped for, he added, "I destroyed my research notes when I fled; no more will ever be made."

"I hope they are all dead," he whispered after a long silence. "We are monsters that were never meant to be. If they lose control like I did, people will die. It is better if they are all dead."

Fenrir suddenly sprang forwards and grabbed Lyncon's hand. Snapped from his thoughts, he rose and tried to pull his hand away but the elf held him fast. They locked eyes, anger and confusion flaring in Lyncon's.

"You lost yourself once but perhaps control is not as far away as you think," Fenrir said calmly as he looked down at Lyncon's hand between them. A hand that had grown claws where the nails had once been.

The next morning Lyncon attacked the challenge of the tree with a new-found confidence and belief. Almost instantly he was able to grow small claws from the tips of each finger, the razor-sharp points morphing from his nails. His elation soon faded when it became apparent that the claws were not big enough to provide the purchase needed for him to reach the arrow. Still, it was progress and his mood was lifted for the rest of the day.

That night a huge storm blew in from the sea carrying rolling banks of thick black clouds, heavy with rain. The wind was fierce, howling through the trees, and the pair made sure to secure anything that might blow away before closing the shutters and retreating inside the hut. As their dinner bubbled and boiled, they sat by the fire drying their sodden clothes and listening to the storm battering the forest around them. Even the huge white tree above them groaned at the force of the storm winds, its branches shaking as if in fear.

Sleep was hard to find with all the noise but Lyncon eventually drifted off after much tossing and turning in his little wooden bed. Once asleep, he dreamt he was standing on a large plain, a flat grassy expanse stretching out around him, never-ending. A huge army was assembled in the distance, thousands of armoured soldiers, slowly advancing towards him, their footsteps rumbling like thunder. Without any hesitation he set off at a run towards the army, taking huge bounding leaps as he hurtled forwards. Only then did he become aware that he was not himself. Instead he was a wolf, a creature of coarse grey fur and huge claws. Around him he saw more like him, huge wolves clad in glittering armour with long swords strapped to their backs. They ran with him, towards the army and certain doom. As he neared the first line of soldiers he could smell their sweat in the air, feel the warmth of their blood and fear. He pulled back his lips in an animal snarl. Bunching his muscles he leapt forwards one last time and crashed into his foes, teeth bared.

He was woken by a sudden bang, frightfully loud, and the deafening roar of the wind swirling around him. Sitting up he saw that the door had been blown open by the sheer strength of the storm and crashed against the wall. Fenrir was already up and grappling with the thin wood, desperately trying to heave it closed against the might of the wind and rain. Around him chaos erupted as the storm threw papers into the air and rattled the pots hanging on the hooks over the fire, which was struggling to stay alight. A smash sounded from the small kitchen area in the corner as several bowls were hurled to the ground.

Jumping up, Lyncon fought his way to Fenrir's side. Rain struck his cheeks as the ferocious air pulled at his limbs and stung his eyes. Several more pots fell from a shelf and smashed onto the floor, the pieces flying into the air to swirl around the room. One struck Lyncon on the thigh, leaving a small trickle of red as it cut through his clothes.

"We need to nail it shut!" the elf shouted over the wind. "You hold it closed while I fetch the wood and nails."

Lyncon nodded and stood behind the door, palms braced flat against the wood as he began to push it back into place. At first it moved with relative ease but, as he kept pushing, the wind grew stronger as it was funnelled through a smaller and smaller gap. Slowly, the door's progress ground to a halt. Lyncon dug his heels into the floor, planting his feet and bracing his legs before pushing with all his strength. The door moved a little more but then stopped a full foot from closing.

Outside, lightning lit up the sky with a flash. The sudden brightness was blinding and Lyncon shut his eyes against the harsh light, grimacing. When he opened them again it was dark, the fire having finally given in to the wind and gone out. As his eyes adjusted he was shocked to find that he could still see almost as well as he had before, making out every detail of the hut around him. His momentary shock distracted him from his task and the wind took full advantage, pushing the door back into Lyncon's face and forcing him to take a step back. Gritting his teeth he resumed his struggle.

Once again he braced his legs and prepared to push. His face and shoulders were soaked from the rain blowing in through the gap and his hands were beginning to turn numb from the cold. Taking a breath to focus, he tensed his muscles and heaved against the wood. From outside, lightning pierced the sky before a deep roll of thunder seemed to shake the whole hut.

As Lyncon pushed he felt an unfamiliar warmth growing in his arms and legs, a heat that seemed to emanate from inside his muscles. The heat grew and with it so did his strength. The door began to swing shut as his body grew more and more powerful, the heat inside him rising to the task, overloading his muscles with a previously unknown strength. He heaved one last time and finally the door closed, jolting against the frame.

Fenrir suddenly appeared from the darkness beside him, wood and tools in hand, and began to nail the door shut. Once it was done, Lyncon tentatively stepped back, afraid it would swing open again. The wood buckled slightly as it settled into its new position but held closed and Lyncon gave a sigh of relief. Outside, the storm howled in anguish. Inside, something howled within Lyncon, a hidden beast that was beginning to emerge.

When dawn broke the duo ripped open the door and ventured outside to assess the damage. Snapped branches littered the clearing and several trees now lay like slaughtered soldiers on the forest floor. The white tree above them seemed undamaged, its bare branches untouched by the winds. The storm itself was long gone, leaving only its memory in the destruction it caused.

As they set about tidying the damage, clearing branches and chopping the fallen trees into firewood, Lyncon spotted something familiar protruding from one of the fallen trunks and laughed. With a grin, he walked over and plucked the arrow from the wood, presenting it to Fenrir with a wink before silently turning away. The elf scowled at first, staring down at the arrow. Then, with a chuckle, he threw it over his shoulder and got back to work, a small smile on his face.

Chapter 9

The Crooked Man

He woke to the peaceful still of dawn after a storm. Gentle light shone through the gap between the shutters over the window and gulls called to each other above the distant waves. The wind had died to nothing, its energy spent in the previous night's fury. He could relate. The storm's power had stirred the last of the Essence from the village and he had spent most of the night feasting, one last time. Now, with the Essence run dry, it was time to move on.

Slowly, the Crooked Man rose from the bed and dressed, donning his familiar faded robes. He left the large bedroom and descended the stairs to the dining room. The whole building had been cleared of bodies and wreckage but here and there patches of red still stained the wooden floor. Here was where the chief had died, his mother too. He could still feel them when he had first arrived, their pain lingering like the smell of smoke after a fire, but now there was nothing. The house was empty, silent.

He stopped at the pail of water that had been left for him beside the door. Looking down he saw no hint of a reflection, only the smooth calm surface of the still water.

Cupping his hands he splashed some water gently onto his face, the cold barely registering against his flesh. After drying himself off he opened the door and stepped out into the day.

The Crooked Man paused just beyond the door and surveyed the village from the hillock where the house stood. The other stone dwellings that fanned out around the rise were all occupied, reclaimed from their deceased owners by his own followers. The others slept in their carts, huddled together with their meagre belongings. The storm had damaged a few of the wooden huts around the village, tearing off roofs or ripping shutters from their hinges. A tree had fallen onto one hut, cleaving it in two as it crushed the wooden structure beneath its weight. It was no concern to him. Those huts were empty. Only the dead resided there now.

Slowly he stretched his shoulders and yawned before making his way down the path towards the rest of the village. He left his staff by the door. After such a feed he had no need for it; his body was young and supple, the wrinkled skin now fresh and smooth, muscles filled with the renewed vigour of new-found youth. He walked tall and proud, back straight. Seacrest had served him well, an almost complete renewal, but now it was gone, the well dry. He knew the aches and pains would return, his strength fading. He would soon be crooked once more. Then he would need a new place to feast.

He crossed the village in silence, picking his way through the wagons towards the furthest stone hut. A few of his followers were awake, cooking or fetching water from the well, and all smiled and bowed as he passed.

Like him they were fresh faced and strong from such a large dose of Essence. Some even wore new clothes they had looted from the houses, nothing too fancy but hard-wearing and clean.

Though no one spoke to him as he passed, his followers each bowed their heads in silent prayer. In their eyes was a deep love, a fanatic devotion to him and everything he offered them, the power he bestowed on their lives. He had no doubt at all that each and every one of them would lay down their life for him. Many already had. Not only did he demand such loyalty but he also deserved it. Without him, these people were nothing. Without him, they would be dust and memory. The eternal life of the Essence was not a gift given lightly.

He entered the house without knocking and was greeted by the sight of a woman's bare backside as she bent down to pick up her fallen clothes. She spun around at the sudden intrusion, dropping the garments once more, and straightened. Her eyes locked with his and he watched the fury and surprise in her gaze mellow almost instantly. She made no move to conceal her nudity as they stared at each other, neither showing signs of embarrassment. The young man sitting in the bed behind her had plenty of that for both of them.

"You're early," she said, her voice laced with its usual playful tone. "Can't you see I'm busy?" She gave a smile that had melted a thousand hearts, her green eyes sparkling like emeralds framed by auburn hair that fell easily over her shoulders and breasts.

"It looks like you are just about done," he replied, refusing to rise to her teasing. "Trisha, it is time."

"Already?" She sighed. "A pity." She turned to the youngster in her bed. "Donnell, I'm afraid we're done for today. Off you go now. The Leeraar and I have work to do."

Donnell nodded and quickly began to dress, desperate to beat a hasty retreat.

"No. He stays." Trisha met his gaze with a questioning one of her own but then shrugged and turned back to her clothes.

The young man stood by the bed, terrified, eyes as wide as saucers. "Please, Leeraar, I… I meant no offence. I… it was…"

"Silence." He uttered the single word and the boy instantly obeyed. He stepped close to him, so close they were almost touching, and raised a gentle hand to the boy's face. Donnell flinched at his touch but did not move away. The Crooked Man could feel the fear oozing out of him, seeping through his skin into his fingers as he gently brushed his cheek. Suddenly, he was hungry again.

He leant forwards and whispered into the young man's ear. "Undress me for her."

At the words, Donnell's breath caught in his throat and it took him several long moments to force himself to obey. With shaking hands, he reached forwards and removed his Leeraar's shirt and belt, causing his trousers to drop to the floor. His job done, he tried to pull away but the Crooked Man caught his wrist.

"Prepare me for her. I need you to help me start." His voice was a gentle whisper, soft and warm, but his face was blank and there was a morbid hunger in his gaze, an eagerness, like a predator stalking its prey, imagining the kill.

"Please… I don't…"

"Enough. Am I not your Leeraar? Your all father?"

Donnell hung his head in shame. "Of course."

"Then do as I command."

Seeing he truly had no choice, Donnell nodded slowly. Tears had begun to trickle down his face and he stank of sweat and fear. The Crooked Man took it all in, feeling the terror, wanting it. His eyes never left the young man's face, unblinking. Slowly, Donnell reached forwards and took his Leeraar's manhood in his hand, whimpering slightly as he began to work it.

The Crooked Man shuddered as pleasure coursed through his veins and a small smile began to form at the corners of his mouth. Trisha watched from across the room with morbid fascination. Slowly, tenderly, he reached up and placed a hand either side of Donnell's face, palms flat against his damp cheeks. Their eyes locked as Donnell continued to move his hand. The Crooked Man saw such fear and loathing in the young man's gaze, a deep disgust in himself and his Leeraar. He smiled then pushed himself forwards and kissed him.

As soon as their lips touched Donnell froze, his movements stopped as every muscle in his body tensed. His eyes began to bulge from their sockets as black tendrils began to grow underneath his skin, emanating outwards from the Crooked Man's palms and lips. They spread quickly, wriggling up into his hair and down over his neck and shoulders. One even popped out of his nostril, wriggling in the air like a thin black worm, before it turned and shot back up the other nostril, forcing its way back inside him. When the tendrils reached his eyes they began to cloud over, the life behind them ebbing away.

As the blackness engulfed Donnell's face, the Crooked Man finally broke away, licking wet lips. He grinned at the sight before him, a terrifying, monstrous grin that split his face and revealed yellow, crooked teeth. Donnell's skin began to sag and flake away, like ash dropping from burning wood. A spasm of terror, primal instinctive fear, pulsed through them and the Crooked Man raised his head to the sky in ecstasy, moaning softly as he devoured all he could. The fear flowed through him, around him, inside him, and he relished its feel, the power it gave him, the life. His breathing came in sharp, excited gasps and his hands began to shake with the excitement of his feast. Then, with one final moan, he pushed his hands together and Donnell's head exploded into a cloud of fine black powder, almost like soot. The powder hung in the air, floating, then surged into the Crooked Man's palms and was gone, disappearing into his pale skin.

Pushing the limp and headless body back onto the bed, he took several deep breaths. Once composed, he dressed and turned to Trisha, offering his wrist.

"Drink."

With lightning speed far beyond any human, she sprang across the room, knelt at his feet and bit deeply into his wrist with freshly formed fangs. She drank greedily, lapping up the Essence that coursed through his veins. After several minutes she stood and staggered back to the bed, giddy from such a rich feast.

"When shall I leave?" she asked as she wiped her mouth with the back of her hand.

"Immediately. I will have Thom pack away your things."

Trisha nodded and took a cloak from a hook by the door. The material was soft velvet coloured a deep black. It made not a single sound as she put it on and fastened it at her shoulders.

"Find us somewhere rich. This place was dead, memories of pain. I want fresh takings, living fear."

"Of course, Leeraar. Your word is wisdom."

The Crooked Man nodded and went to the door, opening it and stepping out onto the porch. Trisha joined him a moment later, closing the door softly behind her, Donnell's corpse still lying on the bed.

She turned and bowed low to him. Her eyes still sparkled from her meal. "I will be as quick as the winds allow."

He smiled and leant forwards to kiss her soft red lips. They were hot against his own. "I know."

She gave him a brief smile before turning away and launching herself into the air, her form changing from that of a woman into a thick, seething mass of black, shifting and contorting like smoke as she rose on the wind. Before long she was out of sight. He watched her go, his precious pet. A nebula was a rare creature, even in Vilantis, and he knew how lucky he was to have her talents at his disposal.

"So we are leaving, then?" Thom asked as he climbed the steps to the porch. He was a skinny man with thinning brown hair. As always he wore a checked shirt, this one blue and red, though there were other colours where it had been patched over the years.

"Yes, it is time. I have found all I can here."

Thom nodded and gave a grin that was as much gap as it was teeth. "Alright. Shall I get everyone rounded up?"

"Yes. Make sure to deal with Trisha's things too. I want us gone by nightfall."

"Your word is wisdom, Leeraar. I'll see to it." He bowed low and strolled off without another word. Thom had been his first ever follower and was by far his most devout. He had been the first to proclaim him Leeraar, God of Shadow, and the first to accept the Essence. Though not the smartest or eldest here, Thom was liked by many and respected by all. He had taken on the role of camp leader without ever being given it.

The Crooked Man stayed on the porch for a while longer, watching as his people began to rouse from their slumber and pack up their lives. They did it all without a single complaint, smiles on their faces, knowing the orders had come from him. His people were wanderers, travellers, accustomed to life on the road, knowing they must always journey from one meal to the next. For most it had not been much of a change from their past lives; many had been homeless or unwanted. He was their life now, their guiding light. Where he went they would gladly follow.

The sun had risen fully and its heat was growing, even against the efforts of a keen wind that blew in from the sea bringing with it a tang of salt. Leaning on the wooden rail he closed his eyes, feeling the sun on his skin. Its heat soaked him but gave no warmth, no joy; such was his curse. He snapped his eyes open as he sensed again something beside him, around him, watching. A shiver passed down his spine and he froze as he probed with his senses, searching for this unseen watcher. Unable to find them he instead blocked them out, forcing them away with all his power.

Slowly, he straightened up and stepped off the porch, moving warily despite knowing whatever had been watching him was no longer there. He shook his head, suddenly concerned, and rubbed his back. Trisha's meal had taken its toll. He would soon need his staff again.

Far away in Astikus, Evanora stood at a window in her chambers and looked out at the rain as it fell on the city below. A ghostly reflection stared back at her from the glass, the face haggard and worn, eyes weighed heavily by lack of sleep. Suddenly she stumbled back from the window as if pushed and crumpled against the wall where she slid to the floor.

Sitting in the mass of her ruffled robes she lowered her head into her hands, images of what she had just witnessed flashing through her mind. She shuddered slightly as she recalled the young man's expression as the black tendrils had enveloped his face and devoured his eyes. She had seen it all, the whole ordeal, and he had let her. Tentatively, she reached out again to try to see through his eyes but saw nothing. The Crooked Man was blocking her, shielding himself from her perversion. He had known she was watching and was afraid. He remembered her. Beneath her hands a thin smile formed.

A knock at the door made her jump and before she could regain her feet Amos had thrown it open and strode in. The huge bald man stared down at her, a smirk forming beneath his thick moustache.

"You know, I find chairs far more comfortable for sitting."

"Stick to killing people, Amos," she said with a scowl. "Your wit isn't half as sharp as your blade. Now help me up."

He reached down a hand and lifted her up with seemingly no effort at all. She flattened her robes with her hands but when she spotted that they were shaking she tucked them behind her back. "What do you want anyway? It is rude to charge into a lady's room without permission. What if I had been bathing?"

"Then you would have had to dry yourself pretty quick," he replied with a smirk. Seeing her unamused expression he sighed. "You are right and I apologise but the king was insistent that I fetched you at once." He shrugged.

She sighed as she strode past him towards the door. "Where is he?"

"The war room," he replied as he joined her in the corridor and led the way.

Though it was the middle of the day, the castle was quiet, the long hallways of red stone mostly empty, filled with a silence disturbed only by the sound of Amos' heavy steps. They passed several doors, all small, identical and probably locked, leading to rooms Evanora had never bothered to investigate. No matter how fancy the prison, she found there was rarely any need to go poking around outside your own cell.

The war room doors were larger and guarded but the soldiers moved aside as their captain approached. The two stepped through the open doorway into a large room with high ceilings and walls lined with tall bookcases, each containing hundreds of books and scrolls. Windows set high into the wall cast rays of light down onto the huge table that dominated the room's centre. The table top was decorated by a map of Petra and Vilantis that had been painted and stained into the wood. That it was an ancient gift given by the elves to a past king had an irony that was never lost on Evanora. How many battles had been planned in this very room? How many elven lives lost?

Seated at the far end of the table was their king, head bowed as he studied a scroll in his hands. More scrolls were stacked untidily around him along with a jug of wine. He did not look up as they approached, nor did he address them until he had finished reading, leaving them standing in awkward silence. Evanora studied his face as he read but could discern nothing about his mood.

"Sit. Both of you," he ordered without looking up. They both did as they were told, seating themselves either side of the king.

"You have news, my lord?" Evanora asked when he did not immediately speak, trying her best to hide her impatience.

"Yes." Finally he looked up at her. His expression was one she could not place. "Earlier today I received an envoy from Vilantis. With them was a letter signed by the Elven High Council. They have asked for peace and an end to the war. They believe, after the Snapping of the Neck and heavy losses on both sides, that peace would be best for all. Now the land border is severed, they have proposed that Vilantis and Petra become separate, independent nations and try to work together for a better future." The king paused, looking at both of them in turn, studying their stunned expressions. "I have been given three days to reply and escort the embassy back to their ship."

While Amos regained some composure and managed a solemn nod, Evanora continued to stare at the king with a blank expression, her wide eyes glazed and distant. Memories shot through her mind, images of her youth in Vilantis, the High Council jeering at her from their thrones. Another life and yet one she would never escape.

Renthor noticed her face and raised a questioning eyebrow. "You do not seem pleased with this news, elf? Why is that?"

"A… apologies, my lord" she muttered as she broke from her trance. "I was not expecting the High Council to ever request peace. After all that has happened… I am shocked."

The king nodded, his chin wobbling ever so slightly. "I too was a little taken aback by the offer but the elves have lost ground steadily over the years and their numbers are dwindling. I think they know the war is lost." He gave a small smile of satisfaction before quickly composing himself.

"Could it be a distraction, my lord?" Amos asked. "Or perhaps a ruse to buy more time to recover?"

"Unlikely. Elves breed, grow and train far slower than we do. They will build, of course, forts and other defences but, now the neck of Corin has broken, I have no desire to move into Vilantis. Let them keep it."

"You mean to accept the peace offer?" Evanora asked in disbelief, fingers gripping the arms of her chair.

The king nodded slowly. "War is expensive and I grow tired of all this killing." As he hung his head and rubbed a hand through his thinning hair he suddenly looked very old. The often bullish and hot-headed king was replaced by a tired man who had ordered more men to their deaths than he could count. Evanora saw for the first time how much that weighed on him. She might have pitied him if she did not already hate him so much. "The elves are right, our numbers are short and, now we have driven them out, I think it is time to look inward, time to rebuild Petra into something greater." He raised a hand for silence as he saw she was about to interrupt. "I know how you feel about your kind, how they banished you, and I am sorry that you will not get the justice I promised when I took you in but I must do what I believe is best for my kingdom and its people."

She was silent for a moment before giving a quick nod, her eyes, fixed on the opposite wall, were clouded by thoughts. The image of the night she had been captured sprang into her mind, the guards dragging her before the king, battered and bruised, as he stared at her with a nasty gleam in his eye. He had worded his speech to sound as if he were helping her but she had always known the truth. She was a trophy, an asset to be used against a bigger foe and perhaps lead the king to something greater. She made a determined effort to relax her grip on the chair. Neither man seemed to have noticed.

"Good," the king said, nodding firmly to each of them. "Now on to the other reason I have summoned you. Amos, is there any news of the old man from the vision?"

"Possibly. Yesterday one of my men reported that a merchant told him of a village he had passed through south of Corin. He did not stop but he noticed that the village seemed to be filled with odd wagons and traveller folk. There were bodies too, lots of them. The village is named… Seacrest. Yes, that was it."

"He is there," Evanora said suddenly, her focus snapping to Amos, thoughts of revenge and hatred forgotten. "How far is the village? I must go."

"Almost a week's march I would think." The big man shrugged. "I have not been there myself."

"Then we must go at once. He is planning to leave the village. We will need to travel light if we are to catch him. We cannot let him slip away."

"Enough!" The king slammed his hand down onto the map table as he puffed out his ample cheeks. His face was an alarming shade of red. His eyes were hard, glazed with his notorious anger. "I am the one who gives the orders around here or have you forgotten?"

"No, Your Grace." The elf bowed her head, her black hair covering her expression.

"Good." He stared at her a little longer before rounding on Amos. "How reliable is your source?"

"He had no reason to lie. He was not paid and offered the information freely."

The king grinned. "Then he is clearly a poor businessman." He paused and stroked his chin in thought. "Evanora is right; we must act quickly if we wish to catch this Crooked Man. Even if we make peace, we do not want the elves finding him first."

"I will go," Evanora offered, trying to keep demand out of her voice. "I must. He is too powerful for any other."

The king was silent for a moment before giving a nod. "Yes, you're right, but I cannot risk anything happening to you either. If anyone recognises you as an elf then there will be a riot. While we are still at war, tensions are high and it only takes one angry drunk with a pitchfork to start a witch-hunt." He let the silence hang as he stared at the sorceress whose earlier enthusiasm had diminished a little.

Renthor, deep in thought, began to stroke his chin again as his subjects waited in silence for him on either side. Around them the scrolls sat on their dusty shelves, voiceless observers. Evanora found herself wondering at the history of this room, the conversations and decisions these scrolls had witnessed. Suddenly the shelves seemed to be drawing closer, leering at her from all sides. She shuddered and forced herself to turn her mind back to the matter at hand.

"Amos, I want you to go with her."

The captain looked shocked. "But, my lord, the elven envoy…"

The king raised a hand for silence, a scowl darkening his face. "I have not forgotten the envoy. The elves will accompany you both, along with an armed guard of course. This Seacrest is on the way to Dentonberg where the envoy's boat is waiting. You can travel under the guise of the envoy's protection and Evanora can then get a look at the village and hopefully track this Crooked Man down." He smiled at his own intelligence but scowled when neither of his companions returned the gesture. "Unfortunately we do not have horses to spare as our cavalry units are still camped near the Neck, so you will be on foot. Leave at first light with as much haste as you can. I suggest you both run along and prepare." With a wave of his hand he returned his attention back to the scroll.

Evanora simply sat for a moment, big round eyes fixed in a vacant stare as her mind worked over everything she had been told. So much was changing, the world shifting beneath her. This had not been part of her plan. The envoy could not jeopardise her search for the Crooked Man. She must adapt and quickly.

Quietly, the two subjects rose and departed the war room. Neither was pleased with the outcome of the meeting but both, like many who had stepped out of these doors before them, shared a foreboding sense of dread.

Chapter 10

A Disturbance in the Forest

Lyncon gripped the sword tightly as he eyed his opponent across the clearing. He paused to push a stray lock of hair from in front of his eyes. After a deep breath he tensed his muscles and exploded forwards, sword held up and ready beside him.

He cleared the distance between himself and Fenrir in three long strides. When he neared the elf he swung his sword at head height with ferocious strength, the blade gleaming in the late afternoon sun as it whistled through the air towards its target. With a casual calm, Fenrir ducked the blade and stepped aside while Lyncon sailed past him, carried on by his own momentum. Grinding to a halt, Lyncon spun on his heel to face his opponent again, turning just in time to catch Fenrir's fist on the left side of his jaw, the punch sending him sprawling backwards into the dirt.

Silently, the elf loomed over him, looking down with impassive eyes. "Too slow." He turned and paced away. "You can do better. I have seen it."

With a huff of frustration Lyncon hauled himself to his feet, rubbing his jaw with his free hand. "Maybe once but that was before."

"Wrong! Training is never forgotten. It is not a memory but an instinct, in your body as much as your mind. Your muscles will remember. You just have to make them. Less thinking and more doing." He turned to face Lyncon and raised his own sword. "Again!"

Still rubbing his jaw, Lyncon reset his stance and adjusted his sword grip. Then he began his approach, cautiously this time, in slow, measured steps. He kept his sword close to him, hands just above hip height. When he was almost in range of the elf he stabbed forwards, driving at his opponent's gut. Fenrir deflected the blow with a dull clang, pushing Lyncon's sword aside before launching an attack of his own. Lyncon just had time to duck the cut that was aimed for his head, the blade whistling through the air above him. The two foes stepped apart and readied themselves to go again.

Fenrir lunged suddenly into an attack. His blade cut through the air in a series of vicious slashes and thrusts that Lyncon could only just manage to parry as he was forced backwards under the onslaught. The speed was frightening, ferocious, and Lyncon had to concentrate as hard as he could to block or dodge every strike. The sound of their swords meeting rang through the clearing, disturbing the tranquillity of the forest around them.

Finally Lyncon's back struck a tree and he could retreat no further. Now he was trapped at the elf's mercy, desperately fending off blow after blow as his arms began to ache and sweat formed on his brow. As Fenrir raised his blade to strike down, Lyncon clenched his jaw and pushed off from the tree with one foot, driving his shoulder into his teacher's midriff. Both fell to the floor in a heap, rolling across the grass. It was the elf who regained his feet first and stood over his opponent once more, sword tip aimed at his throat. Lyncon, who had been trying to retrieve his own weapon, instantly froze.

"That was better," Fenrir said between ragged gasps, his pale face slick with sweat. "A little… unorthodox perhaps but good. Thinking on your feet is key. If you weren't so slow to get back up I would almost be impressed." He twirled his sword and stepped back, allowing Lyncon to stand.

A sudden rustling in the undergrowth made them both turn just in time to see a horse appear bearing an aged-looking man on its back. Upon spotting them the rider reined in immediately and studied them with a wary gaze. From behind him another horse appeared, this one being led by a huge man who, despite his immense size, seemed little older than a boy. Clearly intent on looking where to tread, he did not notice his companion's horse had stopped in front of him and walked straight into its rear, causing the animal to neigh and skitter away, almost unseating its rider.

"Henrik you oaf! Watch where you are walking!" cursed the older man as he got the beast back under control.

"I was," replied the boy in defiance. "I just didn't see you stop." He paused, scratching his chin with one huge hand. "Why did you stop?"

"Because we have company," the rider replied before turning towards the duo. "Good day, friends, our apologies for disturbing you. We are not well acquainted with these woods and seem to have lost the path we were travelling on. My name is Ser Dallan Tan and this is my son and squire Henrik." He indicated the boy, who had finally noticed them and was now staring intently at Fenrir, his mouth hanging slightly open.

At first neither Fenrir nor Lyncon responded. Both had swords in hand and were watching the knight very closely, unsure how to react. Lyncon had immediately spotted the sword dangling from the old man's hip as well as the shield strapped to the side of his saddle. Though Henrik was unarmed, his limbs were as thick as tree trunks and Lyncon spied a second sword stowed on the horse the boy was leading. At least one of them knew how to fight.

"The road is that way," Fenrir said in an even tone as he pointed over the knight's shoulder with one slender finger. "Go as straight as you can for almost half a mile and you will find it."

"Thank you, good ser." The old man bowed his head, his long silver hair falling over his shoulders. "Tell me, to whom do I owe my thanks?" He smiled at them to reveal several missing teeth. Beside him the boy continued to stare at Fenrir with a mixture of confusion and wonder.

Lyncon gripped his sword tighter. Though the old man did not look too threatening, he was a knight and had the advantage of both a shield and a mount. He studied the way the old man looked at Fenrir, searching for anything that may give away his thoughts. Had Lyncon been alone he would have expected no trouble but with an elf beside him things were different. He knew enough about the war to know Fenrir was not wanted in Petra and most would need little excuse to be rid of him.

"We are nobodies. Just folk who live in the quiet of the woods." Fenrir's voice remained calm but Lyncon noticed his knuckles were white as he gripped the handle of his own sword.

The old knight raised a questioning eyebrow. "Nobodies with good steel in their hands. Not often you come across two woodsmen with such fine blades." With a gentle kick he urged his horse a few steps closer. Lyncon resisted the urge to step back and instead stepped between the old man and Fenrir.

A sudden realisation flashed across the tall boy's face and his mouth dropped open. "F... Father..." he spluttered while pointing to Fenrir. "That... that one, he's an... e... e..."

"An elf. Yes, I can see that, Henrik. My eyes have not failed me just yet." The old man gave a shake of his head before summoning another gap-filled smile. "Seems you're a long way from home, friend. I know that feeling more than most. I was born on Tuscanto and I haven't seen the island since I was fourteen. As you may have guessed, that was quite some time ago." He winked as he stroked the untidy grey hairs sprouting from his chin. "What's your name, stranger?" The question was meant for Fenrir.

There was a pause as the elf stared at the old man, weighing his options in silence. Lyncon stood between them, still and tense, sweat running down the back of his neck. His heart was thundering in his chest and he focused on trying to slow his breathing and relaxing his muscles. Humans and elves were old enemies. This could surely only end one way. He started when Fenrir placed a gentle hand on his shoulder and moved beside him, giving him a reassuring smile.

152

"My name is Fenrir Moorn of Belanthor and this is Lyncon Baneswood." Fenrir gave a stiff bow. "It is an honour to meet you, Ser Dallan."

The knight nodded slowly, watching them beneath his bushy brow. "Well met." He indicated their swords with a flick of the reins. "It seems we interrupted your sparring. Do you mind if I join you? It is always good for a knight to train, keep their skills sharp." Without waiting for an answer he swung himself down from his horse and began freeing his shield from his saddlebags. Henrik hurried over to take his reins, his eyes never once leaving Fenrir.

With his shield now in place and his hair tied behind his head, Dallan began slowly walking towards them. He drew his sword from its scabbard, the blade giving a gentle hiss as it was freed. "Come now, no need to be shy. Don't worry about numbers; I have a shield, so I reckon I can take you both at once." He grinned at them from above his shield, eyes gleaming in excitement. Then he exploded forwards into an attack.

Ser Dallan was fast for his age. He charged forwards and was on them in seconds, presenting his shield towards Fenrir as he stabbed at Lyncon, who retreated while he deflected the blow. The elf launched two swipes at the old man, vicious strikes that were intended to kill, but neither found their mark as the knight blocked them both and drove his shield into his opponent, pushing Fenrir away. Lyncon tried to strike while his foe was distracted but he parried the attack and lashed out, kneeing Lyncon hard in the thigh. With surprising grace, he spun on the spot and bashed Lyncon with his shield, sending him sprawling to the floor.

As Lyncon lay dazed on the grass, Fenrir and Dallan traded blows, both striking and parrying with practised precision. The elf's features were taut with concentration while the old man's face was etched with an almost childlike glee. Lyncon regained his feet in time to see Dallan block a strike, step inwards and drive his knee up into Fenrir's groin. Winded, the elf collapsed. The knight stood over him, steel glinting in the sun, a strange look passing across his face.

With a snarl of rage, Lyncon launched himself at Dallan, cutting at his head. The old man just had time to duck the strike and turn before Lyncon slammed into him and fell on top of him on the grass.

On the ground both were unable to use their weapons, Ser Dallan's shield caught between their bodies. Lyncon tried to manoeuvre his sword around it but his arm was pinned underneath him by his own weight. As he tried to lift himself up with his free hand, Dallan released his own sword and punched Lyncon hard in the mouth. With a feral snarl, Lyncon released his own weapon and began to rain down strikes upon the old knight, punching at his head and shoulders and neck with wild inaccuracy. His heart pounded in his chest as he fought, striking again and again, his every breath a ragged gasp. Suddenly, strong arms wrapped themselves around him and pulled him upwards, lifting him off his feet and pinning his arms at his sides. Lyncon tried to twist free, lashing out with his legs, but Henrik stood firm, unmoved, his arms locked in place.

Slowly, Ser Dallan rose to his feet. His face and neck were marked where Lyncon had hit him and he had a split lip, blood running down his chin in a steady trickle. He spat and a shower of red splattered the grass between them. When he spat again a tooth fell at his feet. Carefully he bent and picked it up, examining it closely as he turned it between two fingers. Then he looked up at Lyncon and grinned.

"You knocked out my tooth!" He undid his shield and let it fall to the floor before wiping the blood from his mouth with the back of his hand. "Been wanting rid of that little bastard for quite a time. Was getting terribly sore in the cold weather."

Lyncon said nothing, too shocked to react, his pulse only just starting to drop as the red mist of battle faded. He stared, open-mouthed, as Dallan casually threw the tooth away. When he saw Lyncon was still being held, he scowled. "Henrik, let him go. He did nothing wrong. He was just protecting his friend."

"But he could'a killed ya…"

"Probably but he didn't and it was my fault anyway, got carried away." He grinned like a naughty child.

As the giant boy released Lyncon, Dallan walked over to Fenrir, who was kneeling in the grass, still gasping for breath. Lyncon tensed as the old man stepped next to the elf but he only offered Fenrir his hand. After a brief hesitation, doubt flashing across Fenrir's pale face, the elf took the hand offered and let the knight help him to his feet.

"My apologies for my behaviour, friend." He slapped Fenrir lightly on the back. He was at least a foot shorter than the elf. "Restraint has never been my strong point." He gestured towards Lyncon. "Besides, I needed to make it look good to help this one let loose a little."

"What do you mean help me? I could have killed you!" Lyncon said, brow furrowed.

The old man grinned at him. "Oh no, Henrik would have never let that happen." He waved a hand dismissively. "I just wanted to help you get the feel of a real fight, the blood pumping and adrenaline flowing through ya. Nothing else like it." He pointed towards the bushes from where they had appeared. "Truth is we were watching you for some time, watching you train. Your mentor over here is right; you think too much, hesitate. Sometimes caution is good but other times it can get you killed. Battle is all about instincts, being the quickest to react to everything around you." He turned to Lyncon, looking him up and down as he nodded to himself. "You have potential. With the right teacher you could be a formidable fighter."

Henrik nodded behind him, smiling proudly. "Papa has won more tournaments than there are stars in the sky!"

"Quiet, boy, and don't call me that!" The knight shook his head but there was a hint of a smile on his lips. "Fetch my weapons and put them back on the horse."

The giant man straightened and hurried to do as he was told. "Yes, ser; sorry, ser."

"Where are you heading?" Fenrir asked as he stepped up beside Lyncon, still rubbing his groin.

Ser Dallan shrugged. "Not really sure. We were just travelling looking for work."

The elf frowned. "I thought knights served lords? Swore oaths and such?"

"That's right. I served Lord Marcus of Murton for many years until he died last summer, gods bless his soul. His son, Lord Trent, did not deem me fit to serve him and released me from my oaths." He paused, staring down at his boots, a sudden stillness settling over him, making him seem older. "The boy was only doing what he thought was best. Didn't want an old man protecting him, wanted younger knights by his side. It made sense…" He trailed off, still studying his boots.

Lyncon studied Ser Dallan properly for the first time, noticing the scars that laced his thin limbs, pale ridges etched on to the firm muscles beneath his leathery skin. Lyncon knew better than most that each one told a story, of a battle lost or won, a fight for survival or glory. Here was a man who had devoted himself to battle, to the protection of another, but had lost the biggest fight of all. Time had been his downfall, the slow creep of age.

Beside him, Fenrir bowed his head. "I am sorry. I know what it is like to be cast aside after giving only loyalty to those you serve. It is not easy."

Dallan looked up and studied him a second before nodding. "Thank you. I am sorry you know this pain." He sighed before clearing his throat and forcing a smile back onto his face. "Still, it is not all bad. The life of a Militios has its perks."

"Militios?" Lyncon asked, puzzled by the unknown word.

"It is an old term deriving from elvish," Fenrir explained. "It translates to free-sword but many mercenaries or sellswords took it as their own title."

"Huh, few use it nowadays. This war has made such men bold; they feel no shame at being named mercenary, as long as they are paid. It used to be that a Militios would take no side in a conflict, instead using their sword to protect the weak or to slay beasts. Now men will throw in with anyone for the right price." He shrugged and turned to shout to Henrik. "Boy, bring me a rag for this lip. It is dripping all over me."

"Yes, Pa…I mean ser!" came the reply.

The old knight shook his head in frustration. "That boy," he sighed. "Well it had best be time we were leaving. Henrik is not fond of the woods, especially at night, and I would like to reach the road before dark." He extended a hand to them both. "I thank you for your help and your time. It has been too long since I had a good fight. I had forgotten how much I missed it."

Lyncon shook the hand offered. "I didn't mean to hurt you. It is just, with Fenrir, I thought…"

"I know what you thought and I don't blame you. No hard feelings here, lad. You hit hard. Got the makings of a good fighter." He grinned and spat blood onto the grass beside them, his split lip still producing a steady trickle.

Fenrir paused as he moved to shake Dallan's hand, his large eyes studying the old man's craggy face. Finally he grasped the man's hand but did not shake. "Ser Dallan, why don't you and your boy camp with us tonight? This clearing is as safe as any and we can escort you back to the road at first light. Tonight, let us eat together by the fire and share stories. I am keen to hear about some of these tournaments Henrik mentioned."

Dallan paused for a moment, clearly caught in two minds. Then he smiled his gap-toothed grin and placed a hand on Fenrir's shoulder. "An excellent idea and very kind of you." Over his shoulder he shouted, "Henrik, hobble the horses and fetch that cask of ale. Tonight we dine with company!"

By the time the fire was lit and Henrik had erected Ser Dallan's modest tent, the full moon was shining above them in a cloudless night sky smeared with a splatter of stars. The air was cool but not cold and they soon fell to exchanging stories around the fire while roasting the wild mushrooms Fenrir had found. Neither the knight nor his son had made any mention of the lack of meat present when the elf had returned from his foraging but they had looked more than a little disappointed. They had eaten in silence, seemingly happy for a hot meal, while Henrik did his best not to stare at Fenrir's ears.

Lyncon himself had grown used to the elven diet but even he had hoped tonight may be an exception to the old rules. Fenrir had explained to him that elves never hunt animals and only ever eat meat when it is naturally available. Killing for food was deeply frowned upon and only ever a last resort. Instead Lyncon had to content himself with handfuls of nuts and berries washed down with icy water from a nearby stream. He did not touch the ale the men were gleefully guzzling down.

"His spear had punched straight through my shield so I tossed it and faced the big bastard with a sword alone." The ale had made Ser Dallan loud and he was swaying alarmingly as he recounted his tale while perched on a log they had dragged beside the fire. He had removed his armour and now sat in a simple tunic that looked to have seen a few hard winters. He looked older in the firelight, the creases in his weathered skin casting lines of shadow across his face.

"He came at me hard, swinging like a madman, but he was slow and he couldn't get close. I danced and danced, spinning away from his every attack until I could see he was beginning to tire. Then I stepped in and struck him across the back of the knee. He went down like an old oak in a storm wind, such a crash, the ground shook. One good strike against his helm and he was out cold. Victory was mine." The old knight beamed and downed the rest of his drink, ushering for Henrik to refill his cup.

Fenrir smiled back at him. "A most impressive victory. It must've been quite the spectacle. How old were you then?"

"Just turned nineteen. It was only my second tournament. Afterwards Lord Marcus asked me to join his service and of course I accepted." He fell suddenly quiet, his eyes drifting to stare into the fire. Henrik gave his father a sad smile from across the flames.

Lyncon cleared his throat. "I am sorry to hear about Lord Marcus. How did he pass?"

"He was killed in this war. An elven arrow pierced his throat. He bled to death in my arms." The knight's voice was cold, devoid of emotion, the reflection of the flames dancing across his eyes as he spoke.

A tense silence settled over them all, broken only by the crackling of the fire and the distant hoot of an owl. They had removed their weapons to sit and eat but now Lyncon found his eyes drifting to his sword, calculating how quickly he could reach it.

After the silence had stretched on almost to breaking point, Fenrir spoke. His voice was soft and calm, as if trying not to provoke a dangerous animal. "Ser Dallan, why didn't you ride me down when you first saw me?"

More silence followed and for a long time the old knight just stared into the flames, unmoving. Eventually he gave a heavy sigh. "I have never liked killing. In my eyes, being a knight was about justice, upholding the law, bringing security to people. When I lay on that battlefield, cradling Marcus' body in my arms, I looked around and I saw what a terrible waste of life it all was. All those soldiers around me, from both sides, fighting a war fuelled simply by greed and ego. It made me sick." He turned to Fenrir, sorrow clearly written in the aged crags of his face. "From out of all the chaos around me an elf appeared, bloodied sword held in trembling hands. He stopped and stared down at me with those big round eyes and what I saw was my own feelings reflected back at me. Grief. Pain. Sorrow. For that split second we were not enemies, there was no us and them, we were just two living beings sharing the cost of another's war, the pain it wrought. Then he turned and was gone, leaving me alone with my lord."

The others remained silent as they reflected on the tale they had just heard. Despite only just meeting him, Lyncon felt a great empathy for Dallan. He could see sorrow in the old man, weighing at his limbs as he reached for his ale with unsteady hands. He downed the drink in one and Henrik silently took the cup from his father to refill it. The old man gave him a grateful smile and patted the boy's arm.

As Lyncon had heard the tale, images of his own past had flashed into his mind, pictures of the battle he had fought and of the death he himself had dealt. He shivered as he remembered the screams and blood, the heavy smell of death burning in his lungs. The thrill of battle had pumped around his body and he had liked it. It had excited him, fuelled his muscles to move faster, to fight harder. This most of all haunted him. Despite Fenrir's many attempts to convince him that what had happened at Seacrest was an accident, that he was blameless, this memory always told him otherwise.

After another long drink, Dallan spoke again. "Since that day I try not to judge others so quickly. Not all elves are bad as we are told, just as not all men are good." He shrugged. "We are all a little of both."

"A noble sentiment, ser. I wish there were more like you in this war, on both sides." Fenrir gave a sad smile as he drained his cup and stood up. "Now, sleep calls me. Good night, all."

The three men murmured their goodbyes as Fenrir retreated from the fire to find a sheltered spot to sleep. Overhead an owl gave a dismissive hoot as it took to the air, another answering from further into the woods.

Dallan turned his attention to Lyncon. "Tell me, how did you come to be friends with an elf? Especially here."

"It is a long story and I'm not even sure if we are friends."

"Ha, nonsense. Nobody fights as hard as you did unless they are protecting someone." He grinned and nudged Lyncon's arm. "Besides, I might not be an expert on elven behaviour, but I can tell he is fond of you also."

"Perhaps but it is… complicated."

The old knight gave him a puzzled look but did not press the subject. "And you don't drink? Do you not trust us?" He winked to make sure Lyncon knew he was joking.

"Drink does not agree with me, nor I with it."

Henrik gave a deep booming laugh. "Oh I know all about that. First time I had a drink I threw up all over Pa's shield. Had to scrub it for hours to get rid of the smell." He grinned and downed his drink as if to prove it would not happen again.

Ser Dallan ignored his son entirely and instead studied Lyncon more closely. "You're not like us, Lyncon. There is something... different about you. You have an... aura, a presence perhaps, that tells me you are not all that you seem."

He shrugged, feeling his cheeks flush and thankful for the half-light to hide it. "I have certain... differences."

Henrik was now staring at him too. "What do you mean? Are you a wizard? A vampire? A..."

"Enough, Henrik! Do not be rude!"

Lyncon simply smiled. "It is a long story and the night grows dark. I think I too will retire to bed."

Dallan nodded his understanding. "Of course. It is time we all got some sleep." He rose, stretching his limbs. "You fought well earlier; I can tell you have been trained, but you hold back. You fear yourself, fear hurting others. I have seen it before in other men. Often, those men are the first to be killed." He looked down with a kind smile on his lips. "Allow an old man some words of wisdom. Fight every fight as if it will be your last because, if you don't, it will be."

With that the knight nodded and stumbled away into the dark, his footsteps quickly followed by the sounds of urine splattering onto the grass.

Chapter 11

Paths Lost and Paths Crossed

They rose early the following morning as the sun had just begun to rise, its rays giving the forest a gentle green glow. The group broke camp and Fenrir then led the way to the road, weaving between the trees on a path visible only to him. Dallan and Henrik led their horses while Lyncon followed behind. Above them birds whistled and sang, eyeing the small party with obvious interest.

It was not long before they reached the road, two wide dusty ruts separated by a strip of low grass. It was deserted except for a lone squirrel that gave them a cursory glance before disappearing into the bushes. Flies buzzed as they circled the three men and the horses, the air having grown thick and heavy as the canopy above them caged the heat and robbed them of any breeze. Lyncon did his best to swat the insects away but it was futile; there were simply too many.

Fenrir gestured to their left. "This is the way you want to go. Rootun is the next settlement along, in the middle of the Haren. Rootun is a lumber colony but they are no stranger to travellers. After that there is nothing until Oakdale on the far side of the forest."

"A lumber colony?" said Dallan as he nodded slowly and waved absentmindedly at the flies around his ears. "Sounds like as good a place to stop as any. Though probably not much work."

"I hope they have cakes," Henrik muttered. "It has been so long since I ate cake." He was almost salivating at the thought despite having breakfast only hours ago.

Dallan scowled and shook his head. "You will eat what you are given and be grateful for it. Cakes are no good for you." He paused. "Though I must admit I do miss Lady Helga's baking. Her carrot cake was the best in all of Murton and her fruit tarts weren't bad either." He turned back to Fenrir, grinning. "Pardon us, the life of a Militios is not as glamorous as what we were used to. It has taken some adjusting."

"Of course, I understand, perhaps more than most." Fenrir bowed his head. "I only wish I had something to give you for your journey. A parting gift."

"Nonsense! You have done enough, friend. We would not have found the road without you." After shaking hands with Fenrir and Lyncon, the old man climbed nimbly onto his horse. "It has been a pleasure and an honour spending time with you both. I hope we meet again someday."

"As do I," said Lyncon as he smiled up at the knight. Despite only knowing them a short time he had grown fond of father and son and was sad to see them go.

Fenrir raised an arm and a huge raven suddenly swooped from the trees and landed on his arm. Henrik physically recoiled from the bird, who stared at him with one of its beady yellow eyes. "I have asked this raven to watch over you. She will escort you as far as Rootun."

Dallan nodded, though he looked more than a little unsure. "Can't say I have ever been looked after by a bird before but thank you." He turned in his saddle. "Come on, boy, let us go before we are eaten alive by all these flies."

The duo waved one final time and set off at a gentle pace down the road, Henrik leading his horse rather than riding.

"I do hope they have cakes, Pa. I miss the red toffee sponge I used to have after arms training. So sweet and sticky..."

"Enough talk of cakes, Henrik! Although yes, that red cake was good. And the brandy snaps."

"Oh yes! They were delicious!"

Lyncon chuckled to himself as the conversation faded away. "An odd pair but I am glad to have met them."

Fenrir launched the raven up into the air, its wings beating fast to carry it up above the trees, and laughed too. "Yes indeed. It is rare to find men who are willing to talk first and fight later. It was... refreshing. Makes me think about this war..." He frowned and shook his head. "Come. Let us get back home."

"Dallan fought well for an old knight. He must have been formidable in his youth," Lyncon observed as he followed Fenrir back amongst the trees.

"Old?" He paused, puzzled, then shrugged. "Yes, I suppose he is old in your eyes." The elf chuckled. "He is a good fighter, though. Lord Murton is a fool to let him go." He ducked under a branch and dropped down into an old dried-up river bed. Judging by the droppings and various tracks that littered the hard earth, it was a well-used trail by many animals living in the forest.

"What do you mean by my eyes?" Lyncon called as he struggled to keep up.

"Every human is young to me, Lyncon. Dallan has not even reached the age when elves are considered adults."

"Really? So how old are you?"

Fenrir shrugged. "I don't exactly know. Most elves don't bother to count after childhood. After a hundred years of waiting and counting, age is then seen as irrelevant."

"A hundred years!" Lyncon was shocked and stopped dead as he stared at Fenrir's back, trying to discern if the elf was jesting with him. "You mean you have lived more than a hundred years?"

"Oh yes. If I had to guess I would say around the four hundred mark."

Silence descended between them as Lyncon sped to catch up. He could not quite wrap his head around what he had just been told and stumbled twice as his concentration shifted away from his feet. Then another thought struck him and he stopped dead again.

"Wait, what about me? How old am I? I don't… I don't remember my own age."

With a sigh, Fenrir halted and turned to face him. "I don't know. You were human, before I mean, so must have been no more than forty when I found you." He shrugged. "My knowledge of human years is not so good."

"And… what about now? Am I immortal like you?"

"Elves are not immortal; we just age much slower than humans do. In regards to werewargs I have no idea. Werewolves are said to be immortal but it has never been proven and you are one of the first of your kind; we have no data to compare to. Only time will tell us the answers."

Lyncon fell silent again, lost to his thoughts. The talk of his creation made him feel strange, almost dirty, an imposter in someone else's skin. He was something that nature had not intended, bred for an evil and selfish purpose, a creation of war and death. His mind flashed back to the beach, burying the sword handle into the sand, preparing to throw himself down upon the gleaming blade. He shuddered and wrapped his arms around himself, closing his eyes for a moment. Fenrir noted his silence and took a step towards Lyncon, a look of sadness playing across his pale face, but then stopped himself, clenching one fist at his side. Eventually, he turned and continued down the path. After a few moments Lyncon opened his eyes and began to follow.

When Lyncon spoke again, several minutes later, his voice was quiet and laced with sadness. "Is there anything else I don't know? About being a werewarg."

Fenrir stroked his chin as he walked, thinking. "Well, you heal faster, run farther and hit harder than any man or elf can but you already knew all that. Your senses too are sharper than even mine."

"What about the... transformations?"

"What about them?" the elf asked, turning to look at Lyncon over his shoulder with a puzzled expression.

Lyncon stared at the elf, his eyes hard and serious, concern etched into his features. "Will I always be able to control them? To control... me?"

"Of course. What type of terrible design would it be if you turned feral and became a mindless beast? That is exactly the thing we were trying to stop." He stopped and placed a hand on Lyncon's shoulder. "Your body changes but your mind remains the same. Always."

"But Seacrest…"

"Was an accident brought on by drink. Alcohol polluted the process, something my colleagues and I failed to consider."

"So that will never happen again if I avoid alcohol?" Hope sprang up in the man's eyes.

"In theory, yes." Seeing the hope fade, Fenrir quickly added, "It is all theory; none of this has been tested. It is the best I can offer without lying to you. I… I'm sorry that is all I have."

Lyncon nodded slowly. "I know. Thank you, for not lying."

The elf stared at him for a second before turning on his heel and striding away, once again leaving Lyncon to catch him up. They passed in silence for several more minutes, meandering through the trees, before Fenrir suddenly spoke up again.

"Oh, one more thing. You are a eunuch. You will never have children."

For a moment Lyncon was too shocked to reply, eventually spluttering, "I… but why?"

"We do it with all our creations, to stop population growth getting out of our own control. After the incident with the dogs it became elven law."

"You created dogs?!"

"Well, not me personally but yes, elves did. We wanted to have pets and wolves are not fond of playing fetch."

"Will my hair turn white when I grow older?"

Fenrir paused, a mug of tea halfway to his lips, and gave a loud sigh as he rolled his big eyes. "Do you have to persist with all these questions? I grow very weary of them."

Lyncon grinned across the table. "You are welcome to go shoot another arrow into a tree but it won't take me long to fetch it. Then I'll be right back with more questions."

The elf simply glared at him over his cup as he muttered. "Perhaps I'll shoot an arrow at something else instead… or someone…"

Over the past three days Lyncon had finally mastered the ability to summon his claws. In truth, he didn't really know how he had done it but something had just suddenly clicked and the action had become as natural as walking or talking. This afternoon, Lyncon had practised summoning one claw at a time and then used them to write his name in a tree trunk. Fenrir had not been impressed.

"There will be no more need for retrieving arrows. Tomorrow we move on to something new."

Lyncon raised an eyebrow, still grinning. "Really? Such as?"

Fenrir gestured to the door. "There are still trees that need clearing after the storm. You can do that."

"Ha! I'm not sure how chopping wood will be…"

"Who said anything about chopping them?" the elf said with a wry smile.

Lyncon stopped, stared at the elf, trying to discern if he was joking, but before he could reply there came a sharp tapping against the shutters followed by a loud shriek that pierced the still night outside.

Fenrir was on his feet in seconds, tea forgotten, and he threw open the door. Outside stood a huge owl, as tall as Fenrir with large orange eyes that stared at them with rapt attention. Its feathers were a speckled grey that somehow seemed to shine in the moonlight and its beak, as long as Lyncon's forearm, ended in a curved point.

The owl hooted at Fenrir, hopping from one leg to the other as it tried to convey its message. Lyncon had no clue what it wanted but he understood the animal's sense of urgency, a pressing need that emanated from its every action.

Finally Fenrir nodded and turned away from the bird, striding over to his chest and throwing it open. Frantically, he began to remove the contents.

"What is it? What is wrong?" Lyncon asked, rising from the table but still eyeing the owl. It stared back at him intently, its eyes two unblinking orange orbs, before suddenly lurching into the air and landing in a nearby tree.

"Trouble. The forest has asked for my help." Fenrir had finally emptied the chest and now flicked several hidden latches in the base. This released a false bottom, which he carefully removed, and revealed a hidden compartment within. From the compartment, the elf produced a sword Lyncon had not seen before. It was thin and delicate-looking, not like the dented swords they used to train with, and had a gently curved blade with golden etching on the scabbard and handle. The letters were not the common tongue and he guessed were written in some kind of elvish.

Fenrir strapped the sword belt around his waist and turned to face him. "Something foul has entered the forest, a creature of evil. The Haren wants it removed and has asked me to help. I must go." He strode out through the door without waiting for an answer and Lyncon hurried after him.

Outside, the owl circled above them on silent wings. Across the clearing a horse stood waiting, its nostrils flared as it stamped a hoof in the dirt. Fenrir soothed it with a few calming sounds before gracefully leaping onto its back.

"I can come with you! I can help!" Lyncon insisted.

"No! Stay here. This is beyond you. I must go alone." Without any command from its rider, the horse suddenly leapt forwards towards the trees as it began to follow the owl above them. Fenrir bent low over the beast's neck and within seconds they were gone, leaving Lyncon alone in the deep silence of the dark.

His mind raced as he grappled with what had just happened. He knew there was trouble, could tell by the poorly concealed worry on Fenrir's face as he sped off into the trees. Despite the elf's words he did not think he should face the danger alone. Lyncon could help; he could fight. Quickly, he set off at a run, following the horse's trail through the forest under the light of the pale moon.

The horse dashed through the trees with the speed of the swiftest winds, Fenrir crouching low on its back to avoid the branches as they whipped past. Above them Zulara soared, her eyes watching their progress as she beat her great wings. She called, pressing for urgency, and Fenrir felt the horse strain to speed up further. It was already blowing hard.

As they neared their destination, a growing sense of dread formed in the pit of the elf's stomach and fear began to seep through his veins. He shivered. It had been a long time since he had felt like this, heavy with foreboding. He knew the threat he now rushed to face must be grave indeed for the forest to beg for his help as it had. Even Zulara was scared and she was an owl who had seen many hard winters. He could have asked Lyncon to help them but was glad he had left him behind. This would be dangerous and he did not want to risk the young man, powers or not. He closed his eyes and focused on his breathing in an attempt to calm his racing heartbeat.

Suddenly the horse burst out onto the road and slid to a halt. Zulara perched herself on a branch above and stared down at them, silent as shadow. Fenrir turned to follow her gaze. Trundling slowly along the road towards them were a procession of carts and wagons of all manner of shapes and sizes. Many looked very old with obvious signs of ageing and attempted repair. The lead cart was driven by two men, one holding a lamp while the other held the reins of the oxen. They spotted him and quickly brought their cart to a halt, the others rippling to a stop behind them. With the rumble of the wagons silenced a heavy quiet settled over the scene.

Fenrir dismounted, thanked the horse and ordered it to leave. It did not need telling twice and sprang away into the trees as fast as it could. Zulara stayed where she was, ever watchful from her branch above. Flexing his fingers, he placed a tentative hand on the hilt of his sword.

Two men descended from the rear of the first cart, one helping the other down to the road before retreating back into shadow. The smaller figure moved towards Fenrir slowly, leaning heavily on a staff as he went. He was tall but bent, his back hunched and stooping. He wore long faded robes with a hood that covered his face from view.

He stopped some twenty paces from Fenrir, face downcast and hidden. As he approached, the elf's sense of dread grew and a chill ran down his spine. He fought to keep his heart rate steady.

"Who walks this road? I am the guardian of this forest and you will go no further!" Fenrir's voice was firm and he drew his sword slowly, the steel shining slightly in a sliver of moonlight.

"Fenrir?" The voice that came from the hood was little more than a whisper. "Is it really you?" A laugh came from within the hood, cold and humourless. "How strange our paths should cross again here? Fortunate. For me anyway."

"You know me?" the elf asked, voice touched with a new-found uncertainty.

"You don't know me? Ooof, that hurts."

"Perhaps if you showed me your face instead of hiding in your hood."

"Very well." With a flourish the Crooked Man pushed back his hood and revealed himself, smiling up at the elf with malice in his eyes. "Do you know me now?"

Fenrir's eyes bulged as he froze in shock and his breath caught. "You…" he spluttered. "It cannot be."

"Is that all you have to say? After all these years." He stepped closer and Fenrir flinched, retreating, raising his sword between them. The Crooked Man laughed. "You seem uneasy, Fenrir? Something wrong?"

"I thought you died," Fenrir whispered.

The Crooked Man nodded. "Oh I have. Many times, many ways." He stopped, a grin spreading across his face. In his eyes was an evil blackness. "It hurts, you know, so much." He raised his hand. "Let me show you."

Lyncon had run from the hut faster than he had known he could, swerving through the pitch black forest. His vision was flawless, his eyes having unlocked a new-found night vision since the night of the storm. He could see everything around him with perfect clarity and effortlessly skirted trees and bushes as he powered forwards, wind whistling past his ears.

Even with his new-found speed it felt like an age before he finally sensed he was nearing his destination and heard voices up ahead. He slowed as he got closer, listening intently, and became aware of a strange heaviness to the air, almost as if a storm was brewing within the forest itself.

Silently he crept through the undergrowth, barely out of breath, and flattened himself in some ferns. Some primal instinct told him to be cautious, that danger lurked ahead, as he slowly crawled forwards to the edge of the road. Peering out he could see Fenrir talking to an old man leaning on a staff. The elf had his sword in his hand but looked dazed, his round eyes wide with fear as he stared at the man opposite him.

"Let me show you."

With a flick of his hand the man released a strange dark substance from his fingertips that shot straight at Fenrir. It was like smoke or ink, black as the most lightless night and it was never still, shifting and swirling as it powered towards the elf. With it went a sound like the cracking of thunder, deep and powerful. It struck Fenrir in the chest and threw him backwards, several feet down the road, where he landed in a crumpled heap.

Unable to understand what he had just seen, Lyncon turned back to the old man and studied him closely. On second glance he could see that this man was not like other men. He seemed both young and old all at once, strong and yet somehow vulnerable. He would be tall and powerful if he were not so hunched over, and his skin was wrinkled and sagged, brittle with age. An unseen weight seemed to press him into the earth, a heavy burden that bent his body despite the strength he clearly possessed. Worst of all was the malice that gleamed in his eyes, a dark thing that knew no end. Each eye was like a bottomless void, bereft of any trace of feeling.

The Crooked Man smiled. "Come now. I expected better from you, Fenrir. You used to be so strong, so wise." He laughed, a sound as crooked as he was, and launched another attack.

This time Fenrir was ready and, leaping to his feet, he held his sword out in front of him so the blast struck the flat of the blade and dispersed around him. He was pushed back a little, his feet sliding in the grass, but otherwise untouched.

"Haha, that's more like it!" With a shout the old man threw another blast at the elf. When this too was blocked he snarled and twisted his hand, a new darkness now issuing endlessly from the man's gnarled fingers to strike at the elf repeatedly as he tried desperately to stand his ground.

Lyncon watched from the bushes open-mouthed. He had no idea who this old man was but he was clearly incredibly powerful. The darkness he commanded was like nothing Lyncon had ever seen. It twisted and spun as it struck at Fenrir like a living being, sucking in any moonlight foolish enough to touch it and leaving only its own dense black form. Fear swept through Lyncon as he stared at that deep impenetrable dark, so cold and dead.

A cry from Fenrir snapped him back to his senses and he turned to see his friend struggling against the ceaseless attack, his arms shaking as he fought to hold up his sword against the dark. The blackness beat at him like a storm wind, lashing at everything in its path, tugging at his clothes and hair as it was deflected around him. The elf's face was awash with pain, set into a determined grimace as he continued to be driven slowly backwards. Sweat ran down his forehead and Lyncon could see fear in his big round eyes. It was clear Fenrir could not keep this up much longer.

As fear for his friend built in Lyncon's mind and overtook him it brought a sudden burning sensation in his limbs, a violent heat that flooded his veins as if his very blood was boiling inside him. He groaned as the pain intensified, searing every inch of his body, and he stumbled against a tree when he tried to stand. His muscles suddenly began to react and move by themselves, the fibres beneath his skin shifting and straining as they began to grow. Claws had erupted from his fingers, longer than any he had summoned before, and fur now sprouted from his skin as his whole body shook. He fought to breathe when his lungs contracted on their own and when he did manage to take a breath it came out as a deep snarl. A cracking sound filled his ears as his bones began to break and morph into new shapes. His clothes and boots lay in tatters on the grass at his feet.

As quickly as it began, the change ended. The heat died and Lyncon leant against the tree, panting and feeling very sick. Looking down he saw his whole body had transformed. He was covered in coarse brown fur from his head down to each clawed toe. He was taller now, limbs thick and strong with new muscles, while his fingers were all tipped with long sharp claws. His face too had morphed into a muzzle, protruding forwards and split by a huge jaw crammed with sharp white teeth. When he tried to speak it came out only as a guttural growl.

For what seemed like an eternity he was frozen, paralysed by the realisation of what he had become. Now the heat and pain was gone he felt almost normal, his thoughts and feelings unchanged, placed into a body that was not his own. His senses had grown sharper, hearing and smell far more sensitive than ever before, and he felt dizzy from the barrage of new information that came from all around him. Lyncon fought for breath as panic smothered him, knocking his thoughts aside and causing him to sink to the grass. He wanted to throw up but didn't know if he still could. He pawed at his face, his mind spiralling, when a sudden scream rent the air.

In the road Fenrir had crumpled to his knees, sword lying in the grass beside him, as the darkness beat at his face and torso, leaving bloody gashes where it struck. His face was contorted with agony and he screamed again as the black slashed across his ribs. The Crooked Man stood watching, a smile on his lips and something that looked like hunger in his eyes.

With a roar of pure rage Lyncon leapt out from the bushes and sprang at the Crooked Man, covering the ground in one huge bound. With a swipe of his new powerful arm he struck the Crooked Man in the chest and sent him hurtling backwards, tumbling over and over as he rolled down the road back towards the wagons. With the darkness now gone, Fenrir collapsed onto his front and lay still.

Using his staff to lean on, the old man slowly rose to his knees. To Lyncon's surprise he was still smiling when he looked up at him.

"Well this is a day to remember. A werewarg in Petra; a true modern day fable." He chuckled and got unsteadily to his feet. "Fenrir was always so cold with his subjects. Ha, I should know. I'm surprised to see him keeping one as a guard dog."

Lyncon growled and leapt forwards once more, swiping down at his foe with his claws. He had aimed for the old man's face but his attack was stopped as the man lifted his staff and blocked his arm, catching the blow as if it were no effort at all. Sudden fear bloomed in Lyncon's gut as the Crooked Man laughed in his face and pushed him away with ease. Lyncon lunged, snapping at his foe with his jaws, but the old man again blocked with his staff, forcing it between his teeth. In fury Lyncon bit down, hoping to snap the wood, but it didn't yield, the staff as hard as iron.

For a moment the Crooked Man held him there, staff clenched in his jaw, a smile spreading across his time-wrinkled face. He looked into Lyncon's eyes and winked. Then he punched him hard in the ribs with his free hand.

The blow struck him like a war hammer to the chest, sending him back down the road to land on the grass, winded. With a growl he rose quickly onto all fours and eyed his opponent warily, shocked by his foe's impossible strength.

"You know I shouldn't be surprised you're here. I sensed you in Seacrest. That was excellent work, by the way. Clearly you don't share this elf's foolish views on the value of human life." He licked his lips. "Such destruction, such rage. It was delicious. Thank you."

Burning with a new fury, Lyncon dug his claws into the road and surged forwards with teeth bared in a snarl. The Crooked Man sighed, almost as if disappointed, and raised his staff. As he closed on his target, Lyncon sank low, under the staff, and then attacked upwards, knocking the staff aside with one hand while he swiped with the claws of the other. He felt his claws slice through flesh, one piercing the old man's left eye, as they raked his face. The Crooked Man screamed and lashed out in pain, knocking Lyncon away with a wild flurry of blows.

Lyncon retreated, watching his foe but ready to strike again if needed. The Crooked Man was kneeling in the road clutching his face as blood streamed from between his fingers. He was panting and shaking, teeth clenched in a grimace. His staff lay forgotten beside him. Behind, several of his followers had appeared from the wagons with looks of dismay on their faces. Some had swords in their hands.

Lyncon was also panting, pain blooming behind his ribs every time he took a breath. He glanced backwards at where Fenrir lay, unmoving on the grass. He was tempted to go to him, desperate to make sure he was alright, but knew that the danger had not yet passed.

"That… was a mistake." The Crooked Man's words brought Lyncon spinning around just in time to see the blast of darkness that struck him in the chest like a lightning bolt. He was blown clean off his feet and landed with a heavy thud next to Fenrir.

The Crooked Man rose slowly to his feet, one hand still pressed to his face. His one remaining eye fixed Lyncon with a look of pure wrath. "I was considering letting you live. We are, after all, almost brothers. But you know how the old saying goes, an eye for an eye…" He chuckled as a long drip of blood ran down his neck. His grin was one of madness and rage. "Now I will kill you both and enjoy doing it."

With a wave of his staff, the Crooked Man summoned more darkness, an orb that shifted and crackled as it grew to the size of a watermelon. With a twist of his weapon the dark orb shifted and became a long thin blade that hurtled towards Lyncon and sliced into his shoulder as he tried to rise to his feet. He fell back again, howling in pain. His shoulder felt numb. The darkness had disappeared when it had struck him, so the cut now lay open and bleeding. Lyncon's vision swam as he pressed on the wound, trying to stem the bleeding. He knew he had to get up, to keep fighting and protect Fenrir, but every inch of his body hurt. He sucked in deep lungfuls of air, each one sending a shooting pain from his shoulder to the tips of his fingers, and slowly rolled over. Then, using all his focus and strength, he struggled to his feet, swaying alarmingly but somehow managing not to fall. He gave a low menacing growl as he faced his foe once more.

The Crooked Man was approaching him, leaning heavily on his staff. He had let go of his face and a deep red gash where his left eye had been still dripped blood onto the grass at his feet. His face was set in a look of determined fury, his remaining eye a dark orb of wrath that made Lyncon's blood run cold. He stopped, seemingly shocked that Lyncon still stood, then levelled his staff at him and opened his mouth to speak when the forest around them suddenly burst into life.

With a deafening buzz millions of tiny insects burst from the trees all around them and flooded the road, washing over them all like a river. They blanketed the entire convoy in a living cloud that buffered and chirped at all those caught in its grip. Shocked, the Crooked Man yelled out and stumbled backwards, desperately trying to swat the creatures away. Lyncon, too exhausted to care, simply sank to his knees, the bugs noticeably swerving around him. From the bushes beside him a dark shape appeared, a huge brown bear that picked him up gently in its massive jaws and sprang away, carrying him as if he weighed nothing. Beside him he was dimly aware of another bear carrying the fallen elf.

Seeing his prey escape, the Crooked Man screamed in a fury that for a moment split the whirl of bugs. He raised his staff and shouted words nobody but him understood. Immediately the bugs fell back, retreating to the forest and the shelter of the trees. Within seconds silence once more ruled the road.

Seething with rage, the Crooked Man turned and gestured to his nearest followers. He pointed to some bushes beside the road. "There. Start a fire there. Burn it all!"

Chapter 12

Blood and Fire

The lake had been peaceful before their arrival, a place that few people visited, its silent brooding broken only by the breeze or birdsong. Now it was plagued by the grunts of men and the snorts of horses, all settling down at their tents before turning in for the night. Fires burnt and the smell of roasting meat began to drift over the water. The lake watched it all, a silent observer, its unknown depths repelling the fire light, until, one by one, the men put the flames out and retreated to sleep.

In the middle of the night Evanora walked by the lakeside beneath a carpet of stars. She was shrouded in a black cloak, as dark as the lake itself, and padded silently on bare feet like only an elf could. A gentle breeze pulled at her hair as she made her way around the water.

Eventually, she stopped beside a lone tree, its roots extending greedily into the lake in search of nourishment. Directly opposite the camp, she paused for a moment to study it, her eyes drifting over the neat rows of small tents that each of the soldiers slept in. Two larger tents capped the lines, one for Amos and his captain Hans, while the other was her own. Beyond and slightly apart lay a lone tent unlike all the others. This tent was hexagonal, rising almost two storeys high, and was made of an odd grass-like material that seemed to have been woven together in an interlocking pattern. It belonged to the elven envoy, all three elves sleeping under one roof.

The journey here had been a swift one, Amos imposing the need for haste onto his men whenever they started to lag. They had quick marched north from Astikus until the road split in two at the very south of the Haren Forest. From there they had turned east, following the road as it skirted the forest towards the coast. Each night they had wandered away from the road and made camp, keeping themselves tucked out of sight from any unwanted attention. Despite the thirty soldiers Amos had bought, the sight of elves was enough to stir trouble with almost any local Petran.

The envoy made no quarrel with the pace or conditions. They rode on horses that carried them swifter than any seen in Petra, the beasts working with their riders not for them. Evanora herself had never learnt the animal tongue and found it fascinating to watch the other elves instruct the horses with only a gentle word. The elves themselves had kept their distance, preferring each other over the company of Amos and his soldiers. Though she had not asked them, Evanora had a sneaking suspicion that Amos and his men preferred it that way.

There were three envoys, two male elves and a female, all trusted advisors of the Vilantis High Council. They were thin and pale with the usual wide eyes and short, neatly cropped hair. In Astikus, Evanora had been introduced to them as Braxil, Tenos and Amethyst. They had nodded at her with blank expressions, silent. They knew who she was and they no doubt hated her for it. Since that brief encounter the elves had ignored and avoided her, though she had often caught them staring when they thought she could not see. They knew she was a traitor to their kind and they clearly despised her for it.

Reaching silently into her robes she clasped her hand around something small and cold, a slim glass vial. Slowly, she withdrew it from her pocket and stared at it. The vial was empty, no trace of its original contents left. She marvelled at how something so small, so ordinary, could have held contents that would change so much, shape the course of an entire nation. After a moment's indecision she pulled back her arm and hurled the vial into the lake, the black water swallowing it with a sad splash.

Without another glance she turned her back on the lake and began to walk back around its edge to the camp. A flicker of light in the darkness stopped her in her tracks. She pushed back a strand of her ebony hair as she stared off into the distance. Another flicker soon replaced the first, distant but unmistakable. The forest was on fire. She stood and watched as more fingers of flame began to light the sky and a sudden, terrible chill settled over her. Terror flooded her mind, making her drop to her knees; her heart hammered in her chest. But this was not her terror. This feeling came from the forest, pulsing through the air as the trees and earth screamed in pain as the fire consumed them. Taking a steadying breath, she struggled to her feet and, forgetting the camp, ran into the gloom of the trees towards the flames.

Lyncon woke with a start as the huge bear dropped him gently on the grass. At first he could not recall how he had got there, his mind clouded, but then the pain of the fight returned to him in a rush and he curled up, groaning. Closing his eyes he fought back a wave of nausea that wracked his body.

When he had finally got himself back under some sort of control, he sat up slowly and looked around. He was lying in the clearing outside the hut, his naked body now back to human form. The bears had disappeared into the forest but Fenrir lay nearby, face down and motionless. Struggling to his feet, Lyncon hurried over and knelt beside his friend. He let out a relieved breath when he felt a faint pulse at the elf's neck. Slowly, he rolled him over.

Fenrir's skin was ghostly pale, as if all the blood had been drained from his body, and his hands and fingers were covered in hundreds of tiny red cuts. Several large cuts covered his ribs and chest, while a smaller one leaked a trickle of blood down his cheek. Despite his best efforts, Lyncon found he was unable to rouse his friend, so he gathered him into his arms and carried him inside.

He set the elf down on his bed and covered him with a blanket before busying himself with making tea. As he waited for the water to boil, he dressed in spare clothes, wrapping a bandage around his already healing shoulder, and thought about what had happened, the evil he had seen in the old man's eyes as they had fought. He shuddered and pushed the thoughts from his mind. Once the drink was made he brought it back to the elf and propped him up as he touched the cup to his lips.

"Drink, Fenrir. Please." His voice had a desperate edge to it he had not intended.

For what felt like an eternity nothing happened. Fenrir remained unresponsive, his breathing shallow and weak. Lyncon was just about to give up when the elf's lips parted and he took a sip of the warm liquid. Lyncon smiled and let out a relieved breath.

Slowly, the elf's eyes opened. He groaned quietly and tried to shift but Lyncon held him firm and told him to drink more tea. They sat like this together for several minutes, Lyncon cradling Fenrir's head as the elf drank, the tea bringing strength back to him sip by sip.

Finally, when the drink was gone, Lyncon laid Fenrir back down. He was about to leave him to rest when a hand grabbed weakly at his wrist. He turned back to see Fenrir gazing at him intently, his lips moving. Lyncon bent closer to hear the faint whisper.

"What... hap... happened?"

"We fought someone, an old man. He knew you. He tried to kill you." He placed a hand on the elf's forehead. It was icy cold. "You should rest, Fenrir. Please. You are hurt."

"Rest? Yes... I think I wi... ahh!" Fenrir screamed suddenly, his body beginning to convulse in pain. His hands shot up to his temples and pressed down hard against the skin as if he was trying to stop his head from exploding.

"What is it? What's wrong?" Lyncon asked, fear coursing through his body once more.

"Pain, so much pain." The elf panted. "The forest... it... it burns."

"You mean a fire?"

"Yes. It was him… he… it burns." Fenrir groaned, sweat running down his brow. "The forest… it is dying. I must… help." He tried to rise from the bed on unsteady arms but Lyncon pushed him back down.

"No. You are not going anywhere; you're too weak." He glanced between his friend and the door before grimacing. "I will go."

Slowly, the elf nodded. His eyes were tinged with pain but he gave Lyncon a weak smile. "Thank you." He gestured towards one corner of the room. "Take the axe. You must… cut a line… in the trees… a break. It will stop the fire. Understand?" Lyncon nodded and turned to fetch the heavy tool. Fenrir watched him. "You must hurry, Lyncon. Please. Before it… before it all turns to ash."

Even at a distance the heat was near unbearable, a physical force that beat at his exposed flesh, singeing the hairs on his arms. The flames burnt in vivid hues of red and yellow and orange, powerful and hungry, turning night to day. The light was intense, ever shifting, bright as a thousand suns. Swinging the axe he felled a tree in a single stroke before dragging it, as best he could, away from the oncoming fire.

He coughed suddenly and spat ash onto the leaves at his feet. The air around him was dense with smoke, a grey haze that stung his eyes, leaving tears running down his cheeks and his lungs burning with every breath he took. Not far away, the raging inferno continued its relentless push towards him, devouring everything in its path. The strength and power that radiated from the flames was frightening to behold, a true force of nature unleashed upon the forest, feasting on anything living.

Moving to the next tree, Lyncon glanced along the break he had made. The space was roughly ten feet across and now almost a mile long, an empty corridor completely cleared of trees and bushes, devoid of fuel to feed the burning monster that roared towards it. He did not know how long he had been working but his back and arms were sore, his palms rubbed raw from the axe handle. Ash covered him from head to toe, sticking to his clothes and the sweat on his skin.

He planted his feet and stood ready at the base of the tree, a large elm, its trunk perhaps two feet wide. Loosening his muscles he rolled his stiff shoulders, hefted the axe and then swung it as hard as he could into the wood. Within four strokes the tree was teetering and a fifth brought it crashing down to the forest floor. This one was too big for him to drag, its branches a thick tangle, but the bears could move it and they appeared silently from behind him to grip the tree in their huge jaws and pull it away. A crash to Lyncon's right showed another bear had felled a smaller tree itself and was pulling it away. Another beyond was busy uprooting a shrub.

It had been the owl that had shown Lyncon what to do. The huge bird had been waiting for him outside Fenrir's hut and had led him to a small lake that formed the start of a narrow stream that ran north towards the road where he had faced the Crooked Man. On the east side of the lake, various creatures had already begun to clear a break. Several of the large bears that had saved him from the road were working beside smaller animals, including deer and beavers. Lyncon had set to work immediately, the owl surveying from above. Work was helped by the occasional tree that just collapsed on its own, the forest seeming keen to speed up the job and save itself from the flames.

The fire was getting ever closer, the smoke churning the air into a thick grey soup. Shadows danced as the flames lit up the night like an early dawn, a thousand embers falling to earth like tiny burning snowflakes. Lyncon began to cough again as he stumbled to the next tree, leaning against the trunk as he bent double, his body wracked by vicious barks. He dropped the axe and ripped off his shirt, tying the cloth around his mouth and nose to try to filter out the worst of the smog. An explosion of sparks nearby reminded him of the urgency of his task and he hurried back to work.

The heat continued to grow as Lyncon felled tree after tree. It pummelled his now exposed torso, burning the sweat off his skin as he worked. He was exhausted, the heat and thick air sapping his strength with every passing second, the axe growing heavier with every swing. Still the fire crept closer, its appetite unquenchable.

Lyncon raised the axe slowly with arms that screamed at him to stop, the muscles heavy as lead. He swung but his grip was weak and the axe fell to the floor. He bent to pick it up but instead found himself falling forwards, face crunching against the leaf litter. His lungs burnt, every breath feeling as if he were inhaling shards of glass. He coughed into the dirt. His head was spinning and stars flashed in front of his eyes. An image of Fenrir suddenly appeared in his mind, the elf weak and screaming in pain as his precious forest burnt. Gritting his teeth he tried to stand, to keep working, but he only managed to get to one knee before his body failed him and he collapsed again, helpless. Around him the forest was empty. The animals had all fled. Only the fire remained, a hulking red-orange monster prowling towards him.

The flames were only metres away now, the heat unbearable. Lyncon's breath came in ragged gasps, weak and panicked. His mind was groggy, all his thoughts jumbled and messy, only permeated by a nagging, primal urge to get up and flee. Tears formed on his cheeks as the fire began to singe his leg, lapping hungrily at his skin. He closed his eyes and prepared for his end.

A sudden breeze ruffled his hair. In seconds it had grown to a gale, battering everything in its path as it raced along the ground and past him to collide with the fire. The smoke fell back instantly and Lyncon opened his eyes as he greedily devoured lungfuls of cleaner air. The fire still crackled and burnt but now it had been halted, its progress stopped by this sudden gust.

Slowly, Lyncon propped himself up on one elbow. Squinting against the wind he stared into the forest around him. A voice was being carried towards him, sweet and soft, muttering words he did not understand. It drifted to him from amongst the trees, ebbing and flowing. He scanned the gloom for its source but could see nothing, the voice seeming to emanate from everywhere around him all at once. Then, suddenly, it was gone and the rain began.

The rain quickly became a downpour, smothering the fire while the wind died as quickly as it had begun. The flames, while not defeated, began to falter and Lyncon saw some smaller fires gutter and go out. The heat had faded too but only a little. Lyncon was quickly soaked through but welcomed the cool drops, removing the cloth from his face and greedily sipping at any that fell onto his face.

"Who are you?" a voice said abruptly behind him, making him jump and grimace in pain from the burn on his leg. He turned as best he could while not moving too much.

Next to him stood an elf, her large green eyes peering out at him from a sharp, defined face bordered by long black hair that fell over the shoulders of her dark robes and cloak. Her lips were red and full, bright as any flame. She was staring at him intently, clearly impatient for an answer. The fire did not seem to be bothering her.

"L... Lyncon," he muttered.

"Lyncon." She said the name as if trying it out, feeling the taste of it in her mouth. She frowned for a moment then shook her head and pointed towards the fire. "Did you do this?" Her large eyes bored into him, accusing, pale hands clenched into fists at her side.

"No. It... wasn't me." Before he could give any more explanation he was cut short by a fit of harsh coughs.

She stared at him for several seconds longer then turned away and faced the flames. It was only at this point that Lyncon realised she was completely dry, untouched by the water falling around them. She began to mutter in a strange language again, focused intently on the fire. Instantly the rain fell harder, the drops hissing as they beat the flames into submission.

Finally her eyes returned to him, the fire apparently dealt with. She studied him, her gaze drifting up and down his near naked body before eventually resting on his leg. "Are you hurt?"

He shrugged and sat up slowly. "A little singed but nothing serious." He clenched his jaw as he got unsteadily to his feet and winced when he put any weight on his injured leg.

The elf watched him with one eyebrow raised, calculations running behind her blank green eyes. Suddenly she smiled at him and gestured to where she had appeared from. "I have some ointment back at my tent. It will help with the burn. Come. It is not far." Without waiting for a reply she turned and began to stride through the forest. After a moment's pause Lyncon shrugged and began to limp after her.

As they walked, the rain quickly stopped. Away from the fire, the night was cold and Lyncon was soon shivering, his exposed chest and arms quickly riddled with goosebumps. He rubbed his skin, trying to dry himself as best he could but only succeeding in smearing the ash that still clung to him.

"Did you do that? The rain?" he asked as they walked but the elf only ignored him.

While he picked his way carefully through the trees, grimacing as pain shot through his leg, Lyncon eyed the elf in front of him with curiosity. He had no clue where she had come from or where they were going but he got the distinct feeling that she did not belong here. Her robes and cloak were finely made and clearly expensive, her hair too perfect and glossy for life in the woods. Even the way she moved, though still graceful, was completely different to how Fenrir moved through the trees. While he moved with a lithe ease, her steps were measured and unnatural, each taken with precise care.

Eventually, the forest began to thin and then fade entirely and they found themselves on the edge of a small lake, stars twinkling in the dark waters' surface. Lyncon could see tents beyond, clear signs of a camp, and hesitated. Seemingly sensing Lyncon's sudden trepidation, his guide turned to him with a soft smile.

"Do not fear. No harm will come to you while you are with me." Her voice portrayed complete confidence in her apparent authority. Her red lips flashing in the moonlight.

Quietly they approached the camp, moving between the tents. No one stirred, apparently all sleeping. Reaching one of two larger tents, the elf pulled back the entrance flap and gestured for Lyncon to go in, before quickly closing it behind them.

Inside the tent was lavish and spacious. Similar in size to Fenrir's cabin, the fabric room was lit by a single lantern that hung on a hook above a huge mound of thick furs that covered the centre of the space. Two expensive-looking wooden chests sat at the side and Lyncon could see several garments stacked neatly on top. A wooden stool and basin stood opposite.

"Sit," commanded his host, gesturing towards the stool. Lyncon did as he was told while the elf removed her thick cloak and threw it onto the nearest chest. Then she moved the clothes from on top of the second chest and threw it open before rummaging inside. Eventually she returned to Lyncon with some bandages and a small glass bottle.

"I must look at your wounds." She knelt in front of him and began to inspect the burn on his leg, carefully cutting away the material of his trousers with a small knife. As she worked, Lyncon studied her more closely. His eyes wandered over the uneven waves of her dark hair and the shocking red of her lips. Her skin was milky pale, soft in the half-light. Her hands moved delicately, probing, the nails clean and neatly cut.

He grimaced suddenly as she prodded his burn, bringing his attention away from her plunging neckline. "May I ask your name? I owe you my life, after all."

"Evanora," she replied without looking up as she continued to poke his skin. "This burn seems almost healed. I… I don't understand."

"Perhaps you are a better healer than you give yourself credit for."

Ignoring the obvious sarcasm, she stood and locked eyes with his. "Why exactly were you in that fire?"

"Same reason you were, to stop it."

They stared at each other for a time before the elf turned away suddenly and offered him the glass vial. "This will help your wound. Drink it all and the burn should be almost gone by morning." When he reached for it, she pulled it away. "But first, tell me where you are from? Why were you in the forest, so far from the road?"

Lyncon paused, staring up at the elf questioning him. He knew he should just tell the truth, there was no shame in it, but something about this whole situation felt off to him, wrong somehow. He had no idea who this elf was or why she was in a camp surrounded by soldiers. His mind suddenly flashed with images of Seacrest, of the devastation and death he had wrought. Word of his actions would have spread: an entire village massacred. Perhaps these soldiers were hunting him? Evanora was clearly a sorceress, one of great power, so why was she here and travelling with human soldiers? The answers eluded him but he knew he would have to be careful with his words.

"I was travelling," he said with a shrug. "I saw the smoke and decided to try to help."

"Where were you travelling from?"

"North."

"What village?"

"You won't have heard of it."

She smiled. "I know a great deal. Try me."

Lyncon got to his feet. "I feel better; as you said before, the burn is almost healed. I think I will go."

Gently, the elf rested a hand on his chest. "No, no. You need to rest. The smoke may have damaged your lungs. You should sleep."

He raised an eyebrow. "What? Here? Surrounded by soldiers?"

She gave a little laugh. "Safer than the woods, surely?"

"I'll take my chances."

Evanora grew serious again. "No. You need rest and medicine. Drink this and stay here. I promise, no harm will come to you tonight."

She thrust the bottle into his hand, staring up at him with pleading eyes that caught the light of the lantern. Her lips seemed to glow in the half-light and as she moved away Lyncon caught a brief scent of rosewater that mingled with the smell of smoke that seemed to cling only to him. He unstoppered the vial and sniffed its contents. It was odourless, even to his enhanced senses, and crystal clear. If he had not known otherwise he would have guessed it was water. In one quick motion he downed the potion and handed it back. It tasted sharp, acidic, but quickly faded.

Evanora smiled. "See, nothing to worry about. Tomorrow your leg will be as good as new." She gently took the vial from him and took his arm, steering him towards the furs on the floor.

As Lyncon followed he felt his legs suddenly lurch and the world began to spin. He gripped the elf's shoulder for balance while she lowered him onto the furs. He tried to speak but found his mouth refused to work. His fingers were numb and he felt his vision begin to swim.

"Wha... have you... done... me?" he eventually croaked as Evanora bent over him, propping up his head with a pillow.

"Shh!" She placed a finger on his lips. "It's OK, don't fight it. It will all be over soon." Slowly she bent forwards and kissed him once, gently, on the lips. Then she rose and moved away. Lyncon fought as long as he could but eventually his eyes grew heavy and his breathing slow as his mind slipped into a deep darkness.

Chapter 13

Framed

Lyncon opened his eyes slowly and for a minute everything was blurred and unsteady. His head was throbbing and he couldn't get his thoughts straight no matter how hard he tried. An unfamiliar, acrid taste filled his mouth, lingering on his tongue. Slowly, his vision cleared and he began to take in his surroundings.

He was lying on his back staring up at the roof of a tent. His fingers and toes were numb, tingling as if left out in the cold for too long, and his lips were dry and cracked. He coughed and slowly rolled onto his side, groaning as his muscles protested, his body sore. He froze when he saw the knife in his hand. The blade that was covered in blood.

For a moment he did nothing, just stared at the crimson-coated blade. Images of Seacrest rose up in his mind, Julian and Ellen lying in puddles of their own blood, a village murdered at his hand. Memories of death sprang up all around him, the smell of decay clogging up his nostrils, soaking his mind. With a sudden jerk he threw the weapon away from him and vomited all over the floor.

After emptying his stomach he took several deep breaths, trying to calm the hammering heart in his chest, pushing away the images of a massacred village that circled his mind like hungry sharks. His mouth and throat burnt with stomach acid and he longed for a cup of water. Slowly he sat up and rubbed his eyes with his palms, desperate to clear his head. When he had finally managed to gain some of his senses he examined the horror of the scene around him.

He was in the middle of a strange tent, definitely not the tent he had been in when he had been drugged. The walls were a deep green and seemed to be made of thousands of separate strands, all tightly knitted together to form walls. The tent was large but sparse, with no visible furniture of any kind and only a small pile of saddlebags nestled on one side. Three bodies lay on the ground, blood mingling between them, pale skin illuminated by the soft morning sunlight that shone through a large tear in the tent wall. He knew at once that they were dead. There was so much blood, coating their clothes and skin. One had been stabbed in the chest, while another looked to have had their throat slit. The nearest had been stabbed in the neck, the deep wound unmistakably made by a knife. Slowly his eyes drifted to the knife on the floor across from him.

The sound of footsteps made his head snap up as he saw a large bald man push apart the tear in the tent and peer inside. His eyes had to adjust to the change in light and it was that delay that saved Lyncon. He sprang up, leaping shoulder-first towards the hole and the man filling it.

"What the fu…" was all the big man managed before Lyncon slammed into him and sent him sprawling backwards onto the grass. The two men struggled, the bald man trying to grab at his ankles as Lyncon got to his feet. A sharp kick to the chin made a resounding thud and the grip loosened. Lyncon did not stay any longer and jumped up, running as fast as he could between rows of small, triangular tents.

"Intruder! Soldiers, to me!" his pursuer bawled as he began to give chase, wiping blood from his nose.

Lyncon ignored him and kept running. As he did, soldiers began to appear from the tents, most looking groggy and confused, blinking sleep out of their eyes. One had a few more wits about him and stuck out a foot, tripping Lyncon as he flew past. He was up in seconds though and had slipped away before the man could grab him. Another soldier was just rising in front of him but Lyncon shoved him away and he fell back into his tent, tangled in the collapsing structure. Panting, Lyncon sped up, desperate to reach the safety of the forest.

Soon he had reached the edge of the lake and began to follow the waterline around towards the trees. His heart pounded in his ears as he pumped his legs to carry him faster, his breathing coming in short, harsh bursts. A sudden splash to his left made him turn just in time to see an arrow disappear under the surface of the water. A second struck the grass just ahead of him and he leapt over it. Gritting his teeth he sped on, weaving slightly to put off the archer's aim.

Dodging a few more arrows he eventually reached the cover of the trees, powering beneath the shelter of the canopy. Gloom settled over him as the sunlight was blocked by the trees but Lyncon's eyes adjusted immediately and he didn't slow. Behind him the shouts died away a little, muffled by the density of the forest around him. He began to weave between the trees, making the chase harder for his pursuers. Finally, with his chest heaving, Lyncon threw himself to the floor amongst the roots of a big old oak and flattened himself down into the leaf litter.

As he caught his breath he fought to arrange his thoughts. The knife, the blood, the bodies. It all kept swirling around in an order that made no sense. New images flashed in his mind: Julian and Ellen torn to pieces by a monster, Evanora smiling at him with those blood-red lips. Nausea hit him once more and he gagged, his stomach empty. Suddenly he felt dizzy and the world spun around him as he fought for his breath.

"Over here! I heard something!"

The shout was close by and Lyncon immediately froze, peering into the gloom in the direction of the voice. Two men appeared quickly, breathing harder than he was, both with swords drawn. Lyncon pressed himself further into the ground and held his breath, watching from between two thick roots.

The first man was young and thin, the shadow of a beard attempting to bloom on his chin. His head was moving on a swivel, eyes scanning the forest around him, flicking from tree to tree. The second was the big bald man who Lyncon had tackled at the tent. His nose and moustache were coated in dried blood but he seemed not to have noticed.

"I think it was over here, Captain!" the young man said, moving away from where Lyncon was hiding.

The captain sighed and shook his head, putting his sword away. "Perhaps. Keep looking but don't get lost." He dismissed the soldier with a wave. "Go search over there. I must speak to Evanora."

The young man nodded and strode off in the opposite direction to Lyncon's hiding spot. The captain scanned the trees once but then shrugged and turned to meet Evanora as she appeared from the trees, her blue robes gliding silently across the grass. Her expression seemed to be one of annoyance or boredom and she did not once look around.

"They are dead, the elves. All three of them," she declared, her tone matter-of-fact, cold even.

"Fuck!" the big man roared and lashed out at a broken branch with his boot. "Fuck!" He rubbed a hand over his face, looking suddenly tired, his huge shoulders hunched over.

"Do you know who he was, the attacker? Who sent him?"

The soldier shook his head. "No. He wore nothing to mark him out in any way. By the time I found him the elves were already dead."

Her large eyes stared at him, watching carefully. Her face was a pale mask, unmoving and unreadable. "Did he say anything?"

"Nothing." He paused in thought, staring at his boots as he kicked idly at some twigs. "He seemed... dazed, confused almost. He looked just as shocked as I did. When I called out, he charged me. He moves faster than most. I'll give him that."

"The king will need to be told." The statement hung between them, heavy with foreboding.

He sighed. "With the envoy dead I must return to the capital. The king will want an explanation." He bowed his head and strode away, disappearing briefly from Lyncon's view between the roots before reappearing again looking even more stressed. "As his captain I must take responsibility for the failure."

"No, Amos, you can't." The elf leant forwards and gently touched his arm. "There is still the Crooked Man. He is close, Amos. I know it. We have to find him."

"But the envoy... the war." He shook his head, looking up at her. "It is all fucked. The king will have my head. I must go back to Astikus."

"This was in the tent." Evanora suddenly produced the knife that Lyncon had woken up with in his hand. The blade was still coated in elven blood. "This knife is elven-made. I checked the three bodies; it was not one of their weapons. Nor is it mine." When Amos simply stared at her she placed a gentle hand on his arm and continued. "Where else would the killer get an elven knife but from the Crooked Man? A creation of the elves."

The captain seemed confused. "But... why?"

"War is his friend, Amos. Chaos, fear, death. They are what he feeds on. Assassinating a peace envoy would be an excellent way for him to keep that going."

"How would he know we are here?"

She threw up her hands and moved away, anger flashing briefly in her large eyes. "I told you, he is close, at the very heart of the forest. He will sense me just as I sense him. Our powers are greater than you could ever know."

Slowly, Amos nodded. "Then we must find him. The king will want him found."

Evanora gave a flutter of a smile, tucking the knife into her belt. "Then let us go. No point wasting time wandering through these trees like idiots." With that she turned and walked away, back through the trees. After a second, Amos trailed after her.

Rootun was a forgotten place. A small village that stood in the heart of the Haren Forest, it had been built for one thing and one thing only and that was timber. Over three centuries ago two families had found the clearing and made it their home, turning the dense forest around them into a lucrative and thriving business. They had built the timber yards for the work and small wooden houses for living, arranged in neat little rows around a small village green. In over two hundred years it had barely changed at all.

Though a busy place, the village saw very few new faces. The forest road was the only access, cutting straight through the village from east to west, but few travellers wandered the road. The Haren was a place of fearsome reputation with many stories telling of the evil beasts that lurked amongst the whispering trees. The only visitors were the drivers of the wagon trains that came twice a week to collect fresh planks to haul back to the towns and cities beyond. Even these men didn't change much and many were known to the villagers by sight.

Bryn sat quietly on his front porch enjoying the warmth of the late morning sun as he ate his simple meal of cheese and raw onion on freshly baked bread. His wife,

Megan, sat opposite him sipping her ice tea, the leg of his favourite work trousers draped casually over her knee, the patch she was sewing in half finished. Across from them the timber yards were in full swing and the sound of saw blades biting wood filled the air.

Finishing his last bite he reached for his pipe. "Excellen' cheese, dear. Where was it from?"

"Corin," Megan replied as she returned to her repair job on his trousers, head bent over as she peered at the stitching with ageing eyes. "Grant brought it for me special."

Bryn nodded slowly as he lit his pipe. They sat in silence for a while, Bryn blowing smoke rings, before he finally spoke again. "Don't suppose we'll get much now after that big fight."

His wife shrugged. "Maybe not, though I heard the city is still safe. The elves are sticking to their side o' the water." She sighed. "Let's just hope we keep to our side."

Bryn scowled but said nothing, continuing instead to suck on his pipe. He knew all too well his wife's disapproval of the war and knew better than to argue with her. Though small, his woman was fierce when riled. It was part of why he loved her. Despite this he could never quite understand her love for elves. She held them in an almost sacred regard that he could never agree with.

As he exhaled another perfect smoke ring, a cloud passed above them, cutting out the sunlight and making him suddenly cold. Glancing up, he stopped as he spotted a black smudge streak across the sky before disappearing over the tops of the trees in the direction of the road.

Dumbstruck, he turned to his wife. "Did you see that? In the sky up there."

"No. I'm busy" came the curt reply.

"But… what was it?"

"Probably a bird. Stonepecker maybe."

"That weren't no stonepecker! I'm old but I ain't dull!"

Megan said nothing.

With a frustrated shake of his head he got up with creaking knees and emptied his pipe over the side of the porch. As he did, a young man ran towards them waving frantically. He stopped at the edge of the porch, red-faced and out of breath. Bryn raised an eyebrow at the arrival but said nothing. The youngster was dressed in usual working attire but had a sword at his hip and a yellow handkerchief tied around his left bicep. This marked him out as one of the village guards. Though mostly redundant, they were occasionally required to discourage bandits or creatures that strayed from the trees.

Finally, the youth regained his breath enough to speak. "Foreman, ser. We have a convoy at the gates."

The lines on the old man's craggy face deepened further. "Can't. Next one ain't due for three days yet."

"It isn't a logging caravan, ser. Looks like travellers. A strange bunch too. Captain Howe asked me to fetch you, ser."

"Asked or ordered?" Bryn said. When the young man didn't reply he sighed and shook his head. "Alright. Just let me fetch my chain. First a knight and now this. Whatever is this place coming to?"

After disappearing briefly inside the house he reappeared on the porch wearing a thick chain made of smooth wooden links, each one lined with a band of gold. The chain was a symbol of his status, only ever to be worn by the foreman of the yard. After kissing his wife on the head, he stepped down from the porch on achy legs and followed the young man towards the gate.

The distance to the east gate was not far but at Bryn's age nothing happened fast and by the time they neared the scene the guard was visibly frustrated at the lack of speed. Bryn ignored him, instead focusing on the goings-on in front of him and trying to figure out exactly why he had been called for.

As usual the gate stood open, offering a clear view down the long straight stretch of road that led through the forest. Squinting, the old foreman could see the convoy, a mixture of wagons and carts of all shapes and sizes. They had halted some twenty metres from the gate and three people had moved forwards. An old man, leaning heavily on a staff and with a bandage over one eye, stood between a man and a woman. All three looked weary from travel. Captain Howe stood just outside the gate with a guard either side of him. Several other guards stood on the wall above, crossbows in hand.

The talking stopped as the duo arrived and Howe turned to the foreman with a strange expression on his weathered face. "Foreman, these people claim to be travellers. I offered to escort them through the village as is custom but they have asked for shelter and aid. They say some of their people are sick."

Bryn raised an eyebrow as he studied the strangers over Howe's shoulder. The man and woman seemed normal enough, healthy too, but the old man, the crooked one, seemed different. There was something off about him, the way he stared back at Bryn with such an unflinching gaze. His singular eye seemed to eat into him, hungry. He turned away as a shiver passed down his spine.

"What type of sickness?"

"Didn't say."

"And what about these three?" he nodded to the trio who continued to wait patiently.

"Apparently not. The old one seems to be their leader. He spoke for them, anyhow." The captain paused, a strange look passing over his features. "I don't like them. Send them away."

Bryn sighed and gently patted Howe on the arm. "Let's see."

Stepping past the captain he put on his best foreman smile and spread his thin arms out in front of him. "Welcome, strangers, on this fine Haren day. My friend here tells me you seek aid? What ails you?"

The old man hobbled nearer, leaning on his staff. Up close he was smaller than Bryn had realised, a hunched skeleton covered in paper-thin skin, his robes hanging loose off his frame. He reminded Bryn of a fruit that had dried up in the sun, the juice and sweetness gone, leaving only a shrivelled husk behind. However, when the old man looked up Bryn thought he saw a strange energy in his stare and had to fight a sudden urge to step back a pace.

"We are travellers, weary as we pass through this great forest. Some of us are sick and famished. The road has taken its toll." The old man's words sounded genuine enough but Bryn noticed his face did not match. His expression was fixed in a cold smile. There was no pleading in his gaze.

The foreman made a show of examining the other two visitors. The man stood tall and straight, eyes examining the walls in a lazy, carefree manner. The woman, meanwhile, was eyeing the guards with casual interest. She was astonishingly beautiful with long auburn hair and lips of the brightest red. When she caught his eye she gave him a smile that made even his old knees grow weak.

He turned back to the old man. "Pardon me saying but you don't look too sick, nor hungry for that matter. If there are sick in your wagons then bring them forward. I will fetch the surgeon to take a look at them."

The man nodded. "Of course, thank you. They are old and frail; will your surgeon know to be gentle with them?"

Bryn frowned at the question. "Certainly. We got old folk here too as you might well have guessed." He gave a chuckle that was not returned. He shook his head. "The surgeon treats all folks. He's a good man."

"How many old folk?"

"Sorry?"

"How many old people do you have here?"

Bryn was confused by the odd question and felt a sudden surge of unease. The old man simply watched him, waiting. His expression had not shifted. "Erm, twenty or so, I suppose. Why'd you ask?"

The old man nodded enthusiastically. "Excellent. That will do just fine." He waved his hand at the woman, who gave a curt nod and then simply disappeared.

Bryn stood stock still, blinking against the sun as he tried to understand what he had just seen. Only when he heard a sudden scream behind him did he finally break from his shock and turn to look. What he saw did not help to clear his muddled mind any further.

The woman was somehow now up on the wall, a knife in her hand. As he turned he saw her dart forwards and drive the blade into the nearest guard's throat. Then she disappeared again, twisting into a cloud of smoke that shot along the wall to the next man. In panic, the guard fired his crossbow but the bolt sailed through the smoke and moments later she was behind the man, her knife buried in his back. With a swift kick she sent him tumbling over the wall to land with a heavy thud on the road. It all happened so fast he didn't even have time to scream.

Seeing his men dying, Howe gave a shout of alarm and drew his sword. He turned to face Bryn and began to shout something but his words were cut short when the woman appeared beside him, springing from a living cloud of darkness, and drove her knife up under his chin. A horrible gurgling sound replaced his words as blood foamed at his lips. With a twist of the knife the woman removed the weapon and Howe fell forwards, his blood drenching the dry earth around him.

Bryn backed away, horrified, but then felt the old man grab him and spin him roughly with a strength he would not have guessed. He smiled up at Bryn, menace dripping from his gaze.

"Please!" the foreman begged. "There are families here… children." Hot tears stung his cheeks as he sank to his knees, his legs refusing to support him any longer.

The Crooked Man sighed and shook his head. "Why do you humans always have such concern for the children?" He reached forwards and caught a tear on his finger. Gently he placed it onto his tongue and shivered in delight. "Children are worthless, a blank page with no story. But you…" His smile spread wider. "The old have lived their lives. They know pain and sorrow and death. Memories of all that suffering. I want them."

He reached out slowly and placed a hand on either side of Bryn's head. An intense pain suddenly built inside the foreman's skull and he screamed long and loud. He was dead within seconds, black tendrils moving beneath his skin, devouring him.

When Lyncon finally returned to the hut he was tired and hungry, his muscles stiff and his back sore. Though the day was warm, bathed in the fierce glow of the afternoon sun, he felt cold and hollow, exhaustion sapping all his strength. He staggered across the clearing and leant heavily on the doorframe while he caught his breath. He ran a hand through his knotted hair, dislodging several leaves and twigs that had caught there when he had hidden from the soldiers. His clothes were filthy and torn, covered in ash and still reeking of smoke. He gave a heavy sigh before pushing open the door and stepping inside.

The first thing that hit him was the smell. The fire in the hearth was stacked high, burning fiercely, and from a large pot hanging over the flames came the delicious aroma of fresh stew. Lyncon's stomach growled at the scent and he shuffled closer, staring greedily at the meal as it bubbled away above the flames. He licked his lips, hands shaking with anticipation.

"Sounds like you're hungry."

He grinned. "Just a little."

In his obsession with food Lyncon had not even registered Fenrir, who was smiling at him from where he sat at the table, an empty bowl and a half-eaten hunk of bread sitting in a crowd of crumbs in front of him. As Lyncon stepped closer the elf rose slowly, steadying himself against the table. He looked even more pale than usual but his eyes were focused and he had the strength to pass Lyncon a clean bowl and spoon from the shelf. He sat down as Lyncon helped himself to food.

"You look terrible."

"It's been a long few days," he admitted as he set his bowl down and dropped gratefully to the bench. "How are you feeling?"

"By the looks of it, better than you." The elf smirked but then winced and ran a hand over his eyes. "Tired but still in one piece."

"What happened o…"

Fenrir raised a hand. "Eat first. Then we'll talk."

Lyncon nodded and set to work devouring the portion of stew he had spooned into his bowl. He attacked the food with vigour, scooping up mouthfuls with a single-minded determination. The taste was divine, the best thing he had ever eaten, and he shuddered as the warmth filled him from head to toe. Once he was done he threw down his spoon and gave a deep, satisfied sigh. Without a word, Fenrir gathered his bowl and walked slowly to the fire to refill it. He set the bowl down again, full, and gave Lyncon's shoulder a gentle squeeze as he passed.

"I need to thank you," he admitted as he sat down. "For putting out the fire. The forest is very grateful."

Lyncon nodded as he took a sip of tea, staring down at the cloudy liquid. "I didn't do it for the forest."

212

"I know," Fenrir said quietly, fingers idly toying at a loose splinter of wood on the edge of the table. A single tear fell onto the wood next to his fingers but was quickly wiped away. Lyncon pretended not to have seen it.

After a brief silence Lyncon cleared his throat and returned to his stew, eating more slowly this time, savouring every mouthful as he felt strength return to his body. Finally, he pushed the bowl away and set down his spoon. The elf continued to watch him in silence.

"In truth, it wasn't really me that put out the fire." Lyncon shrugged. "I had help."

Fenrir raised an eyebrow. "Help? You mean the bears?"

He shook his head. "No. There was an elf, a sorceress of some kind. She summoned rain and doused the flames."

The elf's big eyes widened in shock before he launched into his questioning. "A sorceress? Are you sure? Who was she?" He drummed his fingers against the table as he spoke, obvious concern etched on his face.

"Her name was Evanora. She appeared as I fought the fire and saved me with the rain. After, she took me back to…" He trailed off as he saw the expression on his friend's face. "What is it? Do you know her?"

At the mention of her name Fenrir's fingers had instantly stilled and he now sat rigid and silent, his face gripped by a mix of shock and something Lyncon recognised as fear.

"Are you sure it was her?" he whispered, finally. His eyes were fixed on Lyncon's with an intensity that scared him.

"That is what she told me. Who is she?"

Fenrir shook his head as his shoulders sank. "Where is she?"

"She has a camp to the south. She travels with soldiers and…." He stopped as he remembered waking up, the knife in his hand, the bodies at his feet.

"What is it? What happened?" the elf demanded, grasping for his hand.

"I don't know. I'm not sure." Lyncon paused as he tried to arrange the thoughts in his tired mind. "She took me to her tent to heal my burns but then gave me something and… when I woke… there was blood everywhere… bodies. I had a knife in my hand."

Fenrir paused, a look of anger passing over his features that was quickly replaced by concern. "Then what happened? After you woke up."

"A guard found me, so I ran, hid in the forest. They chased me but I managed to avoid them and came back here."

Both sat in silence as they processed the events. Lyncon struggled to grapple with the implications of what had happened. Had he really killed those elves? After everything he had learnt was he still just a mindless murderer? A weapon to be wielded? As he set his cup down he noticed his hands were shaking just as much as Fenrir's. He rose and threw a log onto the fire, the flames crackling happily as they lapped at the new fuel. When he sat back down Fenrir had sorrow in his eyes. Abruptly the elf reached across and took his hand.

"Lyncon, you are not to blame for this. Evanora is dangerous."

Lyncon pulled his hand away and shook his head. "You don't know that. You know my past. Seacrest…" He bowed his head as he felt the threat of tears sting the corners of his eyes.

Fenrir was silent for a time, staring at his friend, a pained expression etched into his features. Eventually he spoke, each word slow, as if difficult to form.

"Evanora is a sorceress of the old blood, a descendant of one of the original elven families who are blessed with unique powers. Before the war she was a scholar, studying magic and its relationship to emotions and feelings. Her experiments were cutting edge, her talent applauded by many of her peers, but not everyone liked what she was doing. The High Council opposed her thinking and ordered her to stop her work, and when she was discovered conducting dangerous experiments, she was banished, ordered never to return to Vilantis. For a time she disappeared and many presumed her dead but eventually rumours began to swirl that she had joined with King Renthor and was advising him on matters of elven warfare and tactics, fuelled by her desire for revenge against those that had thrown her out. In Belanthor she was branded a traitor and despised by all."

The elf paused and rubbed at his eyes, suddenly looking older than ever before. Lyncon had never seen Fenrir so upset, so off balance, and his breath caught as he was hit by a sudden realisation.

"You knew her, didn't you?"

Fenrir gave a barely perceptible nod but said nothing further and hung his head to look down at the table. The flickering of the firelight cast shadows that danced across his pale face.

Lyncon sipped the last of his tea and turned his weary mind to the previous day, acutely aware that he needed a long bathe in the stream and some sleep. It had all happened so fast: the fire, the bodies, the flight through the forest. He struggled to remember the details and exactly what Evanora had said to him but no matter how hard he tried he could not put the pieces together. Since waking in the tent his thinking had been muddled and slow, most likely an aftereffect of the potion he had drunk. The food had helped but he still felt lost and used, dirty, as if the blood still coated his hands. He shuddered and ran a hand through his hair.

"Who were they?" Fenrir spoke without looking up. "These people you found dead?"

"Elves. I overheard mention of some sort of envoy."

The elf looked up sharply, studying him. "Elves?" He stroked his chin as he sank deep into thought. "Were the ones who chased you also elves?"

"No, men. I think they were the king's soldiers. They mentioned having to report to him about the deaths."

Fenrir nodded, suddenly more alive than he had been all evening. "Yes… yes that would make sense." He smiled up at Lyncon. "I don't think you killed those elves."

Lyncon was still sceptical. "How can you know that?"

"Elves would not enter Petra lightly. I believe the elves were part of a peace envoy, sent to treat with King Renthor. I also think that Evanora murdered them to stop any kind of peace from happening and then framed you for the deaths."

"Why would she do that?"

The elf raised an eyebrow. "Perhaps the hatred held for her in Belanthor runs both ways. If she holds a powerful enough grudge, as I believe she does, she would want to do everything she could to keep this war going. With the envoy killed on Petran soil then any chance of peace will be gone."

Lyncon nodded slowly as he grasped the logic of what Fenrir said. "But why save me from the fire? She had no reason to do that."

Fenrir frowned. "That is a little harder to explain but it is most likely she didn't know you were there. She may have seen the fire and simply wanted to put it out. All elves have an instinctive love of nature. It can be hard to turn your back on its plight. Or it may be she thought the fire may threaten the camp. Either way I think she stumbled upon you by accident then decided to use you in her schemes. It is very clever. She obviously hoped you would be found and killed and therefore the blame would never pass to her. It is likely only your powers saved you, woke you earlier than she had planned."

"She put an elven knife in my hand and I heard her mention something about someone called the Crooked Man. I think she was trying to blame him…" He trailed off as he noticed Fenrir had frozen, his breath caught in his chest. "Who is he?"

"She wants the Crooked Man… of course." The elf had turned ghostly pale again and had to grip the table to stop from swaying. He shook his head suddenly and jumped to his feet, knocking the bench over behind him and wincing in pain from his wounds. He took a deep breath through gritted teeth before replying. "We have to find her, to stop her. She… she could destroy everything."

"What? How?" Lyncon rose but was cut off from any further questions by a loud knock on the door.

The two friends exchanged a worried glance before Fenrir moved to fetch his sword from the chest. He drew the blade as quietly as he could and shuffled to the door. He leant against the frame with his free hand before throwing the door open and raising his sword, ready to strike. Outside stood Ser Dallan Tan, red-faced and panting. Henrik stood behind him looking even more exhausted. There were no signs of either of their horses.

"Fenrir!" the old knight exclaimed with a broad smile. "Thank the gods it's you. We need help."

"Dallan? How did you find us?" Fenrir asked, stunned.

With a shrug the old man gestured over his shoulder where a large owl circled lazily in the early evening sky.

Chapter 14

A Crooked Tale

Despite all that was going on, Evanora could not take her mind from the strange man she had met in the woods. Lyncon had seemed so ordinary, so perfect for her plans, an unwitting accomplice who had appeared at just the right time, but the more she recalled of him the more uneasy she felt. The fact that he had woken early and evaded capture only worsened her fears. He knew too much to be kept alive.

"You look worried?" Amos said suddenly from his horse beside her.

She raised an eyebrow. "Aren't you?"

The big man shrugged. "A little but I find it rarely helps."

She sighed and shook her head. While she did not dislike Amos she had always found his lack of imagination and ambition secretly unnerving.

"How much further to the village?" she asked, staring down the road ahead.

"Not far. We should reach it just past noon."

The elf cursed under her breath, gripping the reins tightly in frustration. Not for the first time, she wished

Renthor had given his soldiers mounts. As it were they marched behind Amos and her in a long line, four men wide, followed by the wagons carrying the tents and baggage. Even Amos had not originally set out with a horse and had instead taken one from the envoy. From the way he sat in the saddle she could tell he would rather be marching with his men. A feeling that seemed to be echoed by the horse itself.

A movement above caught her eye and she glanced up in time to see an owl swoop across the strip of blue sky before disappearing above the trees. That was the fourth time she had seen the bird in the last hour. They were being watched. She glanced around at the trees either side of them, the trunks rising to form a screen from what lay beyond. Even her elven eyes could not pierce the gloom beyond a few metres and she shivered at the thought of what might be hiding there.

"What exactly is it that you want with this Crooked Man?"

The question startled her and she took a moment's pause to answer. Amos had never shown any interest in the Crooked Man beyond his own orders before now. This sudden change of heart, no matter how seemingly innocent, did nothing to ease her already overworked mind.

"Why the sudden interest? Don't tell me you've finally had enough of soldiering?" She laughed but kept her eyes fixed on his expression.

He ignored her joke. "I want to know what I am leading my men into."

She paused again. "The Crooked Man is powerful,

he can... do things that others can't. The king wants him found before he falls back into elven hands."

"Ironic that he would send you, then."

She turned to face him but he did not look at her, his eyes never leaving the road in front of them. "Is that resentment I detect in your voice, Captain?"

"Only curiosity."

"That can be almost as bad."

"You told me he has taken Rootun, overrun the entire village. I have been there once, many years ago. It is fortified, guarded. How can one man overcome all that?" He ran a hand over his moustache.

Evanora did not like where these questions were leading. "He has... followers," she said simply. "Little more than a rabble of beggars and peasants but they are loyal. They will die for him."

"How many?"

"I don't know but surely nothing fifty soldiers of the Royal Astikus Guard cannot handle? Or are you afraid of a bunch of women and children?"

He ignored her questions and spoke in an icy tone. "First an assassin and now soldiers. Anything else I should know?"

She paused for a moment, her mind straying to images of the nebula tearing the big captain apart. She stifled a smirk as she replied. "No. Nothing."

They fell quiet, the silence of the forest broken only by the sound of their horses and the stomping boots of the men following behind. Above them the owl appeared again, watching as it wheeled through the sky. Somewhere in the gloom of the trees a branch snapped. Evanora's head whipped around, searching for the source of the noise but unable to see anything. Shuddering, she spurred her horse on a little quicker.

"One of my men said he saw you out of your tent on the night the envoys were killed. He told me you were with someone he didn't know. A man."

She had frozen in her saddle, eyes fixed forwards, face an emotionless mask. Amos too looked forwards, his tone casual, his eyes on the horizon. Fear had flared up inside her but she fought to quell it as she had done for so many years.

She gave a snort of derision before replying. "Really? And how much wine had he drunk before this? I told you, I was asleep all night. Your man is mistaken."

The big man rode on in silence, his face blank as stone, unreadable. Evanora found herself holding her breath, awaiting his reply. After what felt like an eternity he nodded slowly.

"Yes. A mistake. That is what I was thinking."

The Crooked Man stared at the line of kneeling figures with barely concealed desire. The six prisoners were the oldest residents in the village, four women and two men, and all knelt naked in the dirt, heads bowed. Half of them were openly crying while the other half stared up at him with silent hatred in their eyes.

Around them Rootun was being ripped apart as his followers went about their tasks. They worked with a practised efficiency, moving from one building to the next searching for anyone hidden inside or any food to take with them when they left. The sound of desperate screams rose occasionally from a hut only to be abruptly cut short. Bodies lay strewn in the mud between the huts, cut down in the chaos of the initial attack and left where they fell, to become food for the crows. The Crooked Man licked his lips. Fear hung in the air like a dense fog, echoes of the slain lingering on the breeze. He could feel it feeding him, feel the strength it gave his body, the power so addictive. He gave a soft sigh of satisfaction as he turned his attention back to those before him.

"Ladies and gentlemen. I really am sorry you had to see all this, the violence, the death. It is never nice but it… helps me. This fresh pain… fresh fear, it makes it all so much clearer. Much more satisfying." He stroked the hair of one of the women, causing her to cry out in alarm. The two men standing nearby stepped closer, hands on their weapons, but he ushered them back. Instead he crouched in front of the woman, gently stroking the side of her face as he stared into her eyes and continued.

"You have all had such lovely long lives, full of joy and sorrow, highs and lows. Be thankful. Look around you; there are many here who did not get to enjoy what you have had. You have been lucky and now you have been chosen."

He stood and walked to a corpse nearby, hitting it with the end of his staff as he looked down with disgust. "Look at them. Their deaths were meaningless. Pathetic. They gave nothing to this world. But you…" He laughed suddenly, grinning. "You can give me… give us, new life. Give us joy."

Stepping back to the kneeling figures he grasped the woman by the hair, pulling her head back. Ignoring the desperate pleas and the sharp tang of urine as the old woman soiled herself, he placed a hand on the old woman's face and quickly drained the life out of her, devouring the misery with his insatiable hunger. He released his grip and the body slumped to the floor. The woman next to him screamed and tried to flee but one of his men grabbed her and shoved her back to her knees.

After a deep breath to calm his racing heart he moved to the next prisoner. He was about to grasp her face and devour her when a commotion behind him made him pause and turn. Thom had appeared from a house dragging another old woman by the arm. Though small and frail-looking she was clearly fierce and spat curses at the man as he forced her along. Her lip was split and blood ran freely down her chin.

"Found this one in the big house, Leeraar. Stabbed two of ours with a hunting knife before we stopped her." He hurled her to the floor at the Crooked Man's feet and shrugged, face blank. "Tough old crow."

The Crooked Man raised an eyebrow as he stepped towards her. When she stared defiantly up at him he only laughed. "Ha, you are a fierce one indeed. That is good. I need that kind of strength."

As he grasped her face the woman's resolve broke and terror flooded her features. She began to thrash against his touch until Thom grabbed her and held her still.

"Please, no! Stop!" she howled. "Why are you doing this?"

He paused, head cocked as he considered the question. "Why?" Images of an elven lab flashed through his mind, needles and potions. So much pain. Pain that never left him. Pain he craved every waking second.

"My husband… he was a good man. He would have helped ya, given you anything you wanted." She sagged in Thom's grip as grief overtook her and tears streamed down her face.

"But he's already helped me." He smiled down at her with an almost genuine joy in his eyes. "And now so will you." Black tendrils appeared beneath her skin as soon as his hands touched it and, gently, he leant forwards and kissed her head. When he released her she fell to the floor, limp and lifeless.

He returned to the other prisoners and devoured each of them one by one, shaking with ecstasy after each feed. Once done, he breathed a huge sigh of satisfaction, tilting his head back to let the fading sun warm his skin. His muscles felt strong from the new power, his back no longer hunched or bent. Reaching up he slowly removed the bandage from his face, revealing that his left eye was now completely healed, his vision perfect. He twirled his staff in his hands, enjoying the ease of his movements, knowing it would fade all too fast.

"Burn the bodies. We will move on at dawn tomorrow." The men did as ordered without question, Thom helping.

Alone now, he looked around the village with a smile on his lips. Almost all of the buildings seem to have been searched and it pained him to see no more elderly had been found. Though he felt good now, he knew this meal would not last him long, especially once he shared the Essence amongst those within his group who needed it.

Thom appeared beside him once more, hands splattered with blood and worry etched across his brow. The Crooked Man paused. It was unlike Thom to worry.

"What is it?"

"Soldiers, Leeraar. Spotted on the road marching towards us. Looks to be at least fifty of them."

The Crooked Man grinned, suddenly eager to feed further, tempted by the prospect of battle and further deaths. "Then you had better find Trisha. Make sure everyone is ready to give them a proper welcome."

Seated at the table, Dallan and Henrik devoured two bowls of stew each before they had energy enough to tell their tale. Lyncon and Fenrir waited in tense silence, the elf looking more worried with every passing minute as he paced back and forth in the small cabin, occasionally stretching to ease his aching wounds. Lyncon had used the time to change and wash and now simply sat, waiting patiently, still trying to pick over what had happened to him and what Fenrir had told him about the sorceress. Neither had yet mentioned her to the men.

Outside, night had descended at last, thick clouds blocking out almost all moonlight and leaving the Haren in a deep, foreboding dark. The trees stood silent and still, untroubled by wind.

Finishing his food with a hefty slurp, Ser Dallan wiped his mouth with the back of his hand and turned to address Fenrir, who was now leaning against the wall behind Lyncon, face half covered in shadow. "I suppose we should start by thanking you for sending that bird. Took us a bit to realise what it wanted but we got there in the end. How did you find us?"

"I didn't," the elf replied in a flat tone. "Now, tell me what happened?"

Dallan raised an eyebrow at the elf's tone and looked at Lyncon, who shook his head wearily. "It's been a long day."

The old knight nodded and ran a hand through his long grey hair. "Might as well start from the beginning, I suppose. After we left you we followed the road and eventually came across Rootun. They were wary of us to begin with but I told them who I was and, lucky for us, the captain had seen me fight in a tournament a few years back. He was keen to get my help training his men, beat 'em into shape a little."

He laughed and gave Lyncon a wink. Beside him Henrik finished the last of his food and gave a huge belch before chuckling quietly to himself. Dallan paid him no mind. "We were given a warm bed and a hot supper and slept like babies, till long after dawn." His expression saddened, the humour suddenly gone. "In the end, I think that is what saved us from the attack."

"Was it him? The Crooked Man?" Fenrir asked impatiently, his big eyes gleaming in the half-light, his words little more than a whisper.

Dallan frowned. "Crooked Man? Never heard of him but if you mean an old man with a staff then yes, it was him. Not just him either, the whole troop of them. The villagers didn't stand a chance..." He trailed off, looking down at his hands.

"Please tell us. We need to know." Lyncon locked eyes with the old man and gave him a sad smile. Slowly, the knight nodded. Even Henrik was listening now.

"We awoke to screams and chaos. Outside we found everyone shouting, some fleeing into the trees while a group of workmen were heading to the gate with their axes in their hands. We followed." He fell silent a moment, shaking his head. Henrik laid a gentle hand on his father's arm and Dallan gave it an affectionate pat. "It was carnage, a massacre. The captain and his guards were all dead, while the old man stood in the gateway, hands clamped against the foreman's head. It looked… almost like he was… draining him, sucking the life out through his hands and laughing while he did it. That laughter. I ain't never heard anything like it…" He picked up his tea with a shaking hand and downed it in one gulp. Beside him, Henrik had gone very pale.

Lyncon turned to Fenrir. "Is it the man we fought on the road? The one who knew you somehow?" When the elf did not respond he continued. "Who is he, Fenrir? We need to know!"

Fenrir ignored him, his focus fixed on the knight across the table. "Did you attack him? You said you were with the workmen. Is he dead?"

Dallan shook his head. "We never reached him. We were attacked by something before we could get at him."

"She was like smoke. A woman of death." It was Henrik who spoke now, his voice seeming very small for such a big man. "It was all a blur. Then the knife and the… the screams."

His father nodded, placing a reassuring arm around the big man's shoulders. Lyncon felt a pang of sympathy for the two men who had clearly been witness to something terrible and seemingly beyond their own comprehension. If he had not seen the Crooked Man with his own eyes he too would have struggled to understand what they had been through.

"Whatever creature attacked us it was not human. It moved faster than anything I have ever seen, even in all my years fighting. Just a blur of smoke and steel and blood. She… it cut down the workers with ease; they never stood a chance. We should'a helped… but… we ran." At the last confession the old knight hung his head in shame and though his long hair covered his face Lyncon guessed the man had tears in his eyes.

"There was nothing you could have done," Lyncon said.

Fenrir nodded. "He's right for once. From what you have described it sounds like you saw a nebula, taking the form of a woman. They are rare and vicious creatures. Evil. You could not have killed it." The three men nodded in silence, unsure how to proceed.

Finally it was Lyncon who spoke, addressing the elf who had moved to stare out of the window at the darkness outside. "Fenrir, tell us who he is? The Crooked Man."

There was another long silence while Fenrir stared off into the dark. Lyncon could tell he was troubled, his shoulders tense and his bony knuckles white as he gripped the window frame. In the flickering firelight his face looked haunted and when he eventually spoke his voice shook a little.

"The Crooked Man is my fault. He is a failed experiment. We created him to use as a weapon, to put an end to the war, but it went wrong and he got out." He turned and looked right at Lyncon. A lone tear ran down his pale cheek. "You asked me once if I thought you were a monster but that was the wrong way around. It should've been me asking you and I already know the answer."

At the mention of experiments Lyncon had tensed, his breath caught in his lungs and his fists clenching of their own accord. Resentment and angry confusion flowed through him. For many nights he had struggled with the thought of being sculpted and designed by others for the sole purpose of doing their bidding and killing whoever they told him to kill. Finding out he had volunteered for the treatment had only deepened the mystery and his lack of memory drove him in endless circles of frustration and despair. There were many times when he had hated Fenrir for his part in it all, resented the elf for what he had transformed him into, but now, seeing the hurt and pain in the elf's eyes, that anger slipped away. In that moment he saw the burden Fenrir carried, the regret and guilt for his past that weighed on his every moment. These were feelings Lyncon himself knew all too well and fleetingly the image of Ellen smiling flashed across his mind. The elf had seen what he had done and forgiven him, even tried to help him. What kind of man would Lyncon be if he did not do the same?

Wordlessly, Lyncon got to his feet and embraced his friend. Fenrir froze in shock but then finally relented and sagged into Lyncon's arms, openly crying now. Dallan and Henrik shared a sad smile as they turned away to give the two a moment. Outside, an owl gave a hoot of relief and took to the air.

Slowly, Lyncon released Fenrir and guided him back to the table. With the elf seated, he gathered his cup and poured his friend some fresh tea before setting it down in front of him. Fenrir nodded his thanks and, after wiping his face with his sleeve, took a hearty glug of the hot drink.

Setting the mug down with a soft thud he began to tell the tale.

"The Crooked Man is not actually a man at all, at least not entirely. He is a moiety, which means he is half-elf and half-human. In Vilantis people like him are treated... poorly, often abandoned or even killed at birth. This particular moiety ended up with us. He had no family and no name. We were told nothing about him and frankly we didn't care enough to ask." He shook his head in shame. "We took the child and began our experiments without a second thought, blinded by our egotistical desire for progress."

"The idea was simple enough. We wanted to create something that could feed on people's fear, consume their pain and panic, and then use it as power. A battleground is naturally rife with all these feelings and we wanted to use them to truly destroy our enemies. The secret lay in something called the Essence. A force that exists all around us, inside every living thing, and feeds into and from our emotions and feelings. We wanted to harness it, create something that could use it against our enemies. After years of experiments and failure we finally got it right. It worked... too well.

"At first he seemed almost unchanged, simply driven by a new hunger for the pain of others but soon he became too powerful. His body grew old, unable to support the power it now held and in constant need of pain to nourish and restore it. Meanwhile, his mind turned to dark places, places of greed and lust, of an unquenchable hunger for hurt. He turned the pain and fear he consumed into power and used it to escape. We sent soldiers after him but they failed to find him. The High Council were furious and shut down all our work, forbidding us to continue with the idea."

He turned to Lyncon. "When I told you I was here to guard the forest, I lied. I was banished from Belanthor until I could return with proof of the Crooked Man's death and now I must complete my task. We have to reach him before Evanora does."

"Why? What does she want with him?"

"She created him, figured out how to harness the Essence." He shuddered as he spoke. "If I am right, I believe she wishes to take his abilities and use them for her own gain. Use them to destroy both men and elves alike."

Chapter 15

To Battle

The four figures crept quietly through the forest, picking their way slowly in the dark, moving towards the noise and commotion ahead. Fenrir led the way, moving silently with Dallan keeping close behind him, while Lyncon led Henrik, cursing the sound of the big man's heavy steps. All four of them had swords strapped to their hips, while Dallan had his shield on his back and Fenrir had brought his bow and quiver slung over one shoulder.

They stopped at the edge of the trees. Fenrir and Lyncon moved forwards slightly, eyes roving the open gateway and the buildings beyond, while Henrik and Dallan hung back, the village barely discernible for them in the darkness. As he watched, Lyncon could make out several figures moving amongst the houses, towards one of the bigger buildings that resembled a barn or large storage shed. The wooden walls that ringed the village were deserted, with no signs of any sentries or lookouts. Even from this distance Lyncon could see several bodies in the gateway and the smell of death and blood hung heavy in the night air. Images of Seacrest flashed into his mind, vivid memories of the death he had wrought, and he shook his head to clear them. Seeing his struggle, Fenrir placed a reassuring hand on his arm before gesturing to return to the others.

"Looks like nobody is watching the road," whispered the elf to his companions. "We'll go closer but stay as low and quiet as you can." The group nodded and followed him out onto the road, grateful for the gentle moonlight that peeked between the clouds.

As Lyncon moved nearer to Rootun his hand went subconsciously to the small pouch of strange leaves that were tied loosely around his neck. Fenrir had given a pouch to each of them to wear, to ward against the nebula and prevent it from coming too close to them in its true form. Though Fenrir had assured them all the leaves would work, Dallan and Henrik had still needed more convincing before they had agreed to come back to the village. The beast had scared them and they were in no hurry to face it again. Lyncon himself did not fully understand what the nebula was but anything that scared the old knight seemed worth preparing against and it had not taken Fenrir long to find the correct plant amongst the trees near the hut.

Reaching the gate they slipped inside the village and paused to survey the scene. Beyond the walls lay a wide straight track that cut the village clean in two. Timber buildings of various sizes stood on each side, arranged in neat and even rows. Several huts had been burnt down and now stood only as charred husks, the embers still glowing hot. Off to their right a larger structure loomed above the buildings and Lyncon guessed that must be the lumber mill he had been told about.

As he glanced around his gaze was drawn to the nearest building on his left, the one he had seen from the road that was now encircled by a group of men. It was a long rectangular building with wooden walls and a thatched roof. There were no windows and the thin end was capped by two huge oak doors that were firmly shut and resisting all attempts at opening them made by the men outside. A bloody path of bodies lay between the gate and the barn. Clearly someone was holed up inside the building and the men outside were keen to get at them.

A corpse nearby caught his eye, the dead man's shield facing towards him, the sigil on the front showing a golden eagle on a black sky, wings outstretched in flight. Realisation dawned on him as he recognised the symbol.

"These are the king's men. The ones Evanora was travelling with."

Fenrir looked around and nodded. "Yes, but they're not." He gestured to the men at the barn doors, who were now lighting several torches under the instructions of a tall man in a ragged checked shirt. As they watched, the men threw the first of the torches up onto the roof, cheering when the thatch caught and began to burn.

"If it is the king's men in there then we need to help them!" urged Dallan, sword already drawn and shield firmly buckled onto his arm.

"Last time I saw them they tried to kill me. Not sure I want to give them a second chance."

Fenrir waved Lyncon's protests away. "Dallan is right; we should help them. The Crooked Man has more followers than I thought; we will not defeat them without help." Gesturing for the others to move closer into the shadow of the nearest hut, he turned to address them. "We will help the soldiers and then find the Crooked Man and perhaps Evanora as well. That means we need to deal with those men."

Lyncon glanced over at the group, who had now gathered in a loose circle around the barn doors, ready and waiting for the men inside to burst out as they fled the fire that raged in the thatch above. They were an odd-looking bunch, wearing a jumble of mismatching clothes and carrying an assortment of weapons including some that had clearly been looted from the soldiers they had already slain. Though not exactly fearsome-looking, they numbered fourteen in total. Against the four of them the odds were not good and Lyncon felt unease grow in the pit of his stomach.

"We will need to hit them hard and fast, take them by surprise." The men nodded to Fenrir as he fitted an arrow to his bow. He looked at each of them in turn before closing his eyes and mouthing a silent prayer. Henrik's hands were shaking and his father gave his shoulder a gentle pat of reassurance as the big man drew his sword. Lyncon rolled his shoulders and steadied his breathing, tightening his grip on his own weapon. He felt strangely calm and at ease. Despite the promise of imminent violence, his body was relaxed, his mind focused, forgotten memories of old battle-training now guiding him.

Fenrir finished his prayer and took a deep breath. "We can do this. Once I fire, charge."

Without waiting for a reply he stepped out of the shadows, raised his bow, took aim and fired. The arrow sailed through the dark on silent wings and sank into the nearest man's throat with a wet thump. Fenrir was already aiming a second arrow and that soon found its target in another man's back.

Lyncon gripped his sword with both hands as he let out a roar and charged at the men, Dallan and Henrik close behind. His heart was pounding, blood thundering in his ears, but a strange calm had suddenly fallen over him, as if his body were now in control of itself, his mind simply observing as his legs carried him into danger. His muscles were beginning to burn as his wolf blood gave him strength and he powered forwards.

An arrow flew past him, striking the man in the checked shirt and sending him tumbling to the floor. Lyncon ignored him, instead homing in on his first foe, an older man with an untidy beard and a sword in one hand. The man turned as Lyncon leapt at him with a snarl, cutting him down before he could react.

Not stopping, Lyncon moved on into the crowd, seeking a second man, who was holding a large hunting knife. As Lyncon neared, the man lunged forwards, fear driving him to make a desperate attack. Lyncon parried the blow easily and rammed his shoulder into the man, sending him sprawling into the dirt. A quick stab silenced him for good.

Having finally halted from his original charge, Lyncon raised his weapon and scanned the area around him. Behind him he could hear the sounds of his friends locked in their own fierce battles. He wanted to help, to turn and make sure they were unharmed, but there was no time as he sensed rather than saw an attack coming from his right and spun away just in time for a pitchfork to whistle past his ear. With a growl at his own lack of concentration, he faced his new opponent.

The man with the pitchfork was young and strong, with a broad face above a muscular torso. He had a shock of bright blond hair that was tied behind his head with a strip of leather and his expression told Lyncon he would not back down from this fight. He stood with feet apart and his legs slightly bent in a practised stance, the pitchfork ready in his hands.

With a grunt Lyncon sliced at the man, aiming for the shoulder, but he was fast and spun away while striking Lyncon on the back with the fork. It was a blunt impact, nothing more, but it pushed Lyncon forwards and he fought to keep his balance. Seeing his opening, the man lunged again, a reckless two-handed stab that was aimed at Lyncon's heart. He just had time to raise his sword to block before the weapons collided, his blade wedging between the prongs of the fork while one pierced the back of his right hand. He cried out in pain as blood dripped down his forearm and his vision swam. Gritting his teeth, Lyncon grabbed the pitchfork with his free hand and forced it back, untangling both his wounded hand and weapon. Then he gave a hard yank towards him, catching the young man off guard and dragging him forwards, straight onto the point of Lyncon's sword. With a snarl of triumph, Lyncon ripped his weapon free and dropped the pitchfork onto the corpse at his feet.

A sudden blow to the back threw Lyncon to the floor. Instinctively he rolled sideways, just in time to avoid the knife that plunged down into the dirt where he had fallen. Yanking the knife back, his attacker sprang nimbly away as Lyncon made a desperate slice towards his ankles. As he hurried to his feet, pain shot down his left shoulder and he let out a groan. His fingers were tingling and he couldn't close his hand.

Seeing Lyncon's pain his foe pressed his advantage, launching another attack with the club he had surprised Lyncon with. Lyncon blocked the strike easily but was too slow for the dagger as it raked a red line across his ribs while he tried to dodge. With a sudden roar of fury, Lyncon smashed the hilt of his sword into the man's face, breaking his nose in an explosion of blood. The man stumbled backwards, dropping the knife as he clutched his ruined nose, dazed. Lyncon followed him, slicing his knee open before finishing him off with a thrust to the throat.

Panting and with blood still dripping from the tear in his hand, Lyncon spun slowly on the spot, sword raised and ready for the next attack. Around him Fenrir and Dallan were battling their own foes while Henrik was hastily trying to secure a strip of cloth around a cut on his left arm. Everyone else was dead, the bodies scattered around them. Behind them all the barn still burnt, the flames casting a dancing red light that twinkled in the blood.

Sudden footsteps rushing towards him made Lyncon spin to face them. He turned in time to see the man in the checked shirt rushing at him, a broken arrow still lodged in his shoulder. He was unarmed but didn't seem to care and slammed into Lyncon at full speed, sending them both to the floor. Instantly, the man's hands were around his neck, squeezing like a vice.

As Lyncon struggled for breath he tried to free his sword but it was pinned beneath him. Desperate, Lyncon let go of his weapon and instead reached up and grasped the arrow protruding from his opponent's chest, forcing the shaft deeper into his shoulder. The man didn't seem to notice and instead simply laughed as fresh blood flowed from the wound. He grinned down at Lyncon and squeezed harder, fingers as strong as iron.

As his lungs burnt Lyncon felt the heat rise inside his body, the flame of his wolf blood filling his veins. With renewed strength he tore the arrow free from the man's shoulder and stabbed it up, deep into his attacker's left eye. Blood erupted over his hands and face as the man screamed, releasing Lyncon as he clawed at the arrow. His cries were abruptly cut short as a second arrow pierced his throat, snapping his head back in the process. With a final shudder he fell sideways and was still.

Gasping for breath, Lyncon sat up, rubbing his throat and wiping blood from his face with the back of his good hand. His shoulders heaved as he sucked in great lungfuls of air and his vision swam while he blinked away tears. The burning in his muscles faded slightly, diminishing to a gentle warmth as his heart rate slowed.

"Are you alright?" Fenrir asked as he knelt beside him, concern etched into his features.

Lyncon nodded and took several more deep breaths before he managed to wheeze a reply. "Yes… are you?"

The elf wiped blood from a cut on his forehead and stood up, offering Lyncon a hand to help him up. "I'll live."

"Thanks." He gestured to the arrow lodged in the man's throat. "I…"

Fenrir gripped his forearm gently and smiled. "Forget

it. I've got your back. Call us even for saving me on the road."

Their smiles were interrupted by a shout from Dallan, who was gesturing towards the barn. "Lyncon! Fenrir! The fire!"

The duo raced over to join the father and son, who were struggling to get the heavy doors open.

"Open up," Dallan shouted as he hammered on the wood. "We are friends. The men that attacked you are dead."

"Fuck off!" came the reply, followed by a succession of coughing.

The old knight shook his head. "They don't believe us. They'll burn before letting us in."

"Then we will have to break the door down," Fenrir declared. "Henrik, Lyncon, over to you two."

As he stepped towards the door Fenrir grabbed Lyncon's arm and pulled him close to whisper in his ear. "The door is thick and Henrik is hurt. You will need all your strength." He locked eyes with Lyncon for a moment then smiled. "You can do it, I know you can. Just focus."

Nodding, Lyncon moved past the elf and stepped up to the door. The wood was already warm as he placed his palms against it and smoke seeped from the gaps at the frame. With a nod to Henrik he pressed his shoulder against the door and began to push. The wood groaned, giving a little before the locking bar inside stopped any further movement. Henrik was already panting with the effort and Lyncon dug deep, calling his inner strength to help power his muscles. Grunting, he shoved harder, feeling his body respond and his strength grow as fire erupted in his veins. Suddenly, with a resounding crack, the locking bar snapped and the doors flew inwards. Henrik and Lyncon were thrown to the floor as smoke enveloped them, stinging their eyes and throats.

Before Lyncon could react, a figure strode out from the gloom and punched him in the face. He fell onto his front and when he tried to rise he felt the cold, hard point of a sword push into his back. Instantly, he froze.

"Amos, wait!"

The shout cut through the air and his attacker paused, giving Lyncon enough time to glance up and see through his tears the face of the big bald captain who had chased him from the envoy's tent. A snarl of rage was just softening on the captain's face as his eyes searched for the voice that had called out. From the darkness, Ser Dallan stepped forwards, arms raised wide in a gesture of peace.

"Dallan?" the big man whispered.

"Yes, old friend. It's me." The knight gave his usual gap-toothed smile. "Tell your men to come out before they roast alive. We are all friends here."

At first he did not move, his eyes instead drifting to Henrik and Fenrir, who were both watching him carefully. Finally, he turned to Lyncon and shock spread across his face, quickly replaced by the familiar snarl. "This man is a murderer. He killed an elven envoy. He must…"

"A misunderstanding," Fenrir said, stepping up beside Dallan. "He was framed, tricked by Evanora. As, I believe, were you."

Amos glared openly at Fenrir but softened as Dallan nodded. "He's right. We are not your enemy. Please, Amos. Let's at least move away from the heat."

After a brief consideration the captain nodded and stepped away, withdrawing his sword from Lyncon's back. Lyncon got to his feet, brushing himself down and eyeing Amos carefully. The captain ignored him and instead turned and called into the barn. "Everyone out. It is safe. They are with us." Immediately a group of soldiers hurried from the burning barn, coughing as they went. Some were clearly injured and had to be helped out by their comrades.

As he strode away from the fire, Amos surveyed the bodies around them. "I see age has not dulled your skills, Dallan."

The old knight shrugged and gestured towards Fenrir and Lyncon. "It was mostly these two." The captain raised an eyebrow but said nothing.

Once they were safely away from the fire and the wounded had been set down as comfortably as they could, Fenrir turned to Amos. "What happened here? Where is Evanora?"

The big man scowled. "Who are you to know her, elf? Are you a friend of hers? Part of her plots and lies perhaps?" The anger in his words shocked Lyncon, flaring with a sudden passion. Having seen the two together in the forest he guessed that the captain had since fallen foul of the elven sorceress one way or another.

Fenrir remained calm and simply nodded, talking slowly. "I was once but I was betrayed. My guess is that you know how that feels."

Amos was silent for a moment and Lyncon saw the anger drain from him almost as quickly as it had appeared. A weight seemed to press the captain down, slumping his shoulders and giving him a haggard, haunted demeanour.

Lyncon noticed the other soldiers were the same. Many were constantly glancing around as if they expected to be attacked at any moment. He was not sure what could have scared elite royal soldiers so badly but he had no desire to find out.

"She led us here, to fetch... him, but when we arrived she disappeared and we were ambushed." Amos shivered. "It looked like... a woman but... it... it was a monster. My men..."

Fenrir nodded. "The nebula."

"It tore my men apart. We had to retreat, flee to the barn. You know the rest."

"Did you kill it? The woman?" Henrik asked hopefully. The others turned to the captain expectantly but the big man only sighed.

Amos shook his head. "No. It's still out there."

Evanora crept through the outskirts of the village, always keeping to the shadows, eyes alert and knife ready in hand. The screams of battle and the clash of weapons had faded away and now an eerie silence clung to her, watching her from the dark. She knew Amos and his men were most likely dead, slain by the nebula. She smiled. Though she held no grudge against the big captain, he was too loyal to his country and his king to ever understand her own goals. His death had been the only answer. It had been too easy to lure them to their deaths, a perfect way to tie up loose ends, and it was a shame she had not been there to witness the killing. She had never seen a nebula up close, only heard the tales of their savagery.

Silently, she moved to the corner of a building and peered around, straining her big eyes to see into the night. When she was satisfied it was safe she moved on, crossing the open space between buildings, making her way towards the village centre. Her heart was hammering in her chest and she could feel sweat on her palms as she gripped the knife. She was nervous, a cold dread gripped her that she was not used to, tapered only by the rush of being so close to her final goal.

"I knew you would come."

The words shattered the silence as she was halfway across the road, exposed in the open. She whirled around, lightning quick, towards the source of the voice but there was no one there, the road was empty. Fear tingled down her spine as a horrid laugh split the night, echoing all around her, seeming to emanate from the very darkness itself. The air grew heavy with a strange static that made her skin crawl and the hairs on her arms stand on end. She gripped the knife tighter still and fought to steady herself.

"Did you think you could spy on me so easily? That I would not notice? Ha, I expected better. You taught me much, I admit, but I have learnt so much more since last we met. Is it not always the fate of a child to outgrow the strength of its parents?"

The words echoed around her, pulsing in her stomach and vibrating inside her skull. She could not help a gasp escaping her lips as she felt the air shimmer and swirl, felt the power that lurked in the darkness. Her own power responded in kind, surging up inside her, filled with lust and longing. Her hands were shaking, the knife trembling in her grasp.

"Now you are here, to face me. Your own creation. Your greatest mistake."

"You are not a mistake." Her words sounded feeble against his.

"So you meant for me to be this way? A crooked parasite. A leech that feeds on pain. No, you wanted more. You still do."

"Show yourself!" she shouted as she whirled around, trying to spot him in the dark.

"Ha, you don't even deny it. I almost admire you for that. Almost."

With a sudden boom like thunder, the tension broke and air surged towards her, striking her like a giant fist. She flew backwards, landing heavily on the grass. Gasping for breath, she climbed to her feet and there he was, standing in front of her, smiling. She shuddered as, despite her fear, excitement coursed through her body, her power calling to his own. After so long searching she finally had him. Slowly she took a breath and straightened to her full height, her free hand smoothing the fresh creases in her robes. The Crooked Man only grinned at her, staff in hand. His eyes were bright orbs in the moonlight, glinting with the maddening hunger within, the curse she had bestowed upon his soul.

With a sudden tilt of his staff he sent a beam of black energy towards her, the dark and twisting power cutting through the air with terrifying speed. Evanora raised a hand to meet it, unafraid, and released a stream of fire from her palm. The two forces collided and exploded into a cloud of smoke, the blast pushing both attackers backwards.

Smoke filled the road, a thick black cloud that obscured her vision and made Evanora's throat burn. Holding her breath, she summoned a keen wind that pummelled the dense smog and drove it away. As her vision cleared she gasped as the Crooked Man suddenly appeared in front of her from the gloom, a wide grin splitting his wrinkled face. He struck out with his staff, driving the point of it into her gut. She cried out in pain and as she bent double he struck again across her back, driving her into the ground.

"I expected better." He sighed as he stood over her. "I have long dreamt of this moment, imagined it in so many ways. I always knew it would come to this, the two of us, righting old wrongs. Our powers are too entwined to stay apart for long. I just always thought you would put up more of a fight."

Evanora rolled over, winded, the taste of blood on her tongue. She spat onto the grass and looked up at him. "You talk too much." With a sudden flurry she snatched up her knife from beside her and drove it down into his foot.

With a piercing, almost inhuman cry, the Crooked Man tore his foot free of the blade and stumbled away, colliding with the wall of the nearest hut. Evanora rose, panting while blood dripped from her knife, and strode after him. She slashed down twice, slicing across his arm and chest. He hissed in pain and lashed out at her, his fist catching her in the shoulder. With a growl she lunged at him but he slipped aside and struck at her with his staff. As she ducked the strike, the weapon smashed the wall above her, raining down splinters onto her head and shoulders. Ignoring them she leapt forwards and plunged her knife into his side, just below the ribs.

For a moment he was still, frozen in shock. Then he groaned and dropped his staff, slumping against the wall as he grasped for the knife. As he collapsed she caught his wrist and held it up, pinning it against the wooden wall. Whispering her spell, she forced the skin against the wood as it suddenly grew soft, pushing his wrist into the wall itself. As quickly as it had softened, the wood hardened again and the hand was stuck, half submerged in the wall. Satisfied with her work, she did the same with the other hand. The Crooked Man made no attempt to stop her, just sagged, limp, against his new restraints. Blood seeped steadily from his wound to run down his leg. His skin was ghostly pale and he looked to have aged by years in the few seconds since he had been stabbed.

Pulling his head back, Evanora slapped him hard. As his eyes flickered open she grinned at him. "I expected better."

Lyncon's ears were filled with the drumming of his own heartbeat as he crept through the village with the others. They had heard shouting and then a clap like thunder that split the still night air. The smell of smoke had bloomed in the air as a brief light had lit up the opposite side of the village and immediately Fenrir had made his way towards it, the others following behind, unsure of what else to do.

Silently, they emerged from the street and out into an open square that seemed to signal the centre of the village. Here the road through the forest met the main thoroughfare of the village at a right angle, forming a wide crossroad. A statue stood at the centre on a stone plinth, a man hefting a huge axe on his shoulders as he stared out in silent judgement.

The group stopped abruptly as Fenrir halted in front of them. He was staring off down the street to their right and Lyncon followed his gaze through the dark, knowing the other men would be unable to make out anything. Halfway down the road stood Evanora pinning the Crooked Man to the wall of a hut. She was saying something to him, mouth moving as she leant in close to his ear, and had one hand on a knife that was embedded in the old man's gut.

Both Fenrir and Lyncon made to move towards her when a sudden scream made them reel around. A woman was standing amongst Amos' soldiers, a knife in hand, green eyes shining in the moonlight. Her red lips were curved into a smile. The red matched the blood dripping from her knife and the severed hand of the soldier next to her.

"The nebula. Lyncon!" Fenrir gripped his shoulder as the men around them scattered, crying out in alarm. From a nearby building other figures began to emerge, followers of the Crooked Man. They charged into the square with a roar and within seconds the sounds of weapons clashing filled the space.

Fenrir looked at him intently. His voice was stern but calm. "You have to kill her. You are the only one who can."

Lyncon watched as the woman shifted, her body bending and twisting into a living smoke cloud. Quickly, she circled two soldiers before she reappeared again, her knife flashing faster than they could react as she slashed open their stomachs. They fell to their knees, screaming and clutching their wounds, while the nebula launched herself at more of the men.

Fenrir shook him. "Lyncon! You can do it. Focus and you can kill her. You must. You are stronger than you know. You think you are a monster but perhaps now it is time for you to be a hero." He looked into Lyncon's eyes, smiling, and nodded. Then he turned and was gone, sprinting up the road towards Evanora and her prize.

Taking a deep breath Lyncon gripped his sword and stepped into the battle. He tried to focus and will his body to change but he was unsure how and felt only a brief flicker of the power within him that quickly died down again. The last transformation had been caused by a longing to protect Fenrir and save his friend, a decision made for him that had happened quicker than he could think. This was not the same and he cursed as his wolf blood refused to listen to his calling.

Suddenly, a young man ran at him from amongst the throng, slashing at his face with a cleaver in a wild and clumsy strike. Lyncon blocked and countered with a slice of his own but the man skipped away, dancing lightly across the grass. Lyncon snarled and bared his teeth, feeling his blood warm in his veins, giving him new strength for the fight ahead. Blocking his foe's next attack he lashed out suddenly with his left hand and slit the man's throat with claws, freshly formed at his fingertips. The young man blinked, hand clutching his neck, before Lyncon cut him down with his sword and moved on.

Panting slightly, his muscles began to sing with the power of his blood. He killed two more men in quick succession, swinging his sword with lethal efficiency.

Stabbing a third attacker, he turned to face his next opponent but faltered when he saw the nebula staring back at him, those green eyes regarding him with open curiosity. Her lips were still stretched in a warm smile, though now blood ran from one corner of her mouth, leaving a scarlet trail down her chin.

"You," she whispered, voice as soft as velvet. "Werewarg. Thom told me about you."

She took a slow step towards him, ignoring the fighting around them. Lyncon raised his sword and tried to focus, to summon the monster he knew lurked within him. Remembering the pouch secured around his neck, he hoped it would slow the creature down a little.

"Your blood smells… wrong. Tainted. You are not meant to be." She shook her head. "I know you have something to repel me, filthy elvish work, but it does not matter. I will end you."

Without warning she surged forwards, a blur of hair and red lips, but still in her human form. He raised his sword high to block the slice aimed at his face and backed away to take the fearsome power out of the blow. Even then the impact of the attack sent a shockwave down his arm, almost jarring the blade from his hands and numbing his fingers.

He swore and pushed the knife away, swinging his sword to clear some distance between himself and his foe, but the nebula was relentless. She charged him again and, while she sped towards him, another knife appeared from nowhere in her left hand. As Lyncon spun away, she sailed past him, slicing thin lines across his thigh and shoulder as she went. Grimacing, Lyncon stepped further back, shocked by the extreme speed of the creature's attacks.

With a high, happy laugh the nebula attacked again, stabbing at him with both knives at once, one aimed high while the other went low. Instinctively, Lyncon deflected the blade aimed at his neck but the other knife stabbed just above his hip and he cried out as blood began to run freely down his left thigh. The creature grinned, splitting her beautiful features with a manic smile that showed the cruelty that lurked within; the monster beneath the mask. She yanked the knife free and skipped away, still laughing.

As pain welled up inside him, Lyncon felt his body finally respond. His blood exploded with heat, burning through him as his body accepted the power and embraced the change. He roared, both in fury and pain, while his body began to twist and change, muscles growing in size while fur sprouted from his skin. The transformation was quicker than before, less painful, and he growled from behind inch-long fangs as he turned his gaze back to his foe. The nebula simply stood watching, head tilted like a dog who had seen something it did not understand. Across the square, he noticed Amos staring at him, a look of shock frozen on his face.

"Finally!" The nebula shrieked as she charged towards him again, knives out.

This time, Lyncon did not wait for her and instead sprang forwards to meet the attack. Their blades met with a ring of steel before their bodies slammed into one another with a heavy thud. The nebula used the close quarters to her advantage, keeping close to avoid his sword and stabbing a blade across his ribs. With a roar, Lyncon slashed at her with his claws, raking them across her neck and breasts, tearing fabric and flesh alike. She screamed and lashed out in anger, her fist striking the cut across his ribs and forcing him backwards. Nimbly, she circled him and leapt up onto his back, driving a knife deep into his left shoulder while she held on with her other hand.

Howling in pain, Lyncon staggered back and forth as he tried to shake her off. The nebula clung on, gripping his fur tightly as she twisted the knife further into his flesh. With a roar, he leapt backwards, slamming the nebula through the wall of the nearest hut with a splintering crash. Still she hung on and, as he stumbled back out into the open, he dropped his sword and began to reach back to grab at her, claws catching and ripping her robes.

Finally, his claws caught flesh and his attacker screamed as he felt her blood flow warm over his fingers. He had hold of her leg and, with all his strength, he tore her from his back and threw her to the ground. Before she could get up he was on her, driving both of his hands down, claws first, into her stomach. The nebula screamed and began to thrash wildly, agony destroying her once beautiful features. Blood sprayed Lyncon and the grass around them, filling the night with its thick, heavy scent. With a snarl, Lyncon reached down and clamped his jaws around her neck, his fangs sinking deep into the soft pale flesh while hot blood flowed into his mouth. With one vicious yank he tore out the monster's throat and the nebula shuddered before falling still.

Lyncon stumbled backwards, spitting blood at his feet, mind reeling in disgust at what he had just done. His jaw and muzzle were covered in blood, his hands too. The nebula's knife still protruded from his back and he reached up and yanked it free, whimpering as he did. He threw the knife down and turned away, coming face to face with Amos, Dallan and Henrik. All three men were staring at him with a mixture of shock and fear on their faces. All had weapons in their hands. Lyncon's eyes narrowed. He gave a low growl and bared his bloodstained fangs.

Chapter 16

Betrayal

Fenrir ran down the road as fast as he could, heart pounding in his chest, long limbs carrying him forwards with powerful strides. Ahead of him, Evanora had pinned the Crooked Man to the wall and had a hand pressed firmly against his forehead while the other fiddled with a set of beads that were wound about her wrist. His eyes widened as he saw the beads. He knew what they were for, a catalyst for an ancient ritual that would allow her to take his powers. He sped up. She had to be stopped.

As he neared Evanora he felt strangely conflicted at seeing her again after so long. Her appearance had not changed, her hair and beauty still as radiant as when he had known her, those red lips still as alluring, but there was something about her that was different, the gleam in her eyes that spoke of hurt and desire in equal measure. Once they had been so close, so alike. Two elves pushing the boundaries of known science, their minds and ideas unparalleled amongst all their peers. They had been an unstoppable team, always friends, sometimes even lovers. Revered and worshipped, they had been held in the highest regard for their intellect and achievements. Until, one day, it had all come crashing down.

Fenrir still remembered the hurt of their last meeting; the pain of the betrayal he had discovered still weighed on his heart. By pure accident he had stumbled across a hidden scroll containing secret research Evanora had been conducting behind his back. Research that showed she wanted to further her experiments with the Essence despite the High Council's ban against it. He had debated not looking at it but few scientists could control their basic curiosity and he had given in to temptation, slowly reading the madness written in his lover's familiar scrawl. He had wept then and, even as he read the scroll a second time hoping he had misunderstood, he had known what he must do, though it would change his life forever.

The High Council had each read the scroll in turn, sitting around him in their high-backed chairs of ivory. There was little debate, the evidence was clear, and their decision was swift and final. A werewarg named Bane, the sworn sword of the council and first successful subject Fenrir had created, was ordered to find Evanora and bring her to them. Fenrir was labelled a hero, thanked for his service, but he felt only shame and heartbreak.

When news reached him that Evanora had escaped, Bane nowhere to be found, he had been secretly thrilled. He had frantically looked for clues at both the lab and her home of where she might be, perhaps something she had left for him, but in the end found nothing. She had gone, fled, alone. He had not seen her since. Rumours had swirled about her being seen in Astikus under the banner of the human king but Fenrir had dismissed them as simple gossip, nothing more.

Now, halting a few metres away, his heart fluttered at the sight of her. Fear chilled him, fear of her power and the madness that drove her, but he also felt elation, an unexpected longing to be with her, to hold her as he once had. He took a deep breath to calm his racing heart.

"Evanora!"

She froze at the sound of her name, body becoming rigid. Slowly, she turned to look at him, her big eyes tinged with cold, hard hatred.

"You!"

"Stop this! Please! I know what you want. I will not let you take it." He gripped his bow tightly.

She glared at him. "How do you know, Fenrir? Perhaps because you read my work and decided to betray me! You told the council and they tried to kill me!"

"I… I had no choice."

"There is always a choice!" she retorted.

"This isn't right. It is madness. I could not let you…" he shouted, his voice quivering.

"Coward! I trusted you!" She pointed to the Crooked Man, still pinned to the wall. "You're just as much a part of this as he is. You even agreed with me once, when you were a braver elf. Now you are nothing!"

With a simple flick of her hand she sent a blast of air at him that catapulted him against the nearest wall. He collapsed in a dazed heap on the grass.

"This world is broken. It is ruled by the few at the cost of the many but once I am done here I will have the power to reshape it. No kings or councils, only freedom and justice." Evanora eyed him with contempt, face split with a snarl of feral rage. "I will have his power, Fenrir, all of it, and then I will kill you with it."

Lyncon growled as he stared at the men around him, the reflections of the burning barn dancing along their swords. Blood dripped from the hole in his shoulder and his head was spinning; he swayed as he crouched on all fours to try to steady himself. Every muscle in his body burnt like wildfire, alive and invigorated by his victory and the wolf blood that pumped through his veins. His senses were alight, the smells and sounds bombarding his brain as he took in everything around him. The battle was over, the last remnants of the Crooked Man's followers fleeing into the forest.

Amos stepped forwards, weapon raised, his face a grim mask of determination covering a layer of fear beneath. Lyncon snarled but did not move, eyes fixed on the big man's sword. He did not want to hurt this man, his wounds already beginning to sap his remaining strength, but he also did not trust him. The captain had a mean look in his eye that told Lyncon he had to be alert.

However, before the captain could do anything more, Dallan stepped forwards. He sheathed his sword and stepped between them, arms raised. "Enough, Amos! Lyncon is not our enemy."

Amos simply stared up at Lyncon. His knuckles were white as he gripped his sword tightly. "He is not human," he muttered quietly.

The old knight nodded patiently, his eyes flicking briefly to the guards huddled behind their leader, ready to follow him into this fight if needed. "I can see that but he is our friend. He killed that evil beast. Without him, we would all be dead by now."

"Dallan, look at him!" the captain shouted suddenly, gesturing with his sword and causing Lyncon to give another low growl. "He... he's a mo..."

"He's a friend. A friend that just risked his life to save ours!" Dallan fixed the men around him with a hard stare as Henrik loomed large beside him. "I will not let you hurt him."

The captain just stared, entranced by the creature Lyncon had become. Lyncon tried to back away but found himself swaying slightly and had to grip the ground with his claws to stop himself falling. The soldiers behind their captain looked terrified but they had a steel in their expressions that told him they would attack him if they had to. If they were ordered to.

Finally, after a long, tense silence, Amos lowered his sword. His shoulders sagged as he gave a slight shake of the head. He turned to face his men, ignoring Dallan and Henrik. "With me, men. We must sweep the village and look for any more of these bastards hiding in the huts."

He began to issue orders to his remaining soldiers and they were soon formed up and marching away down the streets to begin their search. After one more backwards glance in Lyncon's direction, Amos followed them.

With a rumbling sigh, Lyncon sank to the floor. Suddenly, his limbs felt heavy and cold. A wave of tiredness washed over him, drowning out the fire of his blood, and he felt his body begin to change again. The fur he had grown now contracted, disappearing beneath his skin as his muscles shrank and his limbs shortened. His face began to fold inwards, bones cracking and reforming as his jaw shifted back into place, his fangs becoming teeth again. He moaned, the feeling more alien and unnatural than physically painful. Within seconds it was over and he was a man again.

Panting hard, he lay face down in the grass. His clothes were gone, shredded in his transformation, and only the small pouch of leaves remained around his neck, the string having been just long enough to accommodate his increase in size. Blood coated his body and he shivered against the sudden cold of the night air. His eyes drooped closed, exhaustion threatening to overcome him.

"Henrik! Stop staring and get him a cloak from one of the huts!" Dallan ordered as he knelt down next to Lyncon. He placed a gentle hand on his arm as he whispered, "Stay still. We must bind your wounds."

Henrik soon returned with a cloak and his father immediately sent him to find another as he ripped up the first to create makeshift bandages. Slowly, he helped Lyncon to sit up and then began to bind the wounds in his shoulder and hip. The cuts to his thigh and ribs were shallow and had already scabbed over, so Dallan ignored them, focusing on the two deeper wounds.

"Thank you," Lyncon whispered as Dallan draped the thick material over his shoulders. He was shivering hard and felt like his muscles were made of stone, heavy and cumbersome. Every movement was an effort. His wounds ached but the pain was fading as his powers took care of the damage.

"Can you stand?" the old knight asked. "We need to get you somewhere safe to better check your wounds."

"I'll be fine." He glanced around, suddenly animated. "Where is Fenrir?"

"He ran off to find the sorceress and that old man."

"I have to help him." With a grunt he heaved himself to his feet, his body violently protesting his every movement. He swayed alarmingly as he stood and Henrik had to reach out to steady him. His vision swam as pain shot through his hip but, gritting his teeth, he took several deep breaths and managed to ignore it.

"Lyncon, you need to rest."

"No! Fenrir needs me." He stared at the old knight defiantly, pushing away Henrik's hand and standing by himself. His legs were shaking and his hip was ablaze with pain but he took a deep breath and pushed the hurt to one side. Eventually, Dallan sighed and shook his head.

"Fine, we will go together, but put this on first." He handed Lyncon a belt. "Fasten it around the cloak. I have seen quite enough of you for one night."

After doing as he was told, Lyncon followed the others across the square at a slow walk as they headed towards the street Fenrir had run down. Almost immediately they spotted their targets, the Crooked Man still pinned to the wall while Evanora stood beside him. Fenrir was a few feet away, using the wall of a hut to support him as he struggled back to his feet.

Seeing his friend, Lyncon quickened his pace, ignoring the fresh bursts of pain that each step brought and the blood that trickled down his leg. As he drew near, Fenrir saw him and gave a brief, sad smile. Sorrow was etched onto the elf's face and Lyncon stopped, gripped suddenly by a profound sense of dread. Then, in one fluid motion,

Fenrir fitted an arrow to his bow, raised it and fired. The arrow struck the Crooked Man dead between the eyes, snapping his head back to thump against the wall, his mouth sagging open as his body went limp.

Snatching her hand away, Evanora whirled, screaming in rage. A knife appeared in her hand, pointed towards Fenrir, who simply stared at her with sadness in his eyes. Without a word he dropped his bow at his feet.

With a sudden burst of strength, Lyncon charged forwards, desperate to reach his friend but knowing it was all too late. As he ran, the sorceress stepped forwards, the knife raised. He roared, a sound of rage and frustration, but the elf whirled and sent a blast of air that threw him to the floor. With a groan, he raised himself to his knees as the sorceress eyed him for a moment, as if debating something. Then she turned away and grabbed Fenrir, shouting in a language he did not know. A sudden flash ripped through the night, impossibly bright, and Lyncon snapped his eyes shut, shielding them with his hand. When he opened them again, the street was empty. Both Evanora and Fenrir were gone.

Chapter 17

The Road Ahead

L yncon woke with a start, images of the nebula swirling around his mind, her blade cutting through flesh and dreams alike. He took a deep breath to calm himself, immediately regretting it as pain shot from his wounds. He realised he had been sweating and lay still for a moment, trying to calm his racing heart. Once he was certain he was strong enough, he finally swung his legs over the edge of the bed and sat up slowly.

Stretching his aching body, Lyncon noticed a pile of clothes had been left by the bedside. Yawning and blinking sleep from his eyes, he carefully put them on, doing his best not to disturb his wounds and the bandages covering them. He was pleased to find he was already healing. His shoulder complained at every movement but it was an ache now rather than a sharp pain and he could ignore it. His hip hurt when he put weight on his leg but otherwise it did not trouble him. As he buttoned up the shirt, his stomach gave a huge growl and he suddenly realised how hungry he was. Standing on shaky legs, he stumbled out of the little bedroom in search of food.

The hut he had found to sleep in was the least damaged in the village and yet even here there were signs of the previous night's terrors. Bloodstains covered the floor near the remains of the front door, a splintered mass of planks that had evidently been kicked in. The room smelt strongly of smoke, though the barn fire had not reached the building, and most of the furniture was smashed or overturned. There were no bodies. Amos and his men had gathered all they could find last night and placed them on a pyre to be lit before they left.

Making his way to the kitchen, Lyncon was pleased to find that it was full and relatively untouched. Rooting through the cupboards he helped himself to some bread and a thin sliver of cheese. He searched for water to wash it down but found only ale and avoided that with a hostile glare. As he ate he thought about the events of the previous night and the disappearance of Fenrir and Evanora. When he had realised they were gone he had searched the whole street for his friend but there was no sign of him, even his bow was gone. Eventually he had collapsed from fatigue and Henrik had carried him to the hut to rest. The loss of his friend had left a hole inside him, a cold void of hurt. Tears welled at the corner of his eyes and he hurriedly wiped them away with the back of his hand.

Hunger sated, he decided to head outside and find the others. Stepping out he paused to let his eyes adjust to the harsh morning sunlight. It was warm already, and the air was filled with the gleeful flight of birds as they dashed from tree to tree. A gentle breeze shook the trees around Rootun and Lyncon paused to survey the village. There was nothing that the battle had not touched. All the buildings were damaged or burnt, some no more than charred skeletons. Not a single resident of the village had been found alive and Lyncon silently prayed that the workers and their families had simply fled into the trees. Images of Seacrest flashed into his mind, the similarities forcing themselves into his thoughts. He shuddered and closed his eyes, pushing the memories away as best he could. After a long pause, he opened his eyes again and moved on.

Entering the square, he spotted Dallan tending to a wounded soldier. He had clearly been busy; his hands were stained with blood and he looked like he hadn't slept. Henrik stood close by, passing his father items while he worked to stitch a cut to the soldier's sword arm. Though no trained healer, Dallan had been in enough battles to know his way around most wounds and had taken on the role of medic while no better alternative was available. On the other side of the square, Amos was busy instructing his men on where to put the dead and organising construction of the pyre. Some of the Crooked Man's followers had fled when he had fallen but many had fought until their end, dying at the hands of Amos' remaining soldiers.

As Lyncon crossed the grass he heard the unmistakable sound of hooves and turned towards the gate to see a lone rider galloping down the forest road at full speed towards him. The man was clearly a soldier and wore the same armour and colours as Amos, marking him as a soldier of Astikus. The rider flew through the gate and down the street before reining in sharply beside Lyncon.

"Amos. I… I need Amos," the man spluttered, clearly exhausted. His face was caked in dust and his mount was breathing in ragged gasps, flanks heaving.

"Here!" came a reply as the big bald captain strode over.

"Captain, ser." The man dismounted and snapped to attention, wobbling slightly. "I have an urgent message for you from Councillor Hebb." The man removed a sealed parchment from a saddlebag and handed it to Amos. Dallan and Henrik strode over. Both smiled at Lyncon when they saw him and Dallan raised a questioning eyebrow. Lyncon simply shrugged then winced at the pain the movement caused in his shoulder.

Amos, meanwhile, had broken the seal and was now reading the message. Lyncon watched as the colour slowly drained from his face. Emotions danced in his eyes, fleeting flashes of what looked like anger and fear. He read the message several times, gaze darting across the words while the others waited in silence.

"Is… is this true?" he finally asked, staring at the new soldier, who had been avoiding everyone's gaze. He nodded without looking up.

"What is it, Amos?" Dallan asked gently.

The big man turned, glancing around to see who else was nearby before he spoke. "The king… the king is dead."

A stunned silence fell over them all. Even Lyncon, who knew very little about the monarchy, was shocked. King Renthor had been viewed as a firm but fair leader, equal parts loved and respected by all his people. Now he was dead and Petra was left without a ruler.

"How?" asked Dallan. He looked almost as worried as Amos and shook his head slowly in disbelief, his long grey hair dancing across his shoulders.

"Poison." Amos uttered the word as if it were a curse. "Hebb does not go into details but he suspects elves may

266

have been involved." His eyes flickered briefly to Lyncon then back to the knight. "I must get back to Astikus at once. There will be turmoil in the capital if there isn't already."

"Why?" Henrik asked. "Won't they just have a new king?"

Amos sighed. "Normally yes but Renthor has no children, no heir to replace him. Without a direct descendant the rules on who should be king can get a little... hazy." The captain shrugged. "Renthor has three brothers. It could be any one of them."

"Who decides?" Lyncon asked.

"Usually, whoever has the most soldiers," Dallan said.

Amos shook his head and rubbed a hand over his eyes, suddenly looking very tired. The others stood around him in silence, unsure what to say next. Above them a bank of thick grey clouds rolled across the sky, heavy with the threat of rain.

Finally, the captain turned to the messenger. "Wait here. I will fetch you a fresh mount and write you a reply to take back to Hebb." The man was clearly exhausted from days in the saddle but said nothing, just nodded stiffly.

Amos spun on his heel and strode away, bellowing at the nearest man to fetch him parchment and ink. The others remained with the messenger as he began to remove the saddle from his horse.

"Henrik, help this man!" Dallan ordered, slapping his son into motion. He gestured to the soldier to come closer. "What is your name?"

"Tarik, ser."

"How long ago did you leave the capital, Tarik?"

He paused for a moment to think, scratching his chin. "Six days ago, ser."

"And how long had the king been dead when you left?"

"Two days, ser. At least as far as I know."

Dallan nodded. "What was it like, when you left? Who ruled?"

Tarik shrugged his dusty shoulders. "No one. It was chaos for a little while but then Hebb took over the running of the palace and any civil affairs. The Black Hammer had taken over the guards and city watch while Amos was away but he left shortly before I did."

"The Black Hammer?" Lyncon asked, struggling to keep up with it all.

"Renthor's uncle, Lord Brock," Dallan explained. "He was nicknamed the Black Hammer by many after he defended his burning keep alone, against twenty men, with only his war hammer. He slew them all." When he saw Lyncon's raised eyebrows he held up a hand to object. "A true tale. I should know; I was there."

Tarik's mouth fell open. "You were at the Battle of Burning Hollow?"

Dallan waved him away, failing to suppress a smile at the younger man's awestruck expression. "Yes but now is not the time." He paused as he ran a hand through his fresh stubble. "Where did Lord Brock go? Do you know?"

"He didn't say, just rode off without a word to anyone." Tarik paused. "There was rumour he was heading to Lord Henry and plans to name him king."

The old knight nodded slowly. "That would make sense. The two have always been close. Is there anything else you can tell us? About how Astikus was when you left?"

The messenger shook his head. "Not really. As I said, it was mostly chaos. A few minor lords had arrived to pledge to the new king but none had brought more than a handful of men each. Hebb sent me to find Amos but didn't know exactly where he had been sent. I searched around for a while, asking locals, and when I found the tracks leading here I followed them."

Dallan nodded and clapped the soldier on the arm. "Thank you, Tarik. Go rest or perhaps even bathe. There is a well just beyond those huts. You've earnt some rest before you head back to the city."

"Thank you, ser. A wash sounds just right." He smiled at them both before heading off in the direction Dallan had pointed, moving a little awkwardly on saddle-sore legs.

The old man turned to Lyncon with a worried look on his face. His shoulders slumped as he sighed. "This doesn't sound good."

"Why? Tarik said the trouble was over; Hebb has everything under control now."

"Perhaps but Hebb is not the king. It will only be a matter of time before people begin to question his authority and without a clear succession it may be that all three brothers make a play for the throne. I am almost certain that blood will be spilled, sooner rather than later."

Dallan wandered over and sat on the stone plinth that held the lumberjack statue. Lyncon sat beside him, feeling sorry for his friend. He had no connection to the king or the capital but he could see the issue was clearly weighing on the old knight. He thought back to what Amos had said, how the king was killed by poison and that elves were suspected of being involved. Immediately his mind went to Fenrir and he felt the loss of his friend all over again. A weight settled on his shoulders, the feeling of his failure pushing him down into the stone. Fenrir had been his protector, a teacher who had held faith in him when he himself had none. The elf had trusted him and he had failed. Now he was gone and it was Lyncon's fault.

Henrik joined them and the three men sat in silence for several minutes, each lost to their own thoughts. Lyncon idly watched the clouds moving above them, an almost black wave that blocked out the sun turning day into near night. Tiredness settled over him, a great weariness born of fatigue and loss. A sole tear ran down his cheek, unchecked and unwanted.

"Lyncon. What will you do now?" Dallan asked softly without looking at him.

"W... what do you mean?" he spluttered, wiping his cheek.

"Amos will want to leave for the capital as soon as he can. If things are as bad as we suspect, he will ask Henrik and I to go with him, help him keep the peace. I have friends in the royal court, from many years of visits. It is a beautiful city. I think we will go with him."

Henrik nodded. "I would like to see Uncle Wulf."

Dallan nodded, smiling. "Yes. He, amongst others." He turned to Lyncon. "But what about you? With Fenrir... gone, where will you go?"

Lyncon was struck speechless by the question, words drying up in his mouth. He paused, his eyes drifting to the spot where Fenrir had vanished. Grief and confusion welled up inside him in equal measure. Part of him wanted to run back into the woods and forget his problems, to leave everyone behind and live alone, but he knew he couldn't. He had to get answers. He had to know if Fenrir was still alive.

"I… I don't know," he finally managed. "Fenrir, he… he is all I have. If he is alive then I need to find him."

Dallan placed a gentle hand on his arm. "I know he was your friend, Lyncon, but we searched everywhere. He's gone."

"That does not mean he is dead! We don't know what Evanora was capable of. I think they are still alive. I will not give up on him when he never gave up on me!"

A new determination bloomed in Lyncon's heart as he recalled how Fenrir had found him, saved him. The elf could have left him to die but instead he helped him. Now it would be Lyncon's turn. He stood up, filled with a new-found purpose, wincing only slightly at the pain in his hip.

"Fenrir saved my life, gave me a home when even I believed that I did not deserve one. He never gave up on me and I will not give up on him."

The knight rose with him, raising a hand. "Easy, lad. I didn't say give up on him. For what it's worth I think he's still alive too. My question is, what are you going to do about it?"

Lyncon paused, once again caught off guard by the knight's questions. There was no trace of Evanora or Fenrir, no clues at the sight where they had vanished. Even Lyncon's senses had not picked up anything to help tell him what had happened. With nothing to go on, no lead to follow, he was helpless. Helpless and alone.

"I don't know."

"Then perhaps our paths are aligned," Dallan said, smiling his usual gap-toothed grin. "It was the sorceress that took Fenrir; she caused whatever happened. Without anything to help here perhaps Astikus is your best bet. She was the king's pet and lived in the palace for years. Perhaps her chambers will hold a clue to where Fenrir might be?"

Lyncon frowned as he thought it over. Dallan's plan made sense; Lyncon already knew there was nothing in Rootun that could help his quest for answers. A dread had hung over him ever since he had searched the scene, a sense of hopelessness that he had felt at losing his friend. He had felt hollow and afraid, unable to face the possibility of his own failures. Now though, as he considered the knight's words, he felt that dread ease a little as hope began to bloom once more inside him. He turned to his friend and smiled. "You're right. Perhaps Astikus can help. I shall come with you."

Dallan beamed at him. "Excellent. We had better get ready. I know Amos will want to leave soon."

"He does," said a voice and the trio turned to find Amos and Tarik striding towards them, the messenger still drying his hair with a rag. Another soldier walked behind them leading a fresh horse by the reins.

Amos slowly looked over the three of them before turning his gaze to Dallan. "We are leaving now." He gestured to the rest of his men, who were busy gathering provisions for the march. "Will you join us, old friend? I fear I will need every trustworthy blade I can find."

The old man nodded. "Of course, Amos. My boy and I will help you, though I don't intend to cross swords with anyone over who sits on the throne."

Amos shook his head. "Neither do I." He turned to Lyncon, his gaze a little less steady than it had been before. "What about you? What will you do?"

Lyncon stood up straight. "I will join you. If... you will have me."

The captain eyed him warily, rising up to his full height. "First, I need to ask you a question and I want you to answer me honestly and look me in the eye when you do. Did you murder that envoy?"

"No," said Lyncon as he stared up at the bigger man. "Evanora drugged me. I woke up just before you found me with the knife in my hand. She set me up."

Amos stared at him for a long time as he thought it over, his fists clenched. Lyncon tried not to shift under the big man's gaze as he felt sweat trickle down the back of his neck. Finally, he nodded. "Alright. I'm not sure what you are or where you come from but you did save our lives, twice, so we owe you some trust. You may travel with us, for now at least."

Lyncon sighed in relief. "Thank you."

"Tarik, take this." Amos handed the messenger a folded piece of parchment. "There is no seal but I have signed it. Hebb will know it is from me." He clapped the man on the back. "Tell him we are coming as fast as we can."

"Yes, ser." Tarik nodded to the others before mounting his new horse and kicking it into motion. He was a blur as he charged out of the gates and back down the road through the Haren. The men watched him go.

"Get your things ready," Amos ordered. "We leave soon." Then he strode away towards his soldiers, barking orders at them as he went.

Dallan sighed. "Come, Henrik. Let's go saddle the horses."

Lyncon nodded to them as they left and then paused as he found himself suddenly alone in the square. Around him silence loomed, large and foreboding. He took a deep breath, running a calming hand through his untidy hair. His eyes were once again drawn to the spot where Fenrir had disappeared and before he knew it he was walking over to it.

He stopped in the middle of the street. There was nothing here except for the marks on the walls where the Crooked Man had been pinned and the bloodstained wood. He too had vanished, the body disappearing with the elves.

He knelt down and ran his fingers through the grass. It looked unchanged but when he pulled his fingers away he noticed tiny flecks of what looked like some kind of green powder. After he'd stared at it for a moment, a smile spread slowly across his face as he whispered into the wind.

"I will find you."

Epilogue

Salt and Shields

Jormund stood at the top of the slope that led down to the beach and stared out at the sea mist in silence. Beside him, his first mate Dag did the same, his hands restlessly caressing the heads of the two war axes at his waist. Four other warriors stood behind them, hand-picked by Jormund himself, salt-sworn to live and die for their king. A hundred yards further from the slope lay the edge of Ravens Rest, Jormund's village and the seat of his power as king of the Hook Isles. It was not much to look at, a collection of weathered huts surrounded by a wooden palisade in desperate need of repairs, but it was his home and the thought of what was to come set his temper flaring as he squinted into the fog.

As they stared, the only sound that reached them was the crashing of the breakers, constant and rhythmic as they beat against the shoreline, and the distant call of gulls high above the grey clouds that blocked out any hint of the sun. Jormund took a deep breath, filling his lungs with the familiar, salt-tinged air, and tried not to outwardly show his unease. Not for the first time he felt a stab of sorrow as he thought of his lost ship, his pride and joy, the vessel he had captained for over ten years and that now lay at the bottom of the ocean. He thought of the screams and the smell as his ship and crew had burnt around him and bared his teeth at the mist in a feral snarl. He would have his revenge for the loss. This new enemy they now faced would regret provoking the wrath of his people.

Suddenly a call erupted from the fog, too far to tell what was said, then, in answer, the sound of the waves was drowned out by a new noise, a steady rhythm of metal striking metal. It echoed down the beach, pulsing from the mist, vibrating out from the unseen enemy beyond. Despite his burning hatred, Jormund felt a sudden unease bloom in his chest. Beside him, Dag now gripped his axes tightly with white knuckles.

With a growl of frustration, he turned to his first mate. "It is time. Go."

He nodded. "Yes, my king."

Turning, he began to descend the path down the short slope to the golden dunes beyond and the three hundred men that lay in wait hidden amongst them. Soon Dag had found his spot and flattened himself down, almost completely disappearing amongst the long grass that poked stubbornly from the sand.

As suddenly as the uproar had begun, the enemy in the mist fell silent but now the waves were broken by the sound of boats grinding against sand and the splash of men hurling themselves into the surf and up onto the beach. Slowly, Jormund reached up and removed the battleaxe from across his back. One of the warriors stepped up beside him, a war horn ready in hand. He nodded to his king, who held out a hand, telling him to wait.

Still they waited as the sound of splashing stopped and the breakers once more became the heartbeat of the moment. Jormund gripped the haft of his axe, staring intently as he felt the unease grow from the men around him. His own fear now settled in the pit of his stomach, images of the bloody battle that he had fought on his ship returning unbidden to his mind.

Finally, the enemy appeared, the invaders who had sunk his ship and butchered his crew. Hatred flared up in him as he caught sight of them but he steadied himself. Timing would be key and he could not afford to get carried away with bloodlust. The warriors behind him shifted to get a better look at their foes, at the soldiers that slowly marched from the mist in neat, ordered rows. Another shout rang out from their ranks and the formation halted as one.

Jormund cast his eyes over the soldiers, calculating their number to be no more than a hundred. Hope seized him as he thought of the slaughter to come and he smiled to himself, squaring his huge shoulders for the other men to see. His people were seafarers, more comfortable fighting on the deck of a ship than on land, but with the numbers firmly in their favour he knew there was no way they could lose. The trap was set and it was time to avenge those that had been killed. He grinned to himself, eager for the slaughter to commence.

"Shields up!" came the call from the enemy, carried to the king on a sudden breeze, and he watched as the soldiers hefted their large curved shields in front of them in unbroken lines. Weak morning sunlight broke through the clouds above and gleamed on the identical armour and helmets that every invader wore, the metal painted a brazen gold over a pure, polished white. Each man held a sword in his free hand, the short blades so alien to Jormund's people who valued weapons of size and power that could cut a man clean in two. He might have laughed had he not already seen the damage those little blades could do.

"Advance!"

As one, the soldiers moved forwards one single steady step at a time, the wall of their tall shields remaining intact as they rippled up the beach towards the dunes. Jormund let them come, watching closely as they marched slowly forwards. He knew he needed to be patient, that the trap must be sprung at the right moment to prevent the invaders' escape. The waiting dragged on for what felt like forever as he gripped his axe and watched his foes slow progress, frustration beginning to stir his bloodlust. His people had often told him he was a good king, a fierce king or even a ruthless king but he had never once been called a patient king. He licked his lips in anticipation, tasting the salt from the air.

Finally he judged the enemy to be close enough to the dunes and turned to the warrior holding the horn beside him. "Now!"

The man blew one long, low note that echoed across the beach and was almost immediately drowned out by the roar of the attackers as they sprang from the sand and bellowed their war cries as they charged at the invaders from three sides. The men pelted down the dunes and towards the enemy, swords glinting in the growing sunlight as they waved them above their heads, faces contorted in snarls of rage and fury. Jormund just had time to see the invaders halt and change formation slightly before they were met by his own forces and the battle lines became a blur. The king felt pride swell in his breast as his men hurled themselves into the fight, not one showing a single moment of hesitation in defending their homes. He twirled the axe in his hands, itching to join them but knowing he must direct the battle from afar.

As the two forces clashed, the sound of battle cries was immediately joined by the clash of steel and the screams of the dying. His men threw themselves at the invaders' shields, fighting with the vicious fury and bloodlust that had earned them a reputation as the most fearsome warriors in all the seas. The men of the Hook Isles were renowned for their brutal nature and any captain worth his salt knew to turn tail and flee when they caught sight of their ships. Any that failed to escape would quake in their boots as the pirate vessels reeled them in and the men clambered aboard, swinging their war axes at anything that moved. It was a reputation that Jormund had always been careful to nurture. Since the start of his reign his people had gone from sea-scavengers to legends, their reputation winning them many battles before they had even started. None had opposed them, at least until these men had appeared with their short swords and matching armour. Now Jormund was keen for them to find out the legend was more than just stories.

On the beach, the islanders had begun to surround the invaders, moving to their exposed rear to try and get past the shields. As Jormund watched a shout rang out, calm and assertive, and the men at the rear of the enemy lines turned on their heels and faced outwards, presenting their shields so that they now formed an unbroken wall on all four sides. Swords stabbed viciously between the gaps in the shields, cutting down the islanders while they tried desperately to get at the men behind the wall. Jormund's breath caught as he saw the slaughter these foreigners were wreaking upon his men, stabbing again and again without mercy as their small formation held against the superior numbers. Doubt crept up his spine like a winter chill.

Jormund was no stranger to violence and death. He had killed many men for many reasons, not all of them just. He revelled in the feeling of the fight, the sounds and the smells, that knowledge that he could be one tiny mistake away from meeting his end. It was a high like no other, an unmatched thrill, the closeness to death making him feel truly alive. He was a king in title but he was a warrior at heart, born to lay waste to his foes on the battlefield, to swing his axe and laugh as he tore his enemies to pieces. Yet, despite his many battles, he had never seen anything kill like this shield wall did. It was a ruthless, methodical machine. The slaughter was cold and efficient, the invaders utterly detached from all those that died around them. There was no honour here, no glory. Only cold, hard death, screams of agony and blood-drenched sands.

As he stared down at the battle below him, a cold certainty washed over him, settling in the pit of his stomach like a storm anchor. He shuddered, his giant shoulders slumping, and spoke to the men behind him quietly, without turning to look at them. He knew their faces would only mirror the horror that weighed him down. "Go back to the village. Get everyone out. Tell them I failed."

When the battle was over, the shield wall marched in formation up the slope to face the king. He stood alone, waiting for them, axe gripped firmly in calloused hands, shoulders squared again with the last of his pride and courage that he could muster. Behind the invaders the beach was littered with the dead, the gulls already cawing as they descended with greedy eyes onto the bodies. Only a handful of those slain wore white and gold armour.

Jormund stared at the men as the formation halted before him. "Who will speak for the invaders that slaughter my people?"

The shields suddenly broke apart and a man stepped out of line. He was average height and build, his armour no different to the rest of those around him save for a black strip that ran from front to back down the centre of his helmet. A broken black circle was painted onto his cuirass, the two separate ends almost touching but not quite.

The man removed his arm from his large rectangular shield and leant it against his legs while he removed his helm. The warrior had short brown hair and a serious face and Jormund was surprised to see how young he was. As he looked into the man's eyes he saw a calm, hard gaze, watchful.

"I speak for us," said the man, his voice laced with a faint accent Jormund did not recognise. "I am Maxim Berothi, the commander of the First Legion of the Iron Fist of Dram and sworn blade to our lord and prophet Prince Nathaniel. I have been given orders and today I speak as his voice."

"Iron Fist of Dram? I have never heard of such a land." Jormund shrugged, trying to seem unafraid. In truth, he did not like this young man's stare, the unnerving calmness with which he spoke after the violence of the battle he had only just won. There was no hint of bloodlust or rage, only a cold, detached stillness that made Jormund shudder.

"Dram is an island south of here. For years we have kept to ourselves and spurned outsiders, killing any that reached our shores." He shrugged. "Now it is time to reveal ourselves. The Prophet has spoken and so we shall go forth."

"Prophet? Did your prophet tell you to slaughter all my people? To burn my ships?" the king growled, spitting into the dirt as rage flared in his veins.

The young man looked him dead in the eye, face and voice as hard as stone. "The Prophet told us to come here. We did not want violence. It was you that attacked us. Your people died because of your bloodlust, not ours. Surrender now and no more will die."

"Men of the Hook Isles do not surrender!"

The young commander shrugged. "We have almost sixty of your warriors down there on the beach who say differently." He sighed, stretching his shoulders as he ran the back of his hand across his forehead. "I know how this goes, so let's save some time. You do not wish to tarnish your honour, your reputation or perhaps simply your male pride, but you have only two simple options before you. Surrender or die. It is your choice."

The king spat again, stepping forwards and raising his axe. "We do not surrender!"

Maxim shook his head in disappointment and set his shield on the floor, stepping over it and drawing the short sword at his hip. "Your reputation is fierce, King Jormund. I know words will not sway you. I have faced many men like you and bested them all. Let us fight now and get this over with."

Jormund raised his eyebrows, a slow smile spreading across his face. "You wish to fight me? Alone?"

Maxim nodded. "Why not? You are just a man." He spun his right arm, warming his muscles. "If I defeat you then you and your people belong to the empire of Dram. You will serve us, forever."

"And if I win?" he asked, eyeing the men in the shield wall.

"You won't."

The big king laughed. "I like you! It is a shame I'm going to have to split your skull in two."

Without warning the king surged forwards, swinging his axe in a vicious downwards strike, aiming for the younger man's neck. The weapon moved with frightening speed, whistling as it cut through the air, and Jormund grinned as he waited for the satisfying crunch of impact but it never came. Instead the axe sailed through empty air, Maxim having sprung backwards out of harm's way, a wry smile forming on his lips. With a growl Jormund raised the weapon again and went after him.

His next attack was aimed at the invader's hip, intent on cleaving him in two. Maxim met this attack with his own weapon, using his sword to deflect instead of block the axe, pushing it downwards as he spun away behind Jormund. Maxim moved quicker than the king could comprehend, sword stabbing out twice as he spun past him in a blur of fluid motion, like a cyclone of white armour and glistening steel. His axe hit the ground with a heavy thud, Jormund leaning forwards on the handle as blood welled from two fresh wounds in his ribs and back. Pain burnt through him as his vision swam and he fought to keep his balance. Looking down he saw the cuts were flesh wounds, nothing fatal, but his thighs were already slick with blood.

With a sudden shout of desperation, Jormund spun, whirling the axe around him in a wicked spin. Maxim ducked the blow almost casually, the blade passing harmlessly overhead, and lunged forwards, burying his sword into Jormund's left thigh. Pain shot through him and the king bellowed a roar, charging at the younger man and barrelling into him with his shoulder, heedless of the danger. His axe forgotten, Jormund punched at his foe, aiming for the man's ribs. His fist struck armour and he groaned as he felt his left hand break but saw the strike was powerful enough to make Maxim grimace.

The two men fell to the floor, rolling apart and struggling to their feet as quickly as they could. Maxim was up first, stabbing forwards to cut a deep gash across the king's left bicep while he was on his knees. Gritting his teeth and with only one good arm, Jormund grabbed a handful of sand and threw it in the younger man's face, sending him reeling away as he swiped at his eyes.

Sensing his opening, Jormund snatched up his axe and, wielding it one-handed, launched a flurry of clumsy, desperate attacks, calling on all his years of skill as a warrior. He was panting hard and blood dripped from his many wounds, making him feel lightheaded, but he kept attacking as Maxim ducked and spun, dodging every attack as he furiously blinked the grit from his eyes. Jormund roared in frustration, hatred overriding his pain as he swung again and again at the invader who had killed his men and burnt his ship.

Finally, as Jormund launched yet another attack, his strength failed and his legs collapsed beneath him. He sank to his knees, blood painting the sand red as it trickled down his flesh. He tried to rise but Maxim stepped forwards and struck him on the temple with the pommel of his sword. Dazed, he released his axe and collapsed backwards onto the sand. His head spun as he stared up at the clouds above him and he could taste the iron tang of blood in his mouth. He groaned in pain and tried to roll over but froze when he felt cold steel pressed against his neck.

"Perhaps now you will consider surrender?" Maxim said, staring down at him with that impassive gaze. Apart from being out of breath, he seemed unaffected by the fight he had just won.

"Never!" Jormund yelled, spitting blood.

Maxim shook his head. "You fight well but I am better. There is no shame in knowing your place."

The king stared up at him, trying to focus. "There is no honour in accepting second."

The young commander shrugged. "Remember what I said about pride."

Despite himself Jormund flinched, expecting the sword at his neck to open his throat and leave him to bleed into the sand like the rest of his people. Deep down part of him wanted it. The part that could not accept this loss, that would never forgive him for being bested by this foreigner, the part that believed it would be better to die here, alone on this beach, than live in another man's shadow. Instead, he blinked and the sword was gone.

"I have been ordered to keep you alive. We need your skills and your knowledge."

"Knowledge of what?"

For the first time Maxim smiled, his eyes alight with excitement. "The north. We want to know all about Petra."